Ben Jonson's The Staple of News: A Retelling

David Bruce

Published by David Bruce, 2022.

BEN JONSON'S THE STAPLE OF NEWS: A RETELLING

First edition. July 10, 2022.

Copyright © 2022 David Bruce.

ISBN: 979-8201535186

Written by David Bruce.

Table of Contents

Cover Photograph for Ben Jonson's *The Staple of News*: A Retelling
https://pixabay.com/users/victoria_borodinova-6314823/
https://pixabay.com/photos/beauty-woman-knitted-swimsuit-6106924/
https://www.instagram.com/victoriaborodinova/
https://www.facebook.com/victoria.borodinova

Dedicated to Carl Eugene Bruce and Josephine Saturday Bruce

***

Educate Yourself

Read Like A Wolf Eats

Be Excellent to Each Other

Books Then, Books Now, Books Forever

***

In this retelling, as in all my retellings, I have tried to make the work of literature accessible to modern readers who may lack some of the knowledge about mythology, religion, and history that the literary work's contemporary audience had.

Do you know a language other than English? If you do, I give you permission to translate this book, copyright your translation, publish or self-publish it, and keep all the royalties for yourself. (Do give me credit, of course, for the original retelling.)

I would like to see my retellings of classic literature used in schools, so I give permission to the country of Finland (and all other countries) to buy one copy of this eBook and give copies to all students forever. I also give permission to the state of Texas (and all other states) to buy one copy of this eBook and give copies to all students forever. I also give permission to all teachers to buy one copy of this eBook and give copies to all students forever.

Teachers need not actually teach my retellings. Teachers are welcome to give students copies of my eBooks as background material. For example, if they are teaching Homer's *Iliad* and *Odyssey*, teachers are welcome to give students copies of my *Virgil's* Aeneid: *A Retelling in Prose* and tell students, "Here's another ancient epic you may want to read in your spare time."

CAST OF CHARACTERS

PENNYBOY JUNIOR: the son. The heir and suitor. In some ways, he is a prodigal son. He has long legs.

PENNYBOY SENIOR: the uncle, a usurer.

CANTER: a beggar. A user of cant, specialized language used by people such as beggars and thieves. A canter can also be a singer, aka chanter. The Canter wears ragged clothing. Pennyboy Junior calls him his "founder." In a way, the Canter is the founder of Pennyboy Junior's fortune. He brought Pennyboy Junior the news that his father had died. Pennyboy Junior becomes wealthy through inheritance.

CYMBAL: Master of the Staple of News Office. He deals with empty gossip and is named after a tinkling cymbal.

Note: A Staple is an export commodities market. Also, it is a warehouse full of the commodity, or it is the commodity itself.

FITTON: Emissary Court and jeerer. The rare word "fitten" means "lie." He dresses ostentatiously.

Note: Emissaries are news seekers. Emissary Court means that the person seeks news at Court.

ALMANAC: Doctor in physic (medicine) and jeerer. Also he compiles almanacs. He is a small man.

SHUNFIELD: Sea-captain and jeerer. A person who shuns the field of battle is not a brave person.

MADRIGAL: Poetaster and jeerer. A madrigal is a form of poetry. A poetaster is a petty and poor poet.

Note: Jeerers are sneerers.

PICKLOCK: Man of Law and Emissary Westminster. The Courts of Law were held at Westminster Hall. Someone who picks locks unethically engages in subterfuge.

PIEDMANTLE: Pursuivant-at-arms and heraldet. Pursuivant-at-arms is the lowest grade of heralds. This lowest grade has four members, which are named Rouge Dragon, Rouge Croix, Portcullis, and Blue Mantle, the name which Jonson burlesques in the name Piedmantle. A heraldet is a petty herald.

"Pied" means "motley," and "mantle" means "coat," so Piedmantle is wearing the motley clothing of a fool.

REGISTER: Of the Staple of News Office. A register is a senior book-keeper or clerk.

Note: The Staple of News Office is also called the Staple of News and the News Office and the News Staple and the Staple Office and the Office. It is a business place that gathers and publishes news. In addition, it has a residential section where Cymbal and others can live. This author of this retelling usually calls it the Staple of News Office or the News Office to avoid confusion.

NATHANIEL: First Clerk of the Staple of News Office. Nathaniel Butter published the first edition of Shakespeare's *King Lear*, and he was one of the first publishers of a newspaper in English. The Nathaniel in this book is not Nathaniel Butter, but Ben Jonson is playing with the idea that Butter has become a lowly clerk instead of being a big-shot publisher.

THOMAS BARBER: Second Clerk of the Staple of News Office. Physically, he is a little man.

AURELIA CLARA PECUNIA: Infanta of the Mines. *Pecunia* is Latin for "money." She is wealthy. The word "Infanta" loosely means "great lady." Throughout the play, she is literally a woman and figuratively money. Sometimes, she plays an allegorical role in the play.

MORTGAGE: Lady Pecunia's nurse. A nurse takes care of children or takes care of and chaperons young women.

STATUTE: Lady Pecunia's first serving-woman.

BAND: Lady Pecunia's second serving-woman. A band is a bond, aka security. Bands were also ribbons used to tie official documents.

ROSE WAX: Lady Pecunia's chambermaid. Wax often becomes pliant with little effort; the same is true of some chambermaids.

BROKER: Secretary and gentleman-usher to Her Grace (Lady Pecunia). A secretary is a knower of secrets: a trusted attendant who attends to the personal business of the employer. A gentleman-usher acts as an usher to a gentlewoman. He escorts her to places she needs to go. The word "broker" means a person who acts as a middleman in business deals between other people. To gain access to Lady Pecunia, some people attempt to bribe Broker. He has a beard.

LICKFINGER: A master-cook. A good cook is able to lick his fingers.

FASHIONER: The tailor. A fashioner is a tailor.

LINENER: A shirt-maker and dealer in linen goods.

HABERDASHER: A hatter.

LEATHERLEG: A shoemaker.

SPURRIER: A maker of spurs.

CUSTOMERS: Male and female (including DOPPER, a she-Anabaptist).

PORTER.

DOGS: Two, named LOLLARD and BLOCK, belonging to Pennyboy Senior.

Musicians.

NICHOLAS (NICK): A boy singer.

PROLOGUE: One who speaks the prologue of the play.

GOSSIP MIRTH.

GOSSIP TATTLE.

GOSSIP EXPECTATION.

GOSSIP CENSURE, or Curiosity.

Note: Gossips are godmothers. The word "gossip" when applied to a person may be a term of endearment used by women, or it may mean "an idle chatterer." A gossip can be a confidante.

BOOKHOLDER: A stage prompter.

A COUNTRY WOMAN.

TIREMEN: Stagehands.

The Scene: LONDON

NOTES:

An intermean is a passage of dialogue between acts.

Ben Jonson often regards the word "news" as plural.

THE INDUCTION

The scene is a stage in London in 1626, and the King of England is Charles I.

The Prologue steps on stage. Following him are audience members Gossip Mirth, Gossip Tattle, Gossip Expectation, and Gossip Censure. All four are gentlewomen, and they are dressed like ladies. At this time, audience members were sometimes seated on the stage. Sometimes, badly behaved (and loud) audience members caused problems.

The Prologue began to address the audience: "For your own sake, not ours —"

Gossip Mirth said loudly to Gossip Tattle, "Come, gossip, don't be ashamed. The play is *The Staple of News*, and you are the mistress and lady of Tattle; let's have your opinion of it."

Gossip Tattle had been hanging back, a little abashed.

Gossip Mirth then said to the Prologue, "Do you hear me, gentleman? Who are you? Gentleman-usher to the play? Please, help us to some stools here."

The Prologue was not an usher, but the speaker of the prologue of the play. Nevertheless, he wanted the women to be seated quickly so that he could do his job.

He answered, "Where do you want some seats? On the stage, ladies?"

"Yes, on the stage," Gossip Mirth said. "We are persons of quality, I assure you, and women of fashion, and we have come to see and to be seen — my Gossip Tattle here, and Gossip Expectation, and my Gossip Censure, and I am Mirth, the daughter of Christmas and spirit of Shrovetide. They say, 'It's merry when gossips meet.' I hope your play will be a merry one!"

People often go to the theater to see and to be seen. Many people wear their best clothing at such times.

Shrovetide is a period of revelry before Lent.

"Or you will make it such, ladies," the Prologue said.

He then said to a stagehand, "Bring a bench here."

The stagehand brought a bench and placed it on stage, and the ladies sat down.

The Prologue said to them, "But what will the noblemen think, or the grave wits here, to see you seated on the bench thus?"

Usually men, not women, had seats on stage.

"Why, what should they think?" Gossip Mirth said. "But that they had mothers, as we had, and those mothers had gossips, aka godmothers (if their children were christened), as we are, and such as had a longing to see plays and sit upon and judge them, as we do, and arraign and censure both them and their poet-playwrights."

"Oh, is that your purpose?" the Prologue said. "Why, Mistress Mirth and Madam Tattle, enjoy your delights freely."

"See that your news is new and fresh, Master Prologue, and untainted," Gossip Tattle said. "I shall find them to be otherwise, if they are stale or fly-blown, quickly!"

The Prologue began, "We ask no favor from you, only we would entreat of Madam Expectation —"

Gossip Expectation interrupted, "— what, Master Prologue?"

"That Your Ladyship would expect no more than you understand," the Prologue answered.

"Sir, I can expect enough!" Gossip Expectation said.

"I fear too much, lady," the Prologue said, "and do you teach others to do the like?"

"I can do that, too, if I have cause," Gossip Expectation said.

"I beg your mercy," the Prologue said. "You never did wrong, but with just cause."

Ben Jonson believed that if a play of his failed, the cause was the lack of understanding of the audience.

The Prologue then asked, "Who's this lady?"

"She is Curiosity, my Lady Censure," Gossip Mirth answered.

"Oh, Curiosity!" the Prologue said. "You come to see who wears the new suit today? Whose clothes are best feathered, whatever the part may be? Which actor has the best leg and foot? What king plays without cuffs and his queen without gloves? Who rides post in stockings and dances in boots?"

Feathers were decorations for hats.

"To ride post" meant "to ride on horseback quickly." Post-riders wore more than stockings on their feet.

Dancing in boots can be clumsy.

"Yes, and which amorous prince makes love in drink, or does overact prodigiously in embroidered satin and, having got the trick of it, will be monstrous still, in despite of counsel!" Gossip Censure said.

"Makes love" meant woos or flirts.

Looking at and criticizing actors' costumes and actions were part of seeing and being seen.

The book-holder, aka prompter, entered the scene and said, "Mend your lights, gentlemen. Master Prologue, begin."

The tiremen, aka stagehands, entered and attended to the lights, which were candles whose wicks needed to be trimmed.

"Ay me!" Gossip Tattle said.

"Ay me" is an expression indicating concern.

"Who's that?" Gossip Expectation asked.

They were a little worried about the tiremen. Some plays used firecrackers and other such effects to excite the audience.

"Nay, don't be startled, ladies," the Prologue said. "These men carry no fireworks to frighten you, but a torch in their hands, to give light to the business. The truth is, there are a set of gamesters within in travail — in labor — of a thing called a play, and they are eager to be delivered of it, and they have entreated me to be their man-midwife, the Prologue, for they are likely to have a hard labor of it."

Giving birth to a play can be difficult, indeed.

"Then the poet-playwright has abused himself, like an ass, as he is," Gossip Tattle said.

"No, his actors will abuse him enough by acting badly, or I am deceived," Gossip Mirth said.

She began to talk about Ben Jonson, the writer of the play they were about to see:

"Yonder he is within (I was in the tiring-house — dressing room — for a while to see the actors dressed), rolling himself up and down like a large barrel in the midst of them, and he was foaming with sweat. Never did a vessel of unfermented beer or wine work and begin to ferment so! His sweating put me in mind of a good shroving dish (and I believe it would be taken up for a service of state somewhere if it were known) — a stewed poet!"

A good shroving dish is rich food for Shrovetide. A service of state is a rich banquet.

"He sits like an unbraced drum — a drum with no tension on the drumhead — with one of his heads beaten out. For that you must note: A poet has two heads, as a drum has, one for creating, the other for reciting, and his reciting head is all to pieces — they may gather it up in the dressing room — for he has torn the play's script in a poetical fury and put himself to silence with bad wine, which, even if there were no other vexation, would be sufficient to make him the most miserable emblem of Patience."

Gossip Censure said, "The Prologue. Quiet!"

THE PROLOGUE FOR THE STAGE (AND READERS OF THIS BOOK)

For your own sakes, not his, he bade me say,
Would [The playwright Ben Jonson wishes] you were come to hear, not see, a play.
Though we his actors must provide for those
Who are our guests, here, in the way of shows,
The maker hath [poet-playwright has] not so; he'd have you wise
Much rather by your ears than by your eyes,
And prays you'll not prejudge his play for ill,
Because you mark it not and sit not still,
But have a longing to salute [greet] or talk
With such[-and-such] a female, and from her to walk [move on]
With your discourse to what is done, and where,
How, and by whom, in all the town — but here.
Alas! What is it to his scene [dramatic design, play] to know
How many coaches in Hyde Park did show [appear]
Last spring, what fare today at Medley's [a fashionable tavern that also served meals] was,
If Dunstan [the Devil and St. Dunstan Tavern, whose sign showed St. Dunstan twisting the Devil's nose] or the Phoenix [another tavern] best wine has?
They are things — but yet, the stage might stand as well
If it did neither hear these things, nor tell.
Great noble wits, be good unto yourselves,
And make a difference 'twixt [between] poetic elves [petit poets]
And poets; all that dabble in the ink,
And defile quills, are not those few [who] can think,
Conceive, express, and steer the souls of men,
As with a rudder, round thus [the Prologue demonstrated this with a quill] with their pen.
He [The real poet] must be one that [who] can instruct your youth,

And keep your acme [maturity, high point] in the state of truth,
Must enterprise [undertake] this work; mark but his ways,
What flight he makes, how new. And then he says,
If that not like you [If you don't like] that [play which] he sends tonight,
It is you have left [ceased] to judge, not he to write. [It is your judgment
that is lacking, not the poet-playwright's (Jonson's) skill.]

THE PROLOGUE FOR THE COURT (IF THE PERSON READING THIS IS QUEEN ELIZABETH II, THIS IS YOUR PROLOGUE)

A work not smelling of the lamp [A work that is new], tonight,
> But fitted for Your Majesty's disport [amusement],
> And writ to the meridian [written to suit the taste] of your court,
> We bring; and hope it may produce delight —
> The rather, being offered as a rite [solemn offering]
> To scholars, that [who] can judge and fair report
> The sense they hear above the vulgar sort
> Of nut-crackers, that [who] only come for sight.
> Wherein, although our title, sir, be News,
> We yet adventure here to tell you none,
> But show you common follies, and so known
> That though they are not truths, th'innocent [the innocent] Muse
> Hath [Has] made so like as Fancy could them state,
> Or Poetry, without scandal, imitate.

***

Note: Audience members in Ben Jonson's day used to crack nuts, thus making much distracting noise. Artists still have such problems:

Soprano Frances Alda once was scheduled to give a concert at Versailles in the home of the Marquise de Brou. However, the audience was very noisy, and so she did not start singing even when her accompanist began to play. The Marquise asked her what was the matter, and Ms. Alda replied, "I know I am supposed to have a very strong voice, but even so it would be impossible for me to make myself heard above all this *tohu-bohu*." This shocked the audience into silence, and she sang without distractions. By the way, Mary Garden once told Ms. Alda, "I am always having to explain you to people. Half of them think you're a grand person, and the rest think you're a b*tch." Ms. Alda replied, "They're both right."

Source: Alda, Frances. *Men, Women, and Tenors*. Boston, MA: Houghton Mifflin Company, 1937. Pp. 61-62, 112-113.

Note: David Bruce retold this anecdote in his own words.

CHAPTER 1

— 1.1 —

In the lodging of Pennyboy Junior were Pennyboy Junior himself and Leatherleg the shoemaker.

The shoemaker had just helped Pennyboy Junior pull on a new pair of boots, and now Pennyboy Junior was walking in his gown, waistcoat, and breeches, awaiting his tailor.

"Many thanks, Leatherleg," Pennyboy Junior said. "Get me the spur-maker, and then your part of helping to outfit me will be done."

"I'll do it immediately," Leatherleg the shoemaker said as he exited.

Pennyboy Junior said to himself, "Look to me, wit, and look to my wit, land."

His land was his inheritance, but "land" also meant "compatriots."

"Look to my wit, land" therefore meant "Compatriots, admire my wit," and unintentionally by Pennyboy Junior, "Inheritance, make up for whatever intelligence I lack."

He continued, "That is, look upon me, and look upon me with all your eyes — male, female, and yes, hermaphroditic eyes — and in addition to those bring all your helps and magnifying lenses to see me at best advantage and augment my form as I come forth, for I do feel that I will be one worth looking at, shortly.

"By 'shortly,' I mean now, by and by."

A succession of people were coming in by and by to outfit Pennyboy Junior in new, expensive, fine clothing.

He heard a noise and said, "It strikes!"

Pennyboy Junior drew out of a pocket his watch, which was striking the hours, and he set it on a table.

"One, two, three, four, five, six," he counted. "Enough, enough, dear watch. Your pulse has beaten enough."

The day was starting.

He continued, "Now sleep, and rest. I wish that you could make the time to rest, too. I'll wind you up no more. The hour has come that I have awaited for so long!"

Pennyboy Junior had just attained his maturity: He was now twenty-one years old and had come into his inheritance.

He took off his gown that he had been wearing that night. In this society, such a gown could be informal dress for during the day.

But now that Pennyboy Junior had attained maturity, he would dress differently, and better. He would no longer be a ward, or dependent. He would dress like a great man.

He dropped his gown and said:

"There, there, drop my wardship, my pupil age, and my vassalage and my being in a state of servitude all together with you.

"Liberty and full rights, come, throw yourself about me, in a rich suit, cloak, hat, and band of linen for a collar, for now I'll sue out no man's livery but my own."

The kind of suing he had in mind was a lawsuit as an heir to gain possession of his inheritance: his land and income. But he was also punning: Livery is the distinctive clothing worn by a great man's servants. A glance at the livery would reveal for whom the servant worked. Pennyboy Junior was now no longer a dependent: He had figuratively thrown off that status when he threw off his gown: a nightgown in which he slept. He had come into his inheritance. He would have his own servants.

"I stand on my own feet," Pennyboy Junior said. "I have so much income a year, right, round, and sound, the lord of my own ground, and (to rhyme to it) threescore thousand pounds!"

"Threescore thousand pounds" are 60,000 pounds. Pennyboy Junior was a rich young man. This gave him an income of over 2,000 pounds per year.

Still waiting for his tailor, he went to the door and looked out.

"Not come?" he said. "Not yet? Tailor, you are a vermin, worse than the same you prosecute and prick in subtle — narrow — seam. Bah, I say no more —"

Tailors were traditionally regarded as lecherous, and many people made jokes about a tailor's needle being a tailor's penis, but a real needle could be used to kill lice hidden in seams.

Pennyboy Junior continued, "Thus to retard my longings, on the day I reach manhood, to beat you."

One longing was to be finely dressed on this day of achieving his maturity, and another longing was to beat his tailor — or so he said.

He believed that great men had the prerogative of beating their tailor, and he was looking forward to doing it — or so he said.

Pennyboy Junior continued, "One-and-twenty years of life, since the clock struck, completed! And you will feel it, you foolish animal! I could pity him (if I were not heartily angry with him now) for this one piece of folly he bears about him: to dare to tempt the fury of an heir with an income above two thousand pounds a year, yet hope to have his custom!

"Well, Master Fashioner, there's some must break — a head — for this your breaking your appointment."

One kind of breaking is going bankrupt. A tailor who does not keep his appointments could go bankrupt — or get his head broken.

Seeing the tailor enter the room, he said, "Have you come, sir?"

— 1.2 —

Carrying a suit of clothing, the tailor walked over to Pennyboy Junior and said, "May God give Your Worship joy."

"Joy of what?" Pennyboy Junior asked. "Of your tardiness? And joy of your leaving me to stalk here in my breeches, like a tame heron, for you?"

Herons have long legs, and so did Pennyboy Junior. He was "tame" because he could not leave his house without wearing the proper clothing that his tailor was bringing him.

The tailor said, "I just waited below until the clock struck."

"Why, if you had come a quarter of an hour earlier, would it so have hurt you in reputation to have waited here?" Pennyboy Junior asked.

"No, but Your Worship might have pleaded nonage, if you had got the suit of clothing on, before I could make just affidavit of the time," the tailor replied.

To "plead nonage" meant to plead that one was not responsible for paying a debt because one was underage at the time the debt was incurred.

"That jest has gained your pardon," Pennyboy Junior said. "You would have lived condemned to your own hell otherwise, and you would have never wrought even one stitch more for me or any Pennyboy."

The "jest" was not a jest; it can be regarded as an insult.

14

Despite Pennyboy Junior's words about beating his tailor, he was good-natured.

"Hell" was a place where tailors kept scraps of clothing. Without Pennyboy Junior's custom, the tailor would have no reason to leave his shop and deliver clothing to Pennyboy Junior.

"I could have hindered your career, but now you are mine," Pennyboy Junior said, "for one-and-twenty years, or for the longest length of one of three persons' lives, choose whichever three persons you will. I'll make you a copyholder of land, and I'll pay your first bill without questioning its details."

Pennyboy Junior was promising the tailor to give him his custom for 21 years, or for as long as the longest lived of any three people the tailor named lived.

A copyholder holds land with the permission of the land owner.

He then said, "Help me get this on."

"Immediately, sir," the tailor said. "I am bound to Your Worship."

He helped Pennyboy Junior put on the suit of clothing.

"You shall be, when I have sealed for you a lease of my custom and guaranteed that I will be your customer," Pennyboy Junior said.

"Your Worship's barber is outside, waiting," the tailor said.

"Who?" Pennyboy Junior asked. "Tom?"

He called, "Come in, Tom."

Thomas Barber entered the room.

Pennyboy Junior said to him, "Set your things upon the table and spread your cloths and lay all forth *in procinctu* — in readiness — and tell us what's the news."

"Oh, sir, a Staple of News!" Thomas Barber said. "Or the New Staple, whichever you please."

A Staple of News is a center for news. In this culture, newspapers were just now coming into existence.

"What's that?" Pennyboy Junior asked.

"It is an office, sir, a fine young office set up," the tailor said. "I forgot to tell Your Worship."

"An office set up for what?" Pennyboy Junior asked.

Thomas Barber said, "To enter all the news, sir, of the time —"

The tailor interrupted, "— and vent — publish — it as occasion serves! A place of huge commerce it will be! News will be vended as well as vented."

"Please, be quiet," Pennyboy Junior said to the tailor. "I cannot abide a talking tailor. Let Tom — he's a barber — by his place relate it."

Barbers are known for being talkative. Because they talk so much with their customers, they are purveyors of news — and gossip.

Pennyboy Junior then asked, "What is it? An office, Tom?"

Thomas Barber answered, "Newly erected here in the house you are staying, almost on the same floor, it is a place where all the news of all sorts shall be brought, and there be examined, and then registered, and so be issued under the seal of the Office, as Staple News. No other news will be current."

The Staple of News Office would determine which news was current — that is, authentic.

Pennyboy Junior said, "I say, you are speaking of a splendid business, Tom."

The tailor said, "Nay, if you knew the brain that hatched it, sir —"

"I know you well enough," Pennyboy Junior said to the tailor.

He then said, "Give him a loaf, Tom."

Not only were tailors stereotypically lecherous, they also stereotypically loved bread.

Pennyboy Junior added, "The loaf will quiet his mouth; that oven will be venting otherwise."

The tailor's mouth needed to be closed because what would be coming from it was hot air.

Pennyboy Junior then said to Thomas Barber, "Proceed."

"The tailor is telling you the truth, sir," Thomas Barber said. "Master Cymbal is Master of the Staple of News Office; he came up with the idea of it. He resides here in the house, and the great rooms he has taken for the Office and to set up his desks and bookcases, tables, and his shelves —"

The tailor interrupted, "— he's my customer and a wit, sir, too. But he has splendid wits under him —"

Thomas Barber interrupted, "— yes, four emissaries —"

"— emissaries?" Pennyboy Junior interrupted. "Wait, there's a fine new word, Tom! Pray God it signify anything. What are emissaries?"

Thomas Barber answered, "Men employed outward who are sent abroad to fetch in the commodity."

Emissaries are men sent on a mission to gather information. These particular emissaries were reporters.

The tailor said, "From all regions where the best news are made —"

Thomas Barber interrupted, "— or vented forth —"

The tailor interrupted, "— by way of exchange, or trade —"

Pennyboy Junior interrupted, "— nay, you insist on speaking —"

"— my share, sir," the tailor finished the sentence. "There's enough to say for both the barber and me."

Pennyboy Junior nodded, giving the tailor permission to speak: "Go on, then; speak all you know. I think the ordinaries should help them much."

By "ordinaries," he meant fashionable eating places: upscale taverns.

Misunderstanding what Pennyboy Junior meant by "ordinaries," the tailor said, "Sir, they have ordinaries and extraordinaries, as many changes and variations as there are points in the compass."

In this society, post ordinary and post haste were speeds of delivering messages and letters. Post ordinary were regular letter carriers, while post haste were very quick letter carriers. These letter carriers rode very quickly on horseback.

Thomas Barber began, "But the four cardinal quarters —"

Pennyboy Junior interrupted, "— aye, those, Tom —"

Thomas Barber interrupted, giving the four main places news could and would be gathered: "— the Court, sir, St. Paul's, the Exchange, and Westminster Hall."

The center aisle of St. Paul's Cathedral was a center of gossip.

The Courts of Common Law and of Chancery were located at Westminster Hall, and much gossip occurred there.

The Court and the Royal Exchange were also places of gossip.

"Who is the chief?" Pennyboy Junior asked. "Who has the precedency?"

"The governor of the Staple of News Office, Master Cymbal," Thomas Barber answered. "He is the chief; and after him are the emissaries.

"The First Emissary is at the Court, one Master Fitton. He's a jeerer, too."

"He's a jeerer, too" is ambiguous. It can mean, 1) "Cymbal is a jeerer, and so is Fitton," or 2) "Fitton is an emissary, and he is also a jeerer."

"A jeerer?" Pennyboy Junior asked. "What's that?"

"A wit," the tailor answered.

One kind of "wit" is to jeer at and mock other people.

"Or half a wit," Thomas Barber said. "Some of them are half-wits, two to a wit; there are a set of them.

"Master Ambler is the Emissary at St. Paul's. He is as fine-paced a gentleman as you shall see walk the middle aisle.

"And then my froy — that is, handsome — Hans Buzz, a Dutchman, is Emissary at the Exchange."

The tailor said, "I had thought Master Burst, the merchant, had been made Emissary at the Exchange."

"No," Thomas Barber said. "He has a rupture; he has sprung a leak — he has gone bankrupt."

In fact, the word "burst" meant bankrupt.

Thomas Barber continued, "The Emissary at Westminster Hall is undisposed of yet. That emissary has not yet been named.

"Then the other positions are the examiner, the register, and two clerks — they manage all at home, and sort, and file, and seal the news, and issue them."

Pennyboy Junior said, "Tom, dear Tom, what may my means and wealth do for you? Ask, and have it. I would like to be doing some good — it is my birthday — and I'd do it promptly. I feel a secret longing to be bountiful and generous, and I would not long lie fallow.

"I ask you to think, and speak, and wish for something."

Thomas Barber said, "I wish that I had just one of the clerks' places in this Staple of News Office."

"You shall have it, Tom, if silver or gold will fetch it," Pennyboy Junior said. "What's the rate? At what is it set in the market?"

Masters received payment to take on a new apprentice.

"Fifty pounds, sir," Thomas Barber said.

"Even if it were a hundred pounds, Tom, you shall not lack it," Pennyboy Junior said.

The tailor leapt at and hugged him, saying, "Oh, noble master!"

"What is this now, Aesop's ass!" Pennyboy Junior said.

One of Aesop's fables is about an ass that observed its master favoring a lap dog. Wanting similar attention, the ass decided to act like a lap dog, and it jumped up on its master's lap. Of course, the ass' hooves and weight hurt its master, and the master's servants drove the ass back to its stable with many blows.

Tom Barber was a little man; the tailor was much larger.

Pennyboy Junior continued, "Because I play with Tom, must I necessarily run into your rude embraces? Stand still, sir. Clown's fawnings are like a horse attempting a salutation by curtseying."

He then asked Thomas Barber, "How do you like my new suit of clothing, Tom?"

"Master tailor has hit your measures, sir," Thomas Barber said. "He's molded you and made you, as they say."

Clothes and a tailor make a man.

"No, no, not I," the tailor said. "I am an ass, old Aesop's ass."

"Nay, tailor," Pennyboy Junior said. "I can do you a good turn, too. Don't be musty and peevish, although you have molded me, as little Tom says. I think you have put me in moldy pockets."

He pulled out his pockets.

"Your pockets are perfumed," the tailor said, "with good and right Spanish perfume — the Lady Estifania's. The cost is twelve pounds for a pair of perfumed pockets."

"Your bill will say so," Pennyboy Junior said, drily. "Please tell me, tailor, what authors you read to help your invention? Italian prints? Or tapestries? They are tailors' libraries."

Much English fashion was copied from the fashions of other countries.

"I scorn such helps," the tailor said.

He relied on his own invention for his fashions.

Pennyboy Junior said, "Oh, though you are a silkworm, and deal in satins and velvets and rich plushes, you cannot spin all forms out of yourself; they are quite other things.

"I think this suit of clothing has made me wittier than I was."

"Believe it, sir," the tailor said. "Clothes do much to improve the wit, as weather does on the brain; and thence comes your proverb: 'The tailor makes the man.'"

The right kind of weather can affect the brain and make it alert and sharp, and the wrong kind of weather can affect the brain and make it dull and drowsy. Modern operating rooms are kept at the cold temperature proven to keep surgeons alert and sharp.

Clothes can make the man. Think of the king in Mark Twain's *Adventures of Huckleberry Finn*:

> The king's duds was all black, and he did look real swell and starchy. I never knowed how clothes could change a body before. Why, before, he looked like the orneriest old rip that ever was; but now, when he'd take off his new white beaver and make a bow and do a smile, he looked that grand and good and pious that you'd say he had walked right out of the ark, and maybe was old Leviticus himself.

The tailor continued, "I speak by experience of my own customers. I have had gallants, both court and country, who would have fooled you completely into believing while they were wearing a new suit of clothing that they were the best wits in being. They kept their social acceptability up as long as their clothes lasted and were handsome and neat; but then as their elbows wore out again, or their clothes had a stain or spot, these gallants sank in social respectability most wretchedly."

Pennyboy Junior said, "What you report is but the common calamity, and seen daily. And therefore you've another, answering proverb: 'A broken sleeve keeps the arm back.'"

A person with a broken sleeve would like to keep that fact hidden and so would not move that arm and would avoid drawing attention to the broken sleeve.

"It is true, sir," the tailor said. "And thence we say that such a one plays at peep-arm."

If a sleeve had a tear in it or is worn through, one could peep at the arm inside. Therefore, the person wearing the broken sleeve tried to cover up the tear or worn-through spot.

"Do you say that?" Pennyboy Junior said. "It is wittily said. I wonder that gentlemen and men of means will not maintain themselves fresher in wit — I mean in clothes — to the highest point possible.

"For he who is out of clothes is out of fashion, and to be out of fashion is to be out of countenance, and to be out of countenance is to be out of wit."

A person who is out of countenance is flustered. The word "countenance" refers to appearance, such as the expression on one's face.

He then asked, "Hasn't rogue haberdasher come?"

The haberdasher, the linener, and Leatherleg the shoemaker entered the room. They were carrying apparel and bills. The haberdasher was primarily a hat-maker, and the linener was primarily a shirt-maker.

"Yes, here I am, sir," the haberdasher said. "I have been waiting outside the door this half-hour."

"Give me my hat," Pennyboy Junior said.

Everyone became busy, helping him.

Pennyboy Junior continued, "Put on my belt. Rascal, does my ruff sit well?"

The ruff was a frilled collar.

"In print," the linener said.

"In print" meant "perfectly."

"Slave," Pennyboy Junior said.

He believed that great men could be rude, and he believed that he was a great man. To him, a great man was a rich man.

The linener gave him a mirror and said, "Look at yourself."

Scrutinizing himself, Pennyboy Junior asked, "Is this same hat of the block *passant*?"

He was asking if his hat was in the latest style.

He then said, "Do not answer me; I cannot stay for an answer. I do feel the powers of one-and-twenty like a tide flow in upon me, and I perceive that an heir can conjure up all spirits in all circles.

"Rogue, rascal, slave — give tradesmen their true names, and they appear to them immediately."

By saying the correct name of a spirit along with other words, a conjurer can summon the spirit and keep it safely contained within a protective circle.

"For profit," the linener said.

"Come, cast my cloak about me," Pennyboy Junior said.

He was punning on "casting a spell."

He continued. "I'll go see this Staple of News Office, Tom, and be trimmed afterwards."

"Trimmed" means 1) barbered, and 2) cheated, as in excessive billing for services rendered.

Pennyboy Junior continued, "I'll put you in possession of the clerk's office, my prime work!"

His spur-maker then came into the room, carrying spurs.

"By God, my spurrier!" Pennyboy Junior said. "Put them on me, boy, quickly. I was about to have lost my spurs with too much speed."

The spurrier helped Pennyboy Junior put on his spurs.

Pennyboy Junior had not actually done anything to win his spurs; he had merely purchased them with inherited money.

Singing, the Canter walked over to them. He was wearing a patched cloak, and he was carrying a bag of money. In his song and conversation, he compared Pennyboy Junior and the tradesmen to a military officer and his troops. In his conversation, Pennyboy Junior continued the same comparison.

The Canter sang:

"*Good morning to my joy, my jolly Penny-boy!*

"*The lord and the prince of plenty!*

"*I come to see what riches you bear in your breeches,*

"*The first of your one-and-twenty.*

"*What, do your pockets jingle? Or shall we need to mingle*

"*Our strength both of foot and horses?*

"*These fellows look so eager as if they would beleaguer*

"*An heir in the midst of his forces!*

"*I hope they are sergeants who hang upon your margents!*"

"Sergeants" were 1) officers who arrested debtors, or 2) military personnel.

"Margents" were 1) margins, or 2) military flanks.

Looking at the spurrier, the Canter said, "This rogue has the jowl — jaw — of a jailor!"

The young Pennyboy Junior sang in response:

"*Oh, founder, no such matter, my spurrier, and my hatter,*

"*My linen-man, and my tailor —*"

He then said in his normal conversational voice, "You should have been brought in, too, shoemaker, if the time had been longer, and Tom Barber."

He then asked, "How do you like my company, old Canter? Don't I muster a brave troupe? All are billmen —"

A bill is a weapon — half-ax and half-spear — that is also known as a halberd. Another kind of bill is a document of a debt that must be paid.

Pennyboy Junior said to the tradesmen, "Present your arms before my founder here. This is my founder, this same learnéd Canter!"

The Canter was a pseudo-father for Pennyboy Junior.

Pennyboy Junior continued, "He brought me the first news of my father's death. I thank him, and ever since I have called him my founder.

"Worship him, boys."

The word "worship" means adore.

Pennyboy Junior then took the bills from the tradesmen and said, "I'll read only the sums, and pass them immediately."

Leatherleg the shoemaker said, "Now ale!"

All the other tradesmen said a toast: "And strong ale bless him!"

Pennyboy Junior said, "By God, some ale and sugar for my founder!"

In this society, people used sugar to sweeten ale, which was also often warmed.

Putting the tradesmen's bills in his pockets, Pennyboy Junior said, "They are good bills, sufficient and properly drawn-up bills; these bills may pass."

He meant that he would pay them without challenging any of the items on the bills.

The Canter said, "I do not like those paper squibs, good master."

"Squibs" are firecrackers.

This kind of "master" is a man who has come of age.

The Canter continued, "They may undo your store — I mean, your store of credit — and fire your arsenal, if perhaps you do not in time make good those outer works, your pockets, and take a garrison in of some two hundred to beat these pioneers off who carry a mine that would blow you up at last."

Pioneers are under-miners. They would dig a tunnel — a mine — under a city wall and plant bombs to blow it up.

The bills could be like a bomb that would blow up Pennyboy Junior's line of credit if he could not pay them off in good time. It would be wise for him to have two hundred or so coins in reserve so that he could pay his bills in a timely manner, and it would be wise for him not to spend the two hundred or so coins quickly.

The Canter advised, "Secure your casemates."

Casemates are vaulted chambers used by soldiers defending a fortification. Pennywise Junior could defend his line of credit by keeping money in reserve — and not spending it quickly.

The Canter, who was holding a bag of money, continued, "Master Picklock, sir, your man of law and learnéd attorney, has sent you a bag of munitions."

Taking the bag, Pennyboy Junior asked, "What is it?"

"Three hundred pieces," the Canter said.

The pieces were figuratively bullets and literally gold coins.

"I'll dispatch them," Pennyboy Junior said.

"Do that," the Canter said. "I would have your strengths lined and perfumed with gold as well as ambergris."

The strengths were strongholds. In this case, they were Pennyboy Junior's pockets.

Pennyboy Junior's pockets were already perfumed — ambergris is used in the making of perfume — but he also needed gold coins as a line of defense against becoming impoverished.

A young man who has recently come into a lot of money can be a big spender and too soon discover that he has no money left to spend.

The Canter understood "dispatch" to mean "stow away" (a rare meaning), but Pennyboy Junior meant that he would dispense the gold coins right away.

"Godamercy," Pennyboy Junior said to the Canter. "May God reward you."

He then said to the tradesmen, "Come; *ad solvendum*, boys! Settling-up time! There, there, and there, etc."

He paid all the tradesmen what he owed them.

As he dispensed the coins, Pennyboy Junior said, "I look on nothing but *totalis*."

He did not examine the individual items of the bills to check for inaccuracies, but simply paid their totals.

The Canter said to himself, "Look! See the difference between the covetous and the prodigal: The covetous man never has money, and the prodigal man will have none shortly!"

Misers say that they have no money to spend, give, or lend, and prodigious spenders soon have no money to spend.

"Ha, what does my founder say?" Pennyboy Junior said.

He then said to the tradesmen, "I thank you. I thank you, sirs."

The tradesmen replied, "God bless Your Worship, and Your Worship's chanter."

A chanter is a singer: The Canter had entered the scene singing.

Leatherleg the shoemaker, the linener (shirt-maker), and the haberdasher (hatter) exited.

The Canter said, "I say that it is nobly done to cherish shopkeepers, and pay their bills without examining them, as you have just done."

Chances are, he was being sarcastic. It is good to pay bills in a timely manner, but it is also good to make sure that the bills are accurate.

"Alas!" Pennyboy Junior said. "They have had a pitiful hard time of it, a long vacation from their cheating."

The Inns of Court had a long summer vacation, making tradesmen complain about lack of custom because so many of their customers had left London. In addition, in early 1626, London was still recovering from the plague.

Pennyboy Junior continued, "Poor rascals, I do it out of charity. I want to advance their trade again, and I want to have them make haste to be rich, swear, and forswear wealthily."

One way to become wealthy — many people believe — is to swear and forswear. That is, to swear and then commit perjury, or to make and then break promises.

Pennyboy Junior then asked the spurrier, "Why are you staying here, sirrah?"

"Sirrah" was used to address a man of lower social standing than the speaker. The use of the word by a gentleman to refer to a tradesman was not regarded as impolite.

"I stay because of my box, sir," the spurrier said.

He kept his tips in a money box.

"Your box?" Pennyboy Junior said. "Why, there's an angel."

An angel was a coin worth ten shillings; Pennyboy Junior was a generous tipper.

Pennyboy Junior then said, "If my spurs are not true Ripon —"

Ripon was a town that had the reputation of making very good rowels — pointed spur-wheels.

The spurrier interrupted, "— never give me a penny if I don't strike through your bounty with the rowels."

Ripon rowels were reputed to be so good that they could pierce a coin such as an angel.

The spurrier exited.

Pennyboy Junior asked the Canter, who was wearing a patched cloak, "Do you want any money, founder?"

"Who, sir, I?" the Canter said. "Didn't I tell you I was bred in the mines, under Sir Bevis Bullion?"

These were gold and silver mines.

"That is true," Pennyboy Junior said. "You did tell me, but I quite forgot. You mine-men lack no money; your streets are paved with it. There the molten silver runs out like cream on cakes of gold."

"And rubies grow like strawberries," the Canter said.

"It would be splendid being there!" Pennyboy Junior said.

He then said to Thomas Barber, "Come, Tom, we'll go to the office now."

"What office?" the Canter asked.

"The News Office, the New Staple," Pennyboy Junior said. "You shall go, too. It is here in the house, on the same floor, Tom says."

Actually, Thomas Barber had said it was "almost on the same floor."

Pennyboy Junior continued, "Come, founder, let us indulge in ale and nutmegs."

In this society, ale was sometimes flavored with nutmegs.

The register and Nathaniel, a clerk, were in the Staple of News Office, which was located in the same building in which Pennyboy Junior lodged. A country woman entered the room through another door and stood there.

The register asked Nathaniel the clerk, "Are those desks fit now? Set forth the table, the carpet, and the chair. Where are the news that were examined last? Have you filed them up?"

"Not yet," Nathaniel the clerk said. "I had no time."

The register then asked, "Are those news registered that Emissary Buzz sent in last night? The news of Spinola and his eggs?"

Marquis Ambrosio Spinola was the commander of the Spanish forces in the Netherlands. The eggs were weapons: incendiary egg-grenades.

"Yes, sir, and they are filed," Nathaniel the clerk said.

"What are you working on now?" the register asked.

"The news that our new Emissary Westminster gave us about the Golden Heir," Nathaniel the clerk answered.

The Golden Heir was Pennyboy Junior, who was now a rich young man.

"Dispatch that speedily!" the register said. "That's news indeed, and of importance."

The country woman approached them.

"What would you have, good woman?" the register asked.

'I would have, sir, a groatsworth of any news, I don't care what, to carry down into the country this Saturday to our vicar," the country woman said.

A groat was worth four pence.

"Oh, you are a butter-woman," the register said. "Ask Nathaniel the clerk, who is standing there."

A butter-woman sells butter, but Nathaniel Butter was one of the first news-publishing figures in London.

Nathaniel the clerk said, "Sir, I tell her that she must wait until Emissary Exchange or Emissary St. Paul's send their news in, and then I'll fix her up with what she wants."

"Good woman, have patience," the register said. "It is not now as when the captain lived."

The country woman exited.

The captain was a reference to Thomas Gainsford, who had assisted Nathaniel Butter. Both the register and Nathaniel the clerk wanted to publish reputable news and not just produce "news" to make a buck.

Nathaniel the clerk said, "You'll blast the reputation of the office now, in the bud, if you dispatch these groats so soon."

In other words: If you send out fake news, quickly you will ruin the reputation of the Staple of News Office, almost before the News Office has started its work.

Nathaniel the clerk continued, "Let the customers wait, in the name of policy — it's a good idea to keep them waiting until we have real news to give them."

— 1.5 —

Cymbal and Fitton ushered Pennyboy Junior into the room. Following them were Thomas Barber and the Canter, both of whom stood to the side.

"Truly, they are pleasant rooms," Pennyboy Junior said. "What place is this?"

"This is the outer room, where my clerks sit and keep their sides," Cymbal said. "That is, they look after their own sections. The register is in the midst; the examiner sits in a private office there, within; and here I have my various rolls and files of news by the alphabet, and all put up under their heads."

One function of the Staple of News Office was to examine news and determine its worth and believability.

"But are those various rolls and files of news, too, subdivided?" Pennyboy Junior asked.

"Into authentical and apocryphal," Cymbal replied.

Fitton added, "Or news of doubtful believability, such as barbers' news."

Cymbal and Fitton often interrupted each other and finished each other's sentences.

"And tailors' news, porters' news, and watermen's news," Cymbal added.

Watermen are people who work on the river and do such things as row customers from one side of the Thames to the other.

Fitton said, "Whereto, beside the *coranti* and *gazetti* —"

The *coranti* and *gazetti* are sheets of news.

Cymbal interrupted, "— I have the news of the season."

Fitton added, "Such as vacation-news, term-news, and Christmas-news."

These were news at various times in London, such as when the Inns of Court were in session (term-news).

"And news of the faction," Cymbal added.

Factions can be of various kinds, including religious.

Fitton explained, "Such as the Reformed news, Protestant news —"

Reformed equals Calvinist, Protestant equals Lutheran, and Pontifical equals Catholic.

Cymbal interrupted, "— and Pontificial news. For each of these, the day-books, characters and ciphers, and precedents (from which copies are made) are kept, together with the names of special friends —"

Day-books were records of the day's events.

Fitton interrupted, "— and men of correspondence in the country —"

Cymbal interrupted, "— yes, of all ranks and all religions —"

Fitton interrupted, "— representatives and factors —"

"Factors" are agents.

Cypher interrupted, "— liegers who lie throughout all the shires of the kingdom."

"Liegers" are resident agents. "Lie" can mean 1) reside, or 2) tell falsehoods.

"This is fine and bears a brave relation!" Pennyboy Junior said. "It is worth hearing! But what says Mercurius Britannicus to this?"

Some of Butter's newsbooks of the time contained the phrase "printed for *Mercurius Britannicus.*"

The Latin name means the *British Mercury*. Mercury was a Roman god who was the messenger of the gods, and so a "mercury" is a person who brings news.

Cymbal and Fitton began to talk about and criticize the news endeavors of *Mercurius Britannicus* and other pioneers of the conveying of news.

Cymbal said, "Oh, sir, he gains by it half in half."

In other words, his profits have greatly improved.

"Nay, more," Fitton said. "I'll vouch for it. For where he was accustomed to get in hungry captains, obscure statesmen —"

Cymbal interrupted, "— fellows to drink with him in a dark room in a tavern, and eat a sausage —"

Fitton interrupted, "— we have seen it —"

Cymbal interrupted, "— as obliged to keep so many politic and crafty pens going, to feed the press —"

To get news that would make a profit, rival news publishers used such "sources" as hungry military captains and obscure statesmen. Such sources would tell a tale — often a false tale — to get a meal and a pint.

Fitton interrupted, "— and dish out 'news,' whether true, or false —"

Cymbal interrupted, "— now all that charge is saved the public chronicler —"

The Staple of News Office would use reliable sources and dispense with the cost of paying bad sources.

Fitton interrupted, "— how do you call him there? —"

A man named Edmund Howes was a then-contemporary public chronicler who continued the historian John Stow's *Annals of England* — a series of chronicles of England — after Stow died.

Cymbal interrupted and continued his sentence, "— and gentle reader —"

The newsbooks of the time used this phrase in their prefaces.

Fitton interrupted, "— he who has the maidenhead of all the books."

Cymbal added, "Yes, dedicated to him —"

Fitton interrupted, "— or rather prostituted —"

News purveyors can pander to their readers. Pandering is literally sexual in nature, but Cymbal and Fitton were referring to a metaphorical pandering.

"You are right, sir," Pennyboy Junior said.

Cymbal said, "The gentle readers no more shall be abused.

"Nor shall country parsons of the Inquisition and busy justices trouble the peace, and both torment themselves and their poor ignorant neighbors with inquiries after the many and most innocent monsters that never came in the counties they were charged with."

Sometimes rumors of monsters in the rural areas circulated and were written about in the news-sheets.

"Why, I think, sir," Pennyboy Junior said, "if the honest common people will willfully be hoodwinked, why shouldn't they have their pleasure in believing the lies that are made for them, just as you yourselves in the Staple of News Office take pleasure in making up the lies?"

If people wish to believe made-up stories about Bigfoot and alien abductions, why interfere with that?

"Oh, sir, it is the printing of such made-up stories that we oppose!" Fitton said.

One purpose of the Staple of News Office was to print only real news.

"We do not forbid that any news be made up, but we do forbid that it be printed," Cymbal said, "for when news is printed, it ceases, sir, to be news."

Cymbal seemed to be saying that old news is no news. Once new news is printed, it becomes old news. New news must take its place.

Cymbal continued, "While the news is but written and not printed —"

Fitton interrupted, "— though it be never so false, it runs news still."

News that is not printed but continues to be spread through gossip will remain current although it is false. The same tales about Bigfoot and alien abductions will continue to spread.

"See diverse men's opinions!" Pennyboy Junior said. "To some people the very printing of tales makes them news. Some people don't have the heart to believe anything but what they see in print."

Fitton said, "Aye, that's an error that has abused many; but we shall reform it, as we hope to reform many things besides that have crept among the popular abuses."

It is an error to believe everything you read, and Fitton and Cymbal wanted to reform people so that they would not make that error.

Hmm. One way to reform people so that they would not believe everything they read would be to print news that was unbelievable.

If Fitton and Cymbal were to print news that was completely reliable and believable, they would be training people to believe everything they read.

Cymbal said, "Nor shall the publisher and bookseller cheat upon the time, by uttering over again —"

Fitton interrupted, "— in seven years, as the age dotes —"

Cymbal interrupted, "— and grows forgetful of them, his antiquated pamphlets, with new dates."

Old pamphlets of sensational news stories about such topics as marauding headless bears were sometimes slightly altered and reissued years later as new news.

Cymbal continued, "But all shall come from the mint —"

Fitton interrupted, "Fresh and new stamped —"

Cymbal interrupted, "— with the office seal: Staple Commodity."

Fitton said, "And if a man wants to feel certain of his news, he may. For twopence a sheet he shall be warranted, and have a policy — a written guarantee — for it."

The Staple of News Office would guarantee the certainty and reliability of its news.

"Sir, I admire the method of your place," Pennyboy Junior said. "All things within it are so digested, fitted, and composed that it shows that here Wit has married Order."

Fitton said, "Sir —"

Cymbal interrupted, "— we did the best we could to invite the times and attract contemporary taste."

Fitton said, "It has cost sweat and freezing —"

Cymbal interrupted, "— and some broken sleeps before it came to this."

They had put in much thought and effort before starting their Staple of News Office.

"I easily think it," Pennyboy Junior said.

Fitton said, "But now it has the shape —"

Cymbal interrupted, "— and has come forth."

"It is a most polite — fine — neat thing!" Pennyboy Junior said. "It has all the limbs that sense can taste!"

The Staple of News Office had all the parts that the mind can savor.

Cymbal said, "It is, sir, although I myself am saying it, as well-begotten a business, and as fairly helped into the world."

"You must be a midwife, sir!" Pennyboy Junior said. "Or else the son of a midwife, please pardon me, to have helped it forth so fortunately!

"What news do you have? News of this morning? I would like to hear some fresh from the forge, as new as day, as they say."

"And such we have, sir," Cymbal said.

The register said, "Show him the last roll of Emissary Westminster's: 'The Heir.'"

"Come nearer, Tom," Pennyboy Junior said.

Thomas Barber, who had been standing to the side with the Canter, came forward.

Nathaniel the clerk read the news roll out loud:

"*There is a brave, young heir who has come of age this morning: Master Pennyboy.*"

Pennyboy Junior, pleased that he had made the news, said, "That's I!"

Nathaniel the clerk continued reading out loud:

"*His father died on this day seven nights ago.*"

"True!" Pennyboy Junior said.

Nathaniel the clerk continued reading out loud:

"*At six of the clock in the morning, just a week before Pennyboy Junior was one-and-twenty.*"

"I am here in the news roll, Tom!" Pennyboy Junior said.

He then said to Nathaniel the clerk, "Proceed, please."

Nathaniel the clerk continued reading out loud:

"*An old canting beggar first brought him the news. Pennyboy Junior has employed the beggar to follow him since.*"

"Why, you shall see him!" Pennyboy Junior said.

He called to the Canter, "Founder, come here!"

The Canter stepped forward.

Pennyboy Junior said, "He is no follower; instead, he is my companion."

He then said to Cymbal, "Please put my companion in the news roll, friend."

He then said to Nathaniel the clerk, "There's an angel."

Pennyboy Junior gave an angel — a coin — to Nathaniel the clerk.

He said to Cymbal, "You do not know he's a wise old fellow, although he seems patched thus and made up of pieces."

The Canter's clothing was patched.

Pennyboy Junior said to the Canter, "Founder, we are in, here, in the Staple of News Office!"

Nathaniel the clerk exited.

Pennyboy Junior continued, "We are in this day's news roll, already!"

He then said to Cymbal and Fitton, "I wonder how you came by this information about us, sirs."

Cymbal explained, "A Master Picklock, a lawyer, who has purchased here a place, this morning, of an emissary under me —"

Fitton interrupted, "— Emissary Westminster —"

Cymbal continued, "— gave the news to the Staple of News Office —"

Fitton interrupted, "— for his essay, his masterpiece."

The lawyer had demonstrated his ability to get news by giving the Staple of News Office the news about Pennyboy Junior.

To become a master, apprentices had to demonstrate their mastery of the skill they were studying by creating a master piece of work, aka masterpiece. "Essay" is another word for "masterpiece."

"My man of law!" Pennyboy Junior said. "He's my attorney, and my solicitor, too."

Attorneys do legal work requiring appearances in court, while solicitors do legal work that does not require appearances in court.

He continued, "He's a fine pragmatic man of business! What's his place worth?"

Cymbal said, "A *nemo-scit*, sir."

Nemo scit means "Nobody knows." The job holder would be paid according to the news brought in and printed.

Fitton said, "It depends on the news that come in —"

Cymbal interrupted, "— and as they are issued. I have the just moiety — exactly half — for my part; then the other moiety is parted into seven shares. The four emissaries — whereof my cousin Fitton here's for Emissary Court, Ambler for Emissary St. Paul's, and Buzz for the Emissary Exchange, Picklock for Emissary Westminster, with the examiner and register — they have full parts, and then one part is underparted — subdivided — to a couple of clerks. And there's the just and exact division of the profits!"

"Have you hired those clerks, sir?" Pennyboy Junior asked.

One of the two clerk positions had been filled; Nathaniel had it.

"There is one desk empty, but it has many suitors," Cymbal said.

"Sir, may I present one more suitor for the position and carry — win — it, if his qualities, or gifts, whatever you will call them —"

If Pennyboy Junior were to carry — win — the position of clerk for Thomas Barber, he would carry — bear — the cost.

Cymbal finished the sentence: "— be sufficient, sir."

"What are your present clerk's abilities?" Pennyboy Junior asked. "How is he qualified?"

The present clerk was Nathaniel.

"He was a decayed stationer," Cymbal replied, "but he knows news well and can sort and rank them."

A decayed stationer is a bankrupt publisher or book seller.

Fitton added, "And he can make news when necessary."

Cymbal said, "He's true St. Paul's bred, in the churchyard."

Many booksellers' and publishers' shops could be found at the courtyard of St. Paul's. On the west door of St. Paul's, people posted advertisements for employment.

Pennyboy Junior said, "And this one is true bred at the west door, on the other side. He's my barber, Tom, an apt scholar, and a Master of Arts — he was made, or went out, Master of Arts in a throng at the university, as before, one Christmas, he got into a masque at court by his wit, and the good means of his cittern, holding it up like this" — he pantomimed strumming a cittern — "as he pretended to be one of the musicians."

Barbers often had citterns in the shops for customers to play.

In 1615, King James I of England paid a visit to Cambridge University, which conferred Master of Arts degrees on his entire retinue. Some people, including apothecaries and barbers, got degrees because they crowded in among the members of the entourage when they received degrees.

A cittern is a stringed instrument that is an early forerunner of a guitar.

Pennyboy Junior continued, "Tom's a nimble fellow, and alike skilled in every liberal science, as having certain snaps of all."

Barbers snapped their fingers while plying their trade. The word "snaps" also meant oddments or scraps: Tom Barber knew a little about a lot.

Pennyboy Junior continued, "He has a neat, quick vein in forging news, too."

"Forging" can mean 1) creating, making, or gathering, or 2) counterfeiting.

Pennyboy Junior continued:

"I do love him, and I promised him a good turn, and that I would do it.

"What's your price? What's the value?"

"Fifty pounds, sir," Cymbal said.

Thomas Barber had earlier stated that exact sum: He was a news gatherer, in fact.

Pennyboy Junior said to Thomas Barber, "Get in, Tom; take possession; I install you."

He paid Cymbal the fifty pounds so that Tom could become the second clerk in the Staple of News Office.

Pennyboy Junior said to Cymbal, "Here, count your money."

He then said to Thomas Barber, "May God give you joy, good Tom, and let me hear from you every minute of news while the New Staple stands or the News Office lasts, which I wish may never be less for your sake."

Nathaniel the clerk returned and said to Cymbal, "The Emissaries, sir, want to speak with you and Master Fitton; they have brought in news, three bales altogether."

A bale is a big bundle.

Cymbal said to Pennyboy Junior, "Sir, you are welcome here."

"So is your creature," Fitton said.

The word "creature" meant "creation." Pennyboy Junior had created Tom the Barber's new prosperity by buying for him his position as clerk of the Staple of News Office.

Cymbal and Fitton now said their goodbyes.

"Business calls us off, sir, business that may concern the News Office," Cymbal said to Pennyboy Junior.

"Keep me in your good graces, sir, always in your Staple of News Office," Pennyboy Junior said. "I am here your friend, and I am on the same floor."

"We shall be your servants," Fitton said.

Everyone exited except Pennyboy Junior and the Canter.

"How do you like it, founder?" Pennyboy Junior asked.

"All is well," the Canter said, "except that your man of law, I think, isn't appearing at the time appointed for him to come."

He heard a noise, looked up, saw the man of law approaching, and said, "Oh, here comes Master's Worship."

Picklock entered the room and asked, "How is the heir, bright Master Pennyboy? Is he awake yet in his one-and-twenty?"

Seeing Pennyboy Junior's new clothes, he said, "Why, this is far better than to wear cypress, dull smutting gloves, or melancholy blacks, and have a pair of twelvepenny broad ribbons laid out like labels."

Cypress was a gauzy fabric that was used in mourning veils and other mourning garments after being dyed black. "Smutting" meant "black." "Labels" were strips of cloth that hung from the sides of a bishop's mitre.

Pennyboy Junior's outfit was much different from the clothing that he would have worn at a funeral.

Pennyboy Junior said, "I should have managed to have laughed as heartily in my mourner's hood as in this suit of clothing, if it had pleased my father to have been buried with the trumpeters."

"The heralds of arms, you mean," Picklock said.

Pennyboy Junior said, "I mean, all noise that is superfluous!"

Burial with trumpeters in attendance was expensive, and burial by heralds was very expensive. Fortunately for Pennyboy Junior, his father was frugal and against such expense.

"All that idle pomp and vanity of a tombstone your wise father did, by his will, prevent," Picklock said. "Your Worship had —"

Pennyboy Junior finished the sentence: "— a loving and obedient father of him, I know it: He was a right, kind-natured man, to die so opportunely."

Children should be obedient, more so than fathers.

Did Pennyboy Junior mean that he wanted his father to die, or did he just mean that his father had arranged things so that his death would cause him as little trouble as possible?

"Opportune" can mean 1) convenient, 2) fitting, or 3) advantageous.

Picklock added, "And to settle all things so well, compounded for your wardship the week before, and left your estate entire without any charge upon it."

Pennyboy Junior's father had made sure that Pennyboy Junior would be able to inherit his entire estate without becoming a ward whose estate was managed by someone else. The word "compounded" meant both "arranged" and "made a payment." Pennyboy Junior's father had apparently paid any necessary legal fees before he died.

Pennyboy Junior said, "I must say that I lost an officer of him, a good bailiff, and I shall miss him."

Pennyboy Junior's father had been a good administrator of the estate. A bailiff is a steward or manager of an estate.

He added, "But all peace be with him. I will not wish him alive again, not I, for all my fortune."

He planned to enjoy his new wealth.

Pennyboy Junior continued, "May God give Your Worship joy of your new place, your emissaryship, in the Staple of News Office!"

Picklock was Emissary Westminister. The Courts of Law were held at Westminster Hall.

"Do you know you why I bought it, sir?" Picklock asked.

"No, I don't," Pennyboy Junior said.

"To work for you, and carry a mine — carry out a stratagem — against the master of it, Master Cymbal, who has a plot upon a gentlewoman who was once designated for you, sir," Picklock said.

"For me?" Pennyboy Junior asked.

"Your father, old Master Pennyboy, of happy memory, and wisdom, too, as any in the county, being careful to find a fit marriage match for you in his own lifetime (but he was prevented from doing so), left it in writing in a codicil — an addition — here to be annexed to his will" — he showed the document — "that you, his only son, upon his charge, and blessing, should take due notice of a gentlewoman, sojourning with your uncle, Richer Pennyboy."

Pennyboy Junior's father wanted his son, Pennyboy Junior, to marry well.

Pennyboy Junior's uncle, Richer Pennyboy, was also known as Pennyboy Senior, a miser.

"A Cornish gentlewoman," Pennyboy Junior said. "I know her: Mistress Pecunia Do-all."

A proverb states, "Money can do anything."

"Do-all" can mean "Have sex with all."

Picklock said, "A great lady indeed she is, and not of mortal race. She is Infanta of the Mines. Her Grace's grandfather was duke and cousin to the King of Ophir, the Subterranean, but let that pass."

In 1 Kings 2:28 King Solomon acquires gold from Ophir: "*And they came to Ophir, and fetched from thence gold, four hundred and twenty talents, and brought it to king Solomon*" (King James Version).

Much wealth is subterranean; it comes from mines.

Picklock continued, "Her name is, or, rather, her three names are (for such she is) Aurelia Clara Pecunia, a great princess, of mighty power, although she lives in private with a contracted family — a diminished entourage."

Aurelia Clara Pecunia means "Golden Bright Money."

In this society, the word "family" often meant one's household servants.

Picklock continued, "Her secretary —"

The Canter interrupted, "— who is her gentleman-usher, too —"

Picklock interrupted, "— his name is Broker."

He then listed the rest of Aurelia Clara Pecunia's entourage: "And then two gentlewomen, Mistress Statute and Mistress Band, with Wax, the chambermaid, and Mother Mortgage, the old nurse; two grooms — Pawn and his fellow."

Grooms are man-servants.

Picklock continued, "You have not many to bribe, sir."

Pennyboy Junior could bribe Aurelia Clara Pecunia's entourage in order to gain access to Aurelia Clara Pecunia.

Picklock continued, "The work is feasible, and the approaches easy, by your own kindred."

Because of his late father, and his wealth, Pennyboy Junior could easily find a way to approach Aurelia Clara Pecunia.

Picklock continued, "Now, sir, Cymbal — the master here and governor of the Staple of News Office — thinks by his fine arts and pomp of his great place to attract her. He concludes she is a woman, and that as soon as she hears of the Staple of News Office she'll come to visit it, as women all have longings to see new sights and shows. But your bounty, person, and finery must achieve her."

Pennyboy Junior and Cymbal would be rivals for Aurelia Clara Pecunia.

"She is the talk of the time!" the Canter said. "She is the adventure — and venture — of the age!"

She was a financial venture — whoever married her would marry her fortune, too.

"You cannot put yourself upon an action of more importance," Picklock said.

He felt that Pennyboy Junior could do nothing more important than marry a very rich woman.

"All the world are suitors to her," the Canter said.

"All sorts of men and all professions!" Picklock said.

"You shall have stall-fed doctors, crammed divines pay court to her, and with those studied and perfumed flatteries as no room can stink more elegantly than where they are," the Canter said.

Stall-fed doctors can mean 1) manger-fed or trough-fed (that is, overfed — think of pigs at a trough) doctors, or 2) doctors who have fed their minds with books from the book-stalls.

Divines — preachers — can be crammed with knowledge and/or with food.

"Well chanted, old Canter!" Picklock said. "You sing truly."

"And, by your leave," the Canter said, "good Master's Worship, some of your velvet coat — well-dressed lawyers — make corpulent curtsies to her until they crack for it."

They bowed so low that 1) their backs cracked, and/or 2) they farted.

"There's Doctor Almanac woos her, one of the jeerers, a fine physician," Picklock said.

The Canter said, "Your sea-captain, Shunfield, says that he'll attack head-on the cannon for her —"

Picklock interrupted, "— although his loud mouthing — hot air — gets him little credit."

The Canter said, "Young Master Piedmantle, the fine herald, professes to trace her heritage through all ages, from all the kings and queens who ever were."

Picklock added, "And Master Madrigal, the crowned poet of these our times, offers to her praises as fair as any, when it shall please Apollo, god of poetry, that wit and rhyme may meet both in one subject."

The Canter added, "And for you to bear her from all these, it will be —"

Picklock interrupted, "— a work of fame."

The Canter continued, "— a work of honor."

Picklock said, "It will be a celebration —"

The Canter interrupted, "— worthy your name."

Picklock said, "The Pennyboys to live in it."

The Pennyboys would live in fame.

The Canter said, "It is an action you were built for, sir."

Picklock said, "And none but you can do it."

"I'll undertake it," Pennyboy Junior said.

"And carry it," the Canter said.

"Don't worry about me," Pennyboy Junior said, "for since I came of mature age, I have had a certain itch in my right eye, this corner, here — do you see? — to do some work that is worthy of a chronicle."

Chronicles recorded noteworthy events. In this case, the noteworthy event would be the courting of a rich woman.

THE FIRST INTERMEAN: AFTER THE FIRST ACT

Gossip Mirth said to Gossip Censure, "How are you now, Gossip Censure! How does the play please you?"

"Very scurvily, I think, and sufficiently naught," Gossip Censure said.

"Naught" can mean 1) nothing, or 2) naughty, or evil.

Gossip Expectation said, "As naught as a body would wish. Here's nothing but a young prodigal come of age, who makes much of the barber, buys him a place in a new office — in the air, I know not where — and his man of law to follow him, with the beggar to boot, and those two help him to a wife."

Gossip Mirth said, "Aye, she is a proper piece that such creatures can broke for! With two such scoundrels acting as her agents, she must be quite the woman!"

"Piece" can mean 1) piece of money, aka a coin, 2) woman, or 3) piece of ass. Gossip Mirth does not think that Lady Pecunia is a respectable woman.

Gossip Tattle said, "I cannot abide that nasty fellow, the beggar. If he had been a court-beggar in good clothes, a beggar-in-velvet, as they say, I could have endured him."

The Canter was a beggar who wore patched clothing.

Many courtiers wear velvet and beg for favors from the King.

Gossip Mirth said, "Or a begging scholar in black, or one of these beggarly poets, Gossip Tattle, who would hang upon a young heir like a horse-leech."

Many kinds of beggars and parasites — hangers-on — exist in the world.

Gossip Expectation said, "Or a threadbare doctor of medicine, a poor quacksalver."

A quacksalver is a quack.

"Or a sea-captain, half-starved," Gossip Censure said.

Some ships were shipwrecked or lost their cargo or profit in some way.

"Aye, these were tolerable beggars, beggars of fashion!" Gossip Mirth said. "You shall see some such soon."

They began to talk about what they would like to see in the play.

Gossip Tattle said, "I would like to see the fool, Gossip Mirth; the fool is the finest man in the company, they say, and he has all the wit. He is the very

Justice of the Peace of the play, and he can commit whom he will, and he can commit what he will, such as error and absurdity, as the whim takes him, and no man will say black is his eye, but they will laugh at him."

"No man will say black is his eye" meant "No man will impugn his character."

Gossip Mirth said, "But they have no fool in this play, I am afraid, Gossip Tattle."

"It's a wise play, then," Gossip Tattle said.

"They are all fools the rather, in that," Gossip Expectation said.

"That is likely enough," Gossip Censure said.

Gossip Tattle said:

"My husband, Timothy Tattle (God rest his poor soul), was accustomed to say there was no play without a fool and a devil in it; he was for the devil always, God bless him.

"The devil for his money, he would say: 'I would like to see the devil.'

"'And why would you so like see the devil?' I would say.

"'Because he has horns, wife, and may be a cuckold, as well as a devil,' he would answer.

"'You are even such another, husband,' I would say. 'Was the devil ever married? Where do you read that the devil was ever so honorable to commit matrimony?'

"'The play will tell us that,' he would say. 'We'll go see it tomorrow: *The Devil Is an Ass*. He is an errant learnéd man who made it and can write, they say, and I am foully deceived unless he can read, too.'"

Ben Jonson, the poet-playwright of *The Devil is an Ass*, which featured fools and devils, was an errant — erring — learnéd man, who could read as well as write. He killed a fellow actor in a duel, and he escaped the likely punishment of being executed by pleading benefit of clergy: He proved that he could read Latin, something that the clergy were able to do. The Vulgate Bible is written in Latin.

Gossip Mirth said, "I remember *The Devil is an Ass*, Gossip Tattle; I went with you. By the same token, Mistress Trouble-Truth discouraged us from going, and told us he — Ben Jonson — was a profane poet, and all his plays had devils in them; that he kept school upon the stage, could conjure there above the school of Westminster, and the astrologer Doctor Lamb, too. Not a play he made but had a devil in it; and that he would teach us all to make our husbands cuckolds at plays; by another token, that a young married wife in the company said she could find in her heart to steal thither and see a little of the vanity through her mask, and come practice at home."

One criticism of plays of the time is that by having immoral characters in them, they taught the audience to practice immorality.

Gossip Tattle said, "Oh, it was Mistress —"

Gossip Mirth interrupted, "Nay, Gossip Tattle, I name nobody. It may be it was myself."

Gossip Expectation asked, "But was the devil a proper man, Gossip Mirth?"

"As fine a gentleman of his inches as ever I saw trusted to the stage, or anywhere else, and he loved the commonwealth as well as ever a patriot of them all," Gossip Mirth answered.

"A gentleman of his inches" meant "a gentleman from head to toe." But perhaps Gossip Mirth was referring to the inches of the devil's penis.

Some members of Parliament who were critics of the Crown were called patriots.

She continued, "He would carry away the Vice on his back, quick to Hell, in every play where he came, and reform abuses."

Some old-fashioned plays had a riotous character called the Vice, which the Devil carried off to Hell in a noisy, action-packed scene at the end of the play.

Gossip Expectation said, "There was *The Devil of Edmonton*, no such man, I warrant you."

Gossip Censure said, "The conjurer cozened him with a candle's end. He — the Devil — was an ass."

The Merry Devil of Edmonton was a very popular play (and folktale) in which the conjuror Peter Fabel makes a deal with the Devil. In one version of the tale, in return for granting Fabel certain privileges, the Devil will get his soul when a certain candle burns out. Fabel puts the candle in his pocket so he can keep it safe. The version of the play that has come down to us does not have that incident, but it does contain a comic character named Smug.

Gossip Mirth said, "But there was one Smug, a blacksmith, who would have made a horse laugh and break his halter, as they say."

"Oh, but the poor man had an unfortunate mischance one day," Gossip Tattle said.

Gossip Expectation asked, "How, Gossip Tattle?"

Gossip Tattle said, "Smug the Blacksmith had dressed a rogue jade in the morning that had the staggers, and Smug had got such a dose of the staggers himself by noon that they would not go away but continued all the playtime, do what he could, for his heart."

A jade is a bad horse. The jade described has the disease called the staggers, which made the horse stagger. Dressing a horse means to curry and groom it.

Smug enjoyed drinking to excess. This gave him a case of a different kind of staggers, which made him stagger throughout the play.

A dose is a medicinal drink; many people consider alcohol to be a medicinal drink.

Gossip Mirth said, "It was his part, Gossip Tattle; he was to be drunk, by his part."

"Do you say so?" Gossip Tattle said. "I didn't understand it that way."

Apparently, she thought the comic actor playing Smug had really gotten drunk.

Gossip Expectation said, "I wish we had such another part and such a man in this play! I fear that this play will be an excellent dull thing."

Seeing the actors come back on stage, Gossip Censure said, "Wait. Pay attention to the play."

CHAPTER 2

— 2.1 —

Pennyboy Senior was Pennyboy Junior's uncle, and he was a miser and a usurer. He talked now outside his house with Aurelia Clara Pecunia, Mortgage (Pecunia's nurse), Statute (Pecunia's first serving-woman), Band (Pecunia's second serving-woman), and Broker (Pecunia's secretary and gentleman-usher). They were outside breathing the fresh air.

Pennyboy Senior was an old miser who loved Lady Pecunia and wished to be her minion — her favorite, her lover. Lady Pecunia, however, to her credit, did not wish to romantically enslave such old men.

Pennyboy Senior said to Lady Pecunia, "Your Grace is sad, I think, and melancholy. You do not look upon me with that face as you were accustomed to, my goddess, bright Pecunia.

"Although Your Grace has fallen by two in the hundred in vulgar estimation, yet I am Your Grace's servant still, and I teach this body of mine to bend, and these my aged knees to buckle in adoration and just worship of you."

The Latin word *pecunia* means money. The face of *pecunia* is a coin, and gold is a bright color that does not tarnish. To be "fallen of two in the hundred" refers to a then-recent law against usury that lowered the legally allowed interest rate from ten percent to eight percent.

Pennyboy Senior continued, "Indeed, I confess, I have no shape to make a minion of — that is, I'm not handsome enough to be a lover — but I'm your martyr, Your Grace's martyr.

"I can hear the rogues, as I walk the streets, whisper and point: 'There goes old Pennyboy, the slave of money, rich Pennyboy, Lady Pecunia's drudge, a sordid rascal, one who never made a good meal in his sleep, but sells the delicacies that are sent to him — fish, fowl, and venison — and preserves himself, like an old hoary rat, with moldy pie-crust.'"

A proverb stated, "Beggars and misers may feast in their dreams." Another proverb stated, "Golden dreams make men wake hungry." Pennyboy Senior, however, is so much a miser that he does not feast even in his dreams.

Pennyboy Senior continued, "This I do hear, rejoicing I can suffer this and much more for your good Grace's sake."

"Why do you so, my guardian?" Lady Pecunia said. "I don't bid you to do that. Cannot my grace and favor be gotten, and held, too, without your self-tormentings and your staying up at night, your wasting of your body thus with cares and scantings of your diet and rest?"

Lady Pecunia much preferred that Pennyboy Senior not dote on her and instead enjoy his life.

Misers prefer to have money rather than the good things of life. They will eat inexpensive, not-so-good food rather than spend money to buy much better food.

Pennyboy Senior replied, "Oh, no, your services, my princely lady, cannot with too much zeal of rites be done because they are so sacred."

"But my reputation may suffer, and the respect of my family, when by so servile means they both are sought," Lady Pecunia said.

Money can be a good thing when used correctly. One should avoid the extremes of being a miser like Pennyboy Senior and a prodigal like Pennyboy Junior. An excessive love of money — either for the money itself or for the things that money can buy — gives the love of money a bad reputation.

1 Timothy 6:10 states, *"For the love of money is the root of all evil: which while some coveted after, they have erred from the faith, and pierced themselves through with many sorrows"* (King James Version).

Pennyboy Senior said, "You are a noble, young, generous, gracious lady, and you would be bountiful to everybody, but you must not be so. Only a few know your merit, lady, and can value it.

"You yourself scarcely understand your proper, inherent powers. They are almighty, and we your servants, who have the honor here to stand so near you, know them and can use and exploit them, too."

One way to use and exploit money is usury: to lend it out at an excessive rate of interest.

Pennyboy Senior continued, "All this nether world — world beneath the heavens — is yours. You command it and sway it. You command the honor of it and the honesty, the reputation, aye, and the religion (I was about to say, and I would not have erred) is Queen Pecunia's — for that title is yours, if mortals knew Your Grace, or their own good."

Money does have its gifts. Horace, in his *Epistles*, wrote, "Of course a wife and dowry, credit and friends, birth and beauty, are the gift of Queen Cash." Horace, in his *Satires*, wrote, "Indeed, all things, divine and human, serve the beauty of riches — virtue, reputation, honor; and he who hoards it up will be famous, strong, and just."

Pennyboy Senior also thought that Pecunia and *pecunia* — money — could be adored like the god of a religion. The verb "worship" means adore.

Some people trust in God. Other people trust in money.

Mortgage, who was Lady Pecunia's nurse, and Band, who was one of Lady Pecunia's serving-women, attempted to get her to retire inside.

"May it please Your Grace to retire," Mortgage said.

"I fear Your Grace has taken too much of the sharp air," Band said.

"Oh, no!" Lady Pecunia said. "With my constitution I could endure to take a great deal more, if it were left up to me.

"What do you think about it, Statute?"

Statute, another of Lady Pecunia's serving-women, replied, "A little air now and then does you well, and keeps Your Grace in your good health."

Band added, "And true temper."

Mortgage objected, "But too much, madam, may increase cold rheums, nourish catarrhs, green-sicknesses, and agues, and put you in consumption."

"Cold rheums" are runny noses. "Rheums" are discharges, and catarrhs are buildups of mucus. Green-sickness is anemia, and agues are fevers. "Consumption" is wasting away.

Mortgage was saying that Lady Pecunia might catch a cold.

Pennyboy Senior advised, "It's best to take the advice of your honorable women, noble madam. They know the state of your body, and have studied Your Grace's health —"

Band interrupted, "— and honor. Here will be visitants or suitors by and by; and it is not fitting that they find you here."

"It will make Your Grace too cheap to give them audience immediately," Statute said.

News is a commodity that can make a profit, and Lady Pecunia was being treated by the people around her as a commodity that could make a profit.

"Leave your secretary here to answer them," Mortgage the nurse said.

"Wait here, Broker," Lady Pecunia said to Broker, her secretary.

"I shall stay here, madam, and do Your Grace's trusts with diligence," Broker said.

Everyone except Broker exited.

Piedmantle the herald, who wanted to be a suitor to Lady Pecunia, entered the scene.

"What luck's this?" he said. "I have come an inch too late."

He had caught a glimpse of Lady Pecunia exiting.

Piedmantle then asked Broker, "Do you hear me, sir? Is Your Worship of the family unto the Lady Pecunia?"

Her "family" consisted of her household servants.

"Sir, I serve Her Grace, Aurelia Clara Pecunia, the Infanta," Broker said.

An Infanta is a daughter of the King of Spain or Portugal, although the term came to be used to mean "great lady."

"Has she all those titles, and 'Her Grace' besides?" Piedmantle the herald said. "I must correct that ignorance and oversight before I present myself and my research."

As a herald, he did genealogical research, and he had researched Pecunia's ancestry.

He continued, "Sir, I have drawn a pedigree for Her Grace, although I am yet a novice in that so noble study."

"Are you a herald at arms?" Broker asked.

"No, sir, I am a pursuivant. My name is Piedmantle."

"Good Master Piedmantle!" Broker said, perhaps pretending to recognize the name.

Piedmantle said, "I have traced her lineage —"

Broker interrupted, "— from all the Spanish mines in the West Indies, I hope, for she comes that way by her mother, but by her grandmother she's Duchess of Mines."

"From man's creation I have brought her," Piedmantle said.

He had traced Lady Pecunia's ancestry back to Adam and Eve, he claimed.

"No further?" Broker said. "You must trace her heritage before, sir, long before Adam and Eve; otherwise, you have done nothing. Your Mines were before Adam."

Pecunia is money, and money comes from mines (in the sense of underground deposits of gold and silver), and mines existed before the creation of Adam, the first man.

Broker was mocking Piedmantle by pretending that Mines was a family name.

Broker continued, "Search your office. Search roll five-and-twenty, and you will find it so."

This kind of roll — roll number 25 — was a document at the College of Arms.

Broker continued, "I would have seen you are only a novice, Master Piedmantle, even if you had not told me so."

Pennyboy Senior entered the scene from behind the two men and concealed himself so that he could eavesdrop.

Piedmantle said, "Sir, I am an apprentice in armory — in the story of coats of arms."

Armory deals with blazoning — describing, depicting, painting — coats of arms. It is the science of heraldry.

Piedmantle continued, "I have read the *Elements* and *Accidence*, and all the leading books."

The books Piedmantle referred to were *The Elements of Armories* and *The Accidence of Armory*.

"Accidence" means fundamentals or first principles.

He continued, "And I have now upon me a great ambition to be brought to Her Grace to kiss her hands."

Piedmantle gave Broker a gold coin as a bribe, and Broker now began to give Piedmantle helpful information. Bribes to servants are useful in gaining access to a great lady.

Broker said, "Why, if you have acquaintance with Mistress Statute, or Mistress Band, my lady's gentlewomen, they can introduce you to Lady Pecunia.

"One, Mistress Statute, is a judge's daughter, but somewhat stately and haughty; the other, Mistress Band — her father's only a scrivener, a professional scribe — but she can exert influence almost as much with my lady as the other, especially if Rose Wax, the chambermaid, is willing.

"Do you not know her, sir, neither?"

He was referring to Rose Wax, the chambermaid.

"No, truly, sir," Piedmantle said.

Broker said, "She's a good pliant wench and easy to be manipulated, sir."

Softened wax could be easily manipulated. One way to soften a person is with a bribe.

He continued, "But the nurse, Old Mother Mortgage — if you have a tenement" — an apartment or a land holding — "or such a morsel? Although she has no teeth, she loves a sweetmeat, anything that melts in her warm gums. She could command it — access to Lady Pecunia — for you on such a trifle, a toy."

According to Broker, the entire group of household servants could be bribed, just like Broker had been.

Bribery had worked on him. Why shouldn't it work on the other servants of Lady Pecunia?

He continued, "Sir, you may see how for your love and this so pure complexion, a perfect sanguine, I have ventured thus the straining of a ward, opening a door into the secrets of our family."

"Complexion" meant tinge, and "sanguine" meant red. In this society, gold was said to be colored red. Broker was referring to the gold coin that Piedmantle had used to bribe him.

"The straining of a ward" meant especially "the stretching of a boundary." Broker should have been protecting Lady Pecunia.

A "ward" can be 1) a wardship, 2) a protectorate, 3) a fortification, or 4) a part of a lock.

Piedmantle said, "I ask you to let me know, sir — you to whom I am so much beholden — do but tell me your name."

"My name is Broker. I am secretary and usher to Her Grace."

"Good Master Broker!" Piedmantle said.

"Good Master Piedmantle," Broker said.

Piedmantle said, "Why, you could do me, if you would, now, this favor on your own initiative."

He had already bribed Broker. Why was it necessary to bribe anyone else? Why couldn't Broker introduce him to Lady Pecunia?

"Truly, I think I could," Broker said, "but if I would, I hardly should, unless either Mistress Band or Mistress Statute would lease to endorse it, or the good nurse I told you about, Mistress Mortgage.

"We know our places here. We don't mingle in another's sphere, but all of us move orderly in our own orbs; yet we are all concentrics."

They all had their own duties, and they all revolved around Lady Pecunia.

In order for Piedmantle to be introduced to Lady Pecunia, he would have to get by the servants who were supposed to protect her.

"Well, sir, I'll wait for a better season," Piedmantle said.

"Do, and study the right means — the right way to be introduced to her," Broker said. "Get Mistress Band to urge on your behalf, or little Wax."

Piedmantle turned to go, and Broker made a mocking face at him, but Piedmantle did not see it. Although Piedmantle had bribed him, Broker did not respect Piedmantle.

"I have a hope, sir, that I may, by chance, alight on Her Grace as she's taking the air," Piedmantle said.

As Piedmantle exited, Broker made another mocking face at him.

Broker said, "That air of hope has blighted many an eyrie of kestrels like yourself, good Master Piedmantle."

Broker was comparing Piedmantle's alighting on Pecunia as she took the air to a hawk alighting on its prey in the air. An eyrie, aka aerie, is the nest of a bird of prey. A kestrel literally is a small hawk, and figuratively it is a human fool.

Pennyboy Senior came out of his hiding place and said, "Well said, Master Secretary; I stood behind you two and heard everything you said. I honor your dispatches — I like the way you got rid of him.

"If they are rude, untrained in our method, and have not studied the rule, dismiss them quickly."

Piedmantle did not fit in with Broker and Pennyboy Senior. He gave money; he did not take it.

Pennyboy Senior did not mention the bribe Piedmantle had given to Broker; if he had noticed it, chances are he would have approved of Broker's taking the bribe *and* still getting rid of Piedmantle.

Pennyboy Senior then said, "Where's Lickfinger, my cook? That unctuous, greasy rascal — he never keeps his appointments in a timely manner, that vessel of kitchen stuff!"

The kitchen stuff was Lickfinger's big belly, which was stuffed with food from the kitchen.

56

Lickfinger the cook entered the room.

"Here he has come, sir," Broker said.

"Pox upon him and his kidney — he is always too late!" Pennyboy Senior said.

The word "kidney" meant character and temperament. Lickfinger's character was to be always late.

"Too late to wish that you had them, I confess, who have them already," Lickfinger said.

The pox was smallpox, which left pocks on the victims' faces.

"What?" Pennyboy Senior asked.

"The pox!" Lickfinger answered.

"May the piles, the plague, and all diseases light on him who doesn't know to keep his word," Pennyboy Senior said.

The piles are hemorrhoids.

He continued, "I'd keep my word for sure! I hate that man who will not keep his word. When did I break my word?"

"Or I, until now?" Lickfinger said. "And I am late only half an hour —"

"Half a year," Pennyboy Senior said, "to me who values a minute of time. I am a just man; I love always to be just."

A just man is an exact man; Pennyboy Senior loved always to be on time.

Lickfinger responded, "Why, do you think that I can run like light-foot Ralph, or keep a wheelbarrow with a sail in town here to whirl me to you? I have lost two stone of suet in the service hastening hither."

Light-foot Ralph was a fast runner.

A stone of weight is 14 pounds.

Suet was the greasy sweat dripping from Lickfinger's body as he "hurried" to see Pennyboy Senior.

Lickfinger continued, "You might have followed me like a watering pot and seen the knots I made along the street."

He sweat so much that he was like the spout of a watering pot, and as he "hurried," his dripping sweat made knots — intricate designs — in the dirt he walked on.

Lickfinger continued, "My face dropped grease like the skimmer in a fritter pan."

A skimmer is a slotted utensil used to raise fritters from a frying pan; grease drips from the skimmer.

As he wiped his face, Lickfinger continued, "And my whole body is yet, to say the truth, a roasted pound of butter with grated bread in it!"

He was referring to a kind of rich pastry.

Pennyboy Senior said, "Believe you, he who chooses."

This meant: I don't believe you.

He continued, "You delayed in order to have my venison stink and my fowl mortified, so that you might have them —"

A mortified fowl is one whose carcass is hung until it is tender. Hang it too long and it decays and is worth less money if it is sold, just as stinking venison brings in less money.

Mortified fowl, however, acquired a taste that some people prized and paid more for. It may be the case that Pennyboy Senior, who was not a glutton, cared nothing about taste and simply thought that Lickfinger was costing him money.

Lickfinger interrupted, "— a shilling or two cheaper. That's your suspicion."

Pennyboy Senior sold off gifts of food, and he wanted to receive a good price for them.

"Perhaps it is," Pennyboy Senior said.

He added, "Will you go in and view and value all? Yonder is venison sent to me, and fowl and fish, in such abundance I am sick to see it!

"I wonder what they mean — I have told them about it — to burden a weak stomach and provoke a dying appetite! To thrust a sin upon me I never was guilty of — nothing but gluttony, gross gluttony, that will ruin this land!"

Possibly, some of the people who owed him money were paying their debts with food. Or they were using food to pay for an extension of their loan.

Gluttony is one of the Seven Deadly Sins; it is a sin that Pennyboy Senior was not guilty of.

"And abating two in the hundred," Lickfinger said.

He was referring to the reduction in interest legally allowed to be charged. He knew that Pennyboy Senior believed that the reduction in legally allowed interest would ruin the land.

As a usurer, Pennyboy Senior was against reducing the interest rate. He believed or pretended to believe that lessening the profit of the usurer would make it harder for people — including poor people — to borrow money. Perhaps that is true. Lending to the poor can be risky. Moneylenders take risks to make more money, and they may be willing to risk money at ten percent interest that they would not be willing to risk at eight percent interest.

Pennyboy Senior sounded like a populist, but others could argue that usurious interest rates eat up the poor. Think of Payday Loans in the USA.

Pennyboy Senior said, "Aye, that same — abating two in the hundred — is a crying sin, a fearful damned device. It eats up the poor, devours them —"

Lickfinger said, "Sir, take heed what you give out."

Pennyboy Senior did take care what he lent out; he wanted to get his money back and his interest, too.

Lickfinger's words also meant, Don't be a hypocrite. You care more about money than you do about the poor."

Lickfinger's words also meant for Pennyboy Senior to be careful what he said out loud. The politicians who backed the reduction in interest rates would not like his words.

Pennyboy Senior said, "What words I give out against your grave, great Solons? *Numae Pompilii*, they who made that law to take away the poor's inheritance?"

Solon was an Athenian lawmaker. His name became a word meaning a wise ruler. Numa Pompilius succeeded Romulus as ruler of Rome. His name also became associated with wise rule. *Numae Pompilii* is the plural of Numa Pompilius. Of course, Pennyboy Senior's use of these names for the lawmakers who had reduced the legal interest rate of loans was sarcastic; he did not think that these lawmakers were wise.

Pennyboy Senior continued, "It was the poor's due, I will guarantee it, and the lawmakers have robbed them of it, plainly robbed them. I still am a just man; I tell the truth. When moneys went at ten in the hundred, I, and such as I, the servants of Pecunia, could spare the poor two out of ten, and did it."

This sounds as if he had been charging the poor eight percent interest all along.

If that were true, why is he complaining? Lessening the interest rate two percent from ten percent would have the same effect as charging what the lawmakers allowed — actually, it would be the same thing, at least as far as the poor were concerned.

Pennyboy Senior disliked the fact that charging eight percent interest was now compulsory; now he could get no credit for being charitable.

But also perhaps the ten-percent interest he charged non-poor people allowed him to charge the poor only eight-percent interest.

Pennyboy Senior then asked, "What do you say, Broker?"

Lickfinger said to himself, "Ask your echo."

He thought that Broker was a yes-man to Pennyboy Senior.

"You did it," Broker said.

"I am for justice," Pennyboy Senior said. "When did I leave justice? We knew it was theirs. The poor had right and title to it. Now —"

Lickfinger interrupted, "You can spare them nothing —"

Pennyboy Senior interrupted, "Very little —"

Lickfinger interrupted, "— as good as nothing."

"The legislators have bound our hands with their wise, solemn act," Pennyboy Senior said. "They have shortened our arms."

Short arms are unable to reach deep into pockets to take out money to give to the poor.

Lickfinger said, "Beware lest those worshipful ears, sir, be shortened, and you play Crop in the Fleet, if you use this license."

One punishment of the time was to crop — cut off part of — an offender's ears. Such a punishment could be carried out in Fleet Prison.

"What license have you, knave?" Pennyboy Senior asked. "Are you an informer?"

Some people, such as Fools, have license to mock other people. An informer could have such license: Either let me mock you, or I shall inform the authorities about what you said.

"I am Lickfinger, your cook."

"A saucy jack you are, that's for sure." Pennyboy Senior said.

The word "jack" means "knave." A Jack Sauce is a saucy knave. As a cook, Lickfinger dealt with sauces.

Pennyboy Senior asked, "What did I say wrong, Broker?"

"Nothing that I heard, sir," Broker said.

"I know his gift," Lickfinger said to himself. "He can be deaf when he wishes."

Pennyboy Senior asked Lickfinger, "Have you provided for me my bushel of eggs that I asked you for? I do not care how stale or stinking they are; let them be rotten because they are ammunition here to pelt the boys who break my windows."

Lickfinger said, "Yes, sir, I have spared them for you and not used them for the mayor's custard politic."

At the annual Lord Mayor's Feast in London, a jester would leap into a giant bowl of custard.

"It is well," Pennyboy Senior said. "Go in, take hence all that excess food. Make what you can of it, your best. And when I have friends whom I invite at home, provide me such, such, and such a dish as I ask for, one at a time, no superfluity. Or if you don't have it, return to me the money. You know my ways."

"They are a little crooked," Littlefinger said.

"What, knave?" Pennyboy Senior asked.

Lickfinger explained, "Because you do indent."

Some legal documents were cut into two parts with a crooked line. The two parts could be shown to be a genuine document because the jagged lines of the two parts would fit together. Lickfinger was saying that Pennyboy Senior's ways were crooked.

"It is true, sir," Pennyboy Senior said. "I do indent that you shall return me money —"

One meaning of "indent" is "specify by contract." People gave gifts of food to Pennyboy Senior, and Lickfinger sold them and gave the money to Pennyboy Senior.

Lickfinger interrupted, "— rather than food, I know it. You are just still."

Pennyboy Senior preferred money to the gifts of food.

"I love it — money — still," Pennyboy Senior said. "And therefore if you spend — serve and/or consume — the red-deer pies in your house, or sell them forth, sir, arrange it so that I may have their coffins — the crusts of the pies — all returned here and piled up. I would be thought to keep some kind of house."

He wanted to keep track of household expenses.

"By the moldy signs?" Lickfinger asked.

"Mold" can be 1) a pie-crust, or 2) the earth of a grave.

"Moldy" can mean rotten.

Pennyboy Senior said, "And then remember, meat for my two dogs: fat flaps of mutton, kidneys, rumps of veal, good plenteous scraps. My maid shall eat the leftovers —"

"When you and your dogs have dined!" Lickfinger said. "A sweet remnant."

Pennyboy Senior's dogs ate well — better than the maid, and possibly better than Pennyboy Senior.

Seeing some people coming, Pennyboy Senior said, "Who's here? My courtier and my little doctor, my muster-master — and what plover's that whom they have brought to pluck and cheat?"

The courtier was Fitton. The little doctor was Almanac. The muster-master was Shunfield, who was a sea captain and as such kept a muster-list of sailors. The unknown person — the plover, or dupe — would turn out to be Madrigal, a poetaster, an inferior poet.

"I don't know," Broker said. "Some green plover. I'll find out who he is."

The jeerers wanted Madrigal to borrow money from Pennyboy Senior; if Madrigal got the loan, they would help Madrigal spend the money.

"Do, for I know the rest," Pennyboy Senior said. "They are the jeerers — they are mocking, flouting jacks."

— 2.4 —

Fitton, Almanac, Shunfield, and Madrigal entered the room. All four of them were jeerers, but Madrigal was the newest jeerer. They enjoyed mocking other people.

"How are you now, old money-bawd?" Fitton said. "We're come —"

A money-bawd is a usurer.

Pennyboy Senior interrupted, "— to jeer me, as you are accustomed to do. I know you."

He knew that they were also visiting him to borrow money.

"No, to give you some good security," Almanac said, "and see Pecunia."

"What is the security?" Pennyboy Senior asked.

"Ourselves," Fitton said.

"We'll be one bound for another," Almanac said.

They would guarantee the repayment of each other's loans.

Fitton pointed to Almanac and said, "I will be bound for this noble doctor here."

Almanac pointed to Fitton and said, "I will be bound for this worthy courtier here."

Fitton pointed to Shunfield and said, "This man of war, he was our muster-master."

A muster-master keeps the muster-list of soldiers or sailors.

Almanac said, "But a sea-captain now, brave Captain Shunfield."

Pennyboy Senior held up his nose and sniffed.

"You sniff the air now, as if the scent displeased you?" Shunfield said.

Some sea-goers smell strongly of fish and brine.

Fitton said to Pennyboy Senior, "You need not fear him, man. His credit is sound."

Almanac added, "And seasoned, too, since he took salt at sea — that is, since he took to being a sailor."

"I do not love pickled — brined — security," Pennyboy Senior said. "I wish I had one good fresh-man in for all of you because the truth is that you three stink."

A fresh-man is a novice, someone who can be taken advantage of. Also, a fresh-man is someone who bathes in fresh water.

The three who stank, stank because of bad character in addition to whatever odors they had.

"You are a rogue," Shunfield said.

"I think I am, but I will lend no money on that security, Captain," Pennyboy Senior replied.

Fitton, Almanac, and Shunfield were not good security: They were not people Pennyboy Senior wished to lend money to.

Almanac said, "Here's a gentleman, a fresh-man in the world, one Master Madrigal."

Madrigal was their plover; he was their dupe.

"Of an untainted credit," Fitton said. "What do you say to him?"

According to Fitton, Madrigal would be good security to repay the loan.

Madrigal had stepped aside with Broker.

"He's gone, I think," Shunfield said. "Where is he?"

He called, "Madrigal?"

Pennyboy Senior said, "He has an odd singing — resounding — name. Is he an heir?"

He was punning on "heir" and "air" — a song. A madrigal is a song with parts for many voices.

Fitton said, "An heir to a fair fortune —"

Almanac interrupted, "— and full hopes. He is a dainty scholar and a pretty poet!"

Unfortunately, many poets don't make much money, so their "full hopes" are quite modest, financially. They may have cultural capital without having financial capital. They may be heir to an air: a song.

"You've said enough," Pennyboy Senior said. "I have no money, gentlemen. If he goes to it in rhyme even once, not a penny."

Pennyboy Senior had money, but he had no money to lend to a poet.

He sniffed again.

"Why, he's of years, although he has little beard," Shunfield said. "He is an adult."

"His beard has time to grow," Pennyboy Senior said. "I have no money. Let him still dabble in poetry. No Pecunia is to be seen."

Almanac said, "Come, you love to be costive always in your courtesy, but I have a pill, a golden pill, to purge away this melancholy."

The word "costive" can mean 1) stingy, and 2) constipated. "Courtesy" here means generosity. "Costive generosity" is a contradiction in terms.

The jeerers wanted golden pills — coins, golden coins — to drive away their melancholy — melancholy that was caused by a lack of money.

A golden pill of this kind would drive away Pennyboy Senior's melancholy because he was a miser.

Disappointed at not being able to borrow money, the jeerers began to jeer at Pennyboy Senior.

Shunfield said, "His melancholy is caused by nothing but his keeping of the house here, with his two drowsy dogs."

Fitton said, "A drench — drink — of sack at a good tavern, and a fine fresh pullet, would cure him."

A pullet can be 1) a chicken, or 2) a woman, or 3) a prostitute.

"Nothing but a young hare in white broth," Lickfinger said. "I know his diet better than the doctor."

He may have meant "heir" in addition to "hare." Usurers can devour people they lend money to, including heirs.

Shunfield recognized him: "What, Lickfinger, my old host of the Ram Alley? You have some market here."

Ram Alley was a place with a bad reputation. Cookshops and taverns could be found there.

"Some dosser — pannier, aka basket — of fish or fowl to fetch off," Almanac said.

"An odd bargain of venison to drive," Fitton said.

Lickfinger did sell Pennyboy Senior's food.

Pennyboy Senior said to Lickfinger, "Will you go inside, knave?"

"I must necessarily go," Lickfinger replied.

He then said, "You see who drives me, gentlemen."

Pennyboy Senior shoved him inside the house.

"Not the devil," Almanac said.

A proverb states, "He must needs [necessarily] go whom the devil drives."

"Pennyboy Senior may be, in time," Fitton said. "He is the devil's agent, now."

"You are all cogging jacks — cheating knaves," Pennyboy Senior said. "You are a covey — a set — of wits. You are the jeerers, who always assemble at meals."

Having no money, the jeerers sought free meals where they could find them.

Pennyboy Senior added, "Or rather you assemble at an eyrie, for you are birds of prey and fly at and jeer all — nothing's too big or high for you — and you are so truly feared, but not beloved, one of another as no one dares break company from the rest, lest they should fall upon and insult the man who is absent."

They continued to jeer at Pennyboy Senior.

"Oh, the only oracle that ever squeaked or spoke out of a jacket!" Almanac said.

"How the rogue stinks, worse than a fishmonger's sleeves!" Shunfield said.

"Or currier's hands!" Fitton said.

Horace was once jeered by a man who said that he had often seen Horace's father wipe his nose on his fist.

A currier 1) grooms horses, or 2) dresses leather. Either kind of currier can stink.

"And such a parboiled visage!" Shunfield said.

Fitton added, "His face looks like a dyer's apron, exactly!"

Pennyboy Senior's face was botched red and white.

"A sodden — stewed — head, and his whole brain a posset curd!" Almanac said.

A posset curd is hot milk curdled in hot spiced ale or sack.

"Aye, now you jeer," Pennyboy Senior said. "Jeer on; I have no money."

"I wonder what religion he's of?" Almanac asked.

"No certain species surely," Fitton said. "He's a kind of mule that's half an ethnic Heathen, half a Christian!"

A mule is the impotent offspring of a horse and a donkey.

"I have no money, gentlemen," Pennyboy Senior said.

Shunfield said, "This blockhead — he has no sense of any virtue, honor, gentry, or merit."

Pennyboy Senior replied, "You say very rightly, my meritorious captain — as I take it you are."

Meretrix is Latin for "prostitute." A *meretrix* can make money to pay the bills. One now-obsolete meaning of "meritorious" is "earning money through prostitution."

Another meaning of "meritorious" is "having merit."

A person with the "merit" of a Shunfield cannot make money to pay the bills.

Pennyboy Senior continued, "Merit will keep no house, nor pay no house-rent. Will Mistress Merit go to market, do you think? Set the pot on the stove, or feed the family? Will gentry settle up with the butcher or the baker, fetch in a pheasant or a brace — a pair — of partridges from goodwife Poulterer for my lady's supper?"

A poulterer sells poultry.

"See this pure and utter rogue!" Fitton said.

"This rogue has money, though," Pennyboy Senior said. "My worshipful brave courtier has no money — no, nor does my valiant Captain Shunfield."

"Hang you, rascal!" Shunfield said.

Pennyboy Senior said to Almanac, "Nor do you, my learnéd doctor. I loved you while you did hold your practice and killed tripe-wives, and kept yourself to your urinal."

He liked Almanac when Almanac actually worked as a doctor, killing women who dressed and sold tripe and inspecting the urine collected in urinals.

Medical practices of the time, such as bleeding, often killed patients.

Inspection of urine can show the state of the patient's health; urine is supposed to be clear, and cloudy or bloody urine can indicate bad health.

But now Almanac compiled and consulted almanacs and ephemerides and indulged in astrology. Ephemerides were tables of astronomical data that gave the predicted position of celestial objects such as the planets.

Pennyboy Senior continued, "But since your thumbs have greased the ephemerides, casting horoscopes, and turned over the pages of almanacs for your candle-rents, and your twelve houses in the Zodiac, with your almutens, almacantaras, you truly shall cant — speak — in vain as far as Pennyboy Senior is concerned."

"Candle-rents" are revenue gained from residential properties. Unless a residence is continually well maintained, such property depreciates just like a candle that continually melts away.

People would use the astrological almanacs to help them predict their revenue from rental properties. Imagine a farmer using weather predictions in *The Farmer's Almanac* to predict crop yields.

"Almutens" are the astrological ruling planets.

According to the *Oxford English Dictionary*, an "almucantara" is "A circle on the celestial sphere parallel to the horizon, typically one of a series that cut the meridian at equal angular separations; a parallel of altitude."

Almucantaras are used in astrological almanacs.

Almanac spent his time consulting almanacs and indulging in astrology instead of doctoring.

Shunfield said to the other jeerers, "I told you what we should find him to be: an absolute bawd."

"A rogue, a cheater," Fitton said.

Pennyboy Senior said, "Say what you please, gentlemen. I am of that humble nature and condition never to mind Your Worships, or take notice of what words you throw away like this. I keep house here like a lame cobbler who is never out of doors, with my two dogs, my friends, and as you say, I drive a quick, pretty trade always."

A proverb states, "A cobbler is a king at home."

He continued, "I get money, and as for titles, be they 'rogue' or 'rascal,' or whatever Your Worships fancy, let them pass as transitory things. These titles are mine today and yours tomorrow."

"Hang you, dog!" Almanac said.

"You cur!" Shunfield said.

"You see how I blush and am ashamed of these grossly insulting attributes?" Pennyboy Senior said sarcastically. "Yet you have no money."

Almanac said, "Well, wolf, hyena, you old pock-marked rascal, you will have the hernia fall down again into your scrotum, and I shall be sent for. I will remember then, that; and I will remember your *fistula in ano* I cured you of."

"*Fistula in ano*" means fistula in the anus. An anal fistula is a passage from the inside of the anus to the skin around it.

If Almanac really could cure such hurts, he ought to keep his practice as a doctor of medicine.

"Thank your dog-leechcraft," Pennyboy Senior said.

The word "dog" was used as an insult. "Dog-leechcraft" is quackery. Or perhaps Pennyboy Senior was calling Almanac a dog-doctor.

Perhaps Almanac really did cure Pennyboy Senior's ailments. If he had continued his practice and not become a jeerer, most likely his credit would be good with Pennyboy Senior.

Doctors can do people good, and they can get good money for doing so.

Some people may see astrology as a help in getting rich quick; if it ever works, it works for very few. Famous astrologers, maybe?

"They were 'olesome piles, before you meddled with them," Pennyboy Senior said.

They were wholesome hemorrhoids, and they were hemorrhoids in a hole.

Perhaps Almanac had not cured Pennyboy Senior's ailments.

They continued to jeer at Pennyboy Senior.

"What an ungrateful wretch is this!" Almanac said.

Shunfield said, "He remembers a courtesy no more than London Bridge remembers what arch was mended last."

London Bridge was in a state of disrepair, hence the children's song "London Bridge is Falling Down."

"He never thinks, more than a log, of any grace at court a man may do him, or that such a lord reached him his hand," Fitton said.

A proverb stated, "A friend in court is worth a penny in purse."

Fitton was a courtier, and he was saying that he could do Pennyboy Senior favors at court — if Pennyboy Senior lent him money.

"Oh, yes!" Pennyboy Senior said. "If grace would cancel the brewer's tally, or my good lord's hand would settle the bill; but, sir, they will not do it."

Fitton's good will would not pay Pennyboy Senior's bills.

Pennyboy Senior showed the jeerers a gold coin and said, "Here's a piece — it is my good Lord Piece, and it does everything. It goes to the butcher's and fetches in a mutton, and then it goes to the baker's and brings in bread. It makes fires, gets wine, and does more real courtesies than all the milords I know.

"My sweet Lord Piece! You are my lord; the rest are cogging jacks, under the rose."

"Under the rose," aka *sub rosa*, is an idiom meaning "between you and me" or "confidentially."

"Rogue!" Shunfield said. "I am tempted to beat you now."

"Truly, captain, if you dared to beat any other person, I would believe you," Pennyboy Senior said.

Shunfield was good at threatening, but he was not good at actually fighting.

Pennyboy Senior continued, "But indeed you are hungry. You are not angry, captain, if I know your character rightly, good captain. No Pecunia is to be seen, even if Mistress Band would speak, or little Blushet — Blushing, aka Rose — Wax be never so easy.

"I'll stop my ears with her against the sirens Court and Philosophy."

In Homer's *Odyssey*, Odysseus wanted to hear the song of the Sirens, who used their beautiful voices to lure sailors to their death. He ordered his men to stop their ears with wax so they wouldn't hear the song of the Sirens, and he ordered his men to tie him to the mast so that when he heard the song, he wouldn't jump overboard to go to the Sirens, which would result in his death.

The Sirens whom Pennyboy Senior and Pecunia were stopping their ears against and rejecting were Court and Philosophy: the courier Fitton and the natural philosopher Almanac, who was a doctor and so studied or was supposed to study the effects of natural medicines. Pennyboy Senior had no interest in hearing whatever these jeerers — or any jeerers — said.

"God be with you, gentlemen," Pennyboy Senior said. "If you provide better names, Pecunia is for you."

"God be with you" means "Goodbye."

The jeerers need better names than they have (that is, they need to be different people with better characters than they have) if they want to borrow money from him. They also need to provide better names than they had been using to refer to him — "wolf, hyena, you old pocky rascal" — if they want to borrow money from him.

Fitton said, "What a damned Harpy he is!"

Harpies are mythological creatures that are half-bird and half woman. They are usually nuisances, but sometimes they are oracles.

Fitton then asked, "Where's Madrigal? Has he sneaked away from here?"

Madrigal returned with Broker.

Shunfield said, "Here he comes with Broker, Lady Pecunia's secretary."

Almanac said, "He may do some good with him, perhaps."

Who is he, and who is him?

He may be Broker, who may get bribe money from Madrigal. Or he is Madrigal, who may get access to Lady Pecunia and her women from Broker. But possibly, Madrigal may be able to borrow money from Pennyboy Senior.

Almanac asked, "Where have you been, Madrigal?"

"Above with My Lady's women, reading verses," Madrigal replied.

Apparently, Lady Pecunia was not present.

Fitton said, "That was a favor."

It was a favor for Madrigal to have been admitted into the ladies' presence. Whether hearing Madrigal's verses was a favor to the ladies is open to interpretation.

Fitton then said to Broker, "Good morning, Master Secretary."

"Good morning, Master Usher," Shunfield said to Broker.

Almanac said, "Sir, by both your worshipful titles and your name, Mas' Broker, good morning."

Mas' is short for *Master*.

Madrigal said, "I did ask him if he were Amphibian Broker."

An amphibious animal such as otters can live both on land and water: river otters and sea otters.

"Why?" Shunfield said.

Almanac said, "Because he has two offices, he is a creature of two natures."

Broker was Lady Pecunia's secretary and her gentleman-usher. These were his offices: his jobs.

"You may jeer," Broker said. "You have the wits, young gentlemen, but your hope of Helicon will never carry it here with our fat — dull and complacent — family."

The Muses resided on Mount Helicon. Poets have long attempted to climb that mountain.

Broker continued, "We have the dullest, most unbored — unpenetrated and unenlightened — ears for verse among our females."

He said to Madrigal, "I grieved that you read so long, sir. Old nurse Mortgage snored in the chair, and Statute, if you noticed her, fell fast asleep, and Mistress Band nodded, but not with any consent to what you read.

"They must have somewhat else to chink — clink — than rhymes; if you could make an epitaph on your land — imagine it on the point of departing from you — such a poem would wake them and bring Wax to her true temper."

If Madrigal would sell his land, then he could bribe Lady Pecunia's women servants with gold coins they could clink. That would keep them awake.

"To temper wax" is "to make wax malleable by kneading it." Rose Wax would become pliant through the application of money to her hand.

Madrigal was supposed to be inheriting land — that is why the jeerers were attempting to take advantage of him. If they succeeded, Madrigal could well make an epitaph on the departure of his land.

"Truly, sir, and I will try," Madrigal said.

"It is only earth, fit to make bricks and tiles of," Broker said.

Broker wanted Madrigal to sell his land so that he — Broker — could get bribes.

Madrigal could also get money by mortgaging his land to Pennyboy Senior — and lose his land through non-payment of his debt.

Shunfield said, "A pox upon land. It is only for pots or pipkins — small earthen pots — at the best. If it would keep us in good tobacco pipes —"

Broker interrupted, "— it would be worth keeping."

Fitton added, "Or in porcelain dishes, there would be some hope."

"But this is a poor, hungry soil," Almanac said. "And must be helped."

Fitton said, "Who would hold any land to have the trouble to marl it?"

To marl land meant to improve it with marl, a kind of clayey soil used to improve sandy land.

"Not a gentleman," Shunfield said.

Broker said, "Let rustics and laborers who love plows, carts, and harrows pursue such work; they always are busy in vexing the dull element."

The dull element is earth.

They were working hard to persuade Madrigal that land was not worth having.

Many gentlemen at the time, of course, got their income from land.

"Our sweet songster shall rarify it into air," Almanac said.

They wanted Madrigal to mortgage his land so they could burn through his money, which would go up in smoke and dissipate into the air.

Fitton whispered to Broker, "And you, Mas' Broker, shall have a feeling."

The jeerers would be happy to "borrow" money from Madrigal once he had mortgaged or sold his land, and Broker would have a share for helping to persuade Madrigal to mortgage or sell his land.

A "feeling" is a tip — or a bribe.

Broker said, "So it will gratify or soften, sir, the nerves."

Tips gratify; bribes soften.

"Oh, it shall be palpable," Madrigal said. "It shall make you run through a finger-ring, or a thumb-ring, run through the nose — hole — of a tobacco pipe, and draw your ductile — flexible — bones out like a knitting needle, to serve my subtle turns."

Attendant spirits — familiars — were thought to be kept in a ring.

Madrigal was aware that money had power to turn greedy people into servants.

"I shall obey, sir," Broker said "And run a thread, like an hourglass."

Broker was a greedy person.

He would run continually like a trickle of sand in an hourglass to serve Madrigal and get bribes. Once Madrigal was out of money, the sand in the hourglass would cease to run. No bribes, no service.

Pennyboy Senior entered the room and asked, "Where is Broker?"

Seeing that the jeerers were still present, he asked, "Aren't these flies — these parasites — gone yet?"

He said to the jeerers, of whom Madrigal was now one, "Please, leave my house. I'll smoke you out else."

Smoke is a way to keep unwelcome visitors such as mosquitoes away.

"Oh, the prodigal!" Fitton said. "Will you be at so much charge — expense — with us, and loss?"

The expense would be the cost of the wood — probably juniper wood to cleanse the house.

Madrigal pretended that Pennyboy Senior would be upset at the loss of fragrant smoke escaping from his house.

Madrigal said to Pennyboy Senior, "I have heard you have offered, sir, to lock up smoke, and caulk your windows, spar up — bolt — all your doors, thinking to keep it a close prisoner with you, and wept when it went out, sir, at your chimney."

According to the jeerers, misers don't wish to let go of any possession, even smoke, except in return for money.

"And yet his eyes were drier than a pumice because of the smoke," Fitton said.

Shunfield said, "He is a wretched rascal, who will bind the nose of his bellows lest the wind get out when he's abroad!"

Almanac said, "He sweeps down no cobwebs here, but instead he sells them for cut fingers."

Cobwebs were used to stop cuts from bleeding.

Almanac continued, "And he sells the spiders, which are creatures reared of dust and cost him nothing, to fat old ladies to feed to their pet monkeys."

Fitton said, "He has offered to gather up spilt water and to preserve each hair that falls from him to stuff balls with."

Hair was used to stuff tennis balls.

Shunfield said, "He is a slave, and an idolater to Pecunia!"

Pennyboy Senior replied to the jeerers, "You all have happy memories, gentlemen, in rocking my poor cradle."

Possibly, at one time, the jeerers had money, which they had borrowed from Pennyboy Senior, using their land as security. Pennyboy Senior had slept soundly with such security. Now, possibly, Pennyboy Senior had money *and* the jeerers' lands.

Pennyboy Senior continued, "I remember, too, when you had lands, and credit, worship and honor, friends, yes, and could give security in the form of land.

"Now you have none, or will have none very shortly."

He was thinking of Madrigal, whose new friends would most likely convince him to sell or mortgage his land.

Pennyboy Senior continued, "Time and the vicissitude of things can bring these things about."

He could also have mentioned that having the wrong kind of "friends" can bring these things about.

He continued, "I have all these, and money, too, and do possess them, and I am right heartily glad of all our memories, and both the changes: the change for the better in my case, and the change for the worse in your cases."

Fitton said to the other jeerers, "Let us leave the viper."

Pennyboy Senior had struck a nerve.

Everyone exited except Pennyboy Senior and Broker.

Pennyboy Senior said to himself about Fitton, "He's glad he is rid of his torture, and so soon."

He then said, "Broker, come here. Go up and tell your lady that she must be ready immediately, as well as Statute, Band, Mortgage, and Wax.

"My prodigal young kinsman will straightaway be here to see her. He is the top of our house, the flourishing and flaunting Pennyboy Junior."

The top of the house is the best of the house: the heir who will marry and produce descendants to carry on the family name. The other Pennyboys were unable to have children. Pennyboy Junior's father was dead, and Pennyboy Senior was old.

He continued, "We were but three of us in all the world. My brother Francis, whom they called Frank Pennyboy, was the father to this Pennyboy Junior — Frank Pennyboy is dead.

"This Pennyboy Junior is now the heir.

"I, Richer Pennyboy, not 'Richard,' but old Harry Pennyboy, and (to make a rhyme) close, wary Pennyboy, I shall have all at last, my hopes do tell me."

"Old Harry" was one of the devil's nicknames.

For some reason, Pennyboy Senior thought he would have all the family wealth. Possibly he thought this because Lady Pecunia resided with him.

Pennyboy Senior said to Broker, "Go, see that all is ready, and where my dogs have faulted on the floor, remove it with a broom, and sweeten all with a sprig of juniper — not too much, but sparing. We may be faulty ourselves otherwise, and turn prodigal in the entertaining of the Prodigal."

Fragrant juniper wood was burned to sweeten the air.

Broker exited.

Seeing his nephew approaching, Pennyboy Senior said, "Here he is! And with him — who? A clapper dudgeon!"

A clapper dudgeon is a beggar. "Dudgeon" is a wood used to make bowls and knife handles. A clapper is a lid to a clap-dish or begging-bowl. Beggars could make noise by hitting their wooden begging bowl with a lid or a knife handle. Clappers are also tongues: Beggars ask for alms while holding their begging bowl.

Pennyboy Senior said, "That's a good sign, to have the beggar follow him so near at his first entry into fortune."

Why would that be a good sign?

Pennyboy Senior had just had the jeerers trying to borrow money from him without good security. They were unlikely to ever be able be able to pay the money back.

By contrast, a real beggar was an improvement. A beggar would ask for alms and not make false promises to pay the money back.

A real beggar would also be a reminder to Pennyboy Junior not to waste his wealth.

Pennyboy Junior, Picklock, and the Canter entered the scene. The Canter was the clapper dudgeon whom Pennyboy Senior had seen.

Broker, Pecunia, Statute, Band, Wax, and Mortgage were in a neighboring study, where they could not be seen.

"How now, old uncle?" Pennyboy Junior said. "I have come to see you and the splendid lady here, the daughter of Ophir, they say you keep."

Lady Pecunia was Pennyboy Senior's guest.

Pennyboy Senior said, "Sweet nephew, even if she were the daughter of the sun, she's at your service, and so am I, and the whole family, worshipful nephew."

The family was the household servants.

"Do you say so, dear uncle?" Pennyboy Junior said. "Welcome my friends, then. Here is Domine Picklock, my man of law."

Learnéd professionals were called by the title "Domine," aka "Master."

Pennyboy Junior continued, "He solicits all my causes, follows my business, makes and settles my quarrels between my tenants and me, sows all my strifes and reaps them, too, troubles the country for me, and vexes any neighbor whom I please."

"But with commission?" Pennyboy Senior asked.

A lawyer who worked under commission could cause problems and then receive payment for correcting them.

"Under my hand and seal," Pennyboy Junior replied.

The lawyer definitely got paid.

"A worshipful — honorable — place!" Pennyboy Senior said.

Definitely a profitable job.

"I thank His Worship for it," Picklock said.

Pennyboy Senior pointed to the Canter and said, "But who is this old gentleman?"

The Canter said, "A rogue, a vagrant, a very canter; aye, sir, one who maunds upon the pad — that is, I am one who begs upon the highway."

In using words such as "maunds" and "pad," the Canter was using cant: the specialized jargon used by beggars.

The Canter continued, "We should be brothers, though, for you are nearly as wretched as myself. You dare not use your money, and I have none."

A person who will not use money when it ought to be used is like a person who owns books but does not read them.

Money should be used to make oneself comfortable, and good books ought to be read.

"Not use my money, you cogging jack — you cheating knave?" Pennyboy Senior said, angrily. "Who uses it at better rates? Who lends it for a greater percentage in the hundred than I do, sirrah?"

He used his money in usury.

Pennyboy Junior said, "Don't be angry, uncle."

"What?" Pennyboy Senior said. "To disgrace me with my queen? As if I did not know her value."

His queen was Queen Pecunia and Queen *Pecunia*.

Pecunia is Latin for "money."

He worshiped money, and money can be a quean — a whore.

The Canter said, "Sir, I meant that you dare not to enjoy it."

For example, he could burn more juniper wood than he did to perfume the air in his house.

"Hold your peace," Pennyboy Senior said. "You are a jack."

A jack is a knave.

Now Pennyboy Junior was angry.

He said, "Uncle, he shall be a John — he shall be my servant, And, what's more, for all that, he's as good a man as you are. If I can make him so, he will be a better man. Perhaps I will, too."

He then said to the Canter and Picklock, "Come, let us go."

Pennyboy Senior said, "Nay, kinsman, my worshipful kinsman, and the top of our house, don't do your penitent uncle that affront, because of a rash word to leave his joyful threshold before you see the lady whom you long for, the Venus of the time and state, Pecunia!

"I perceive your bounty loves the man — the Canter — for some concealed virtue that he hides under those rags."

The Canter said, "I owe my happiness to him, the waiting on His Worship, since I brought him the happy news, welcome to all young heirs."

The "happy news" was that Pennyboy Junior's father had died and left him all the father's wealth.

Pennyboy Junior said, "You did it, indeed, for which I thank you yet."

He then said to his uncle, "Your fortunate princess, uncle, is long in coming."

Pecunia was fortunate in that it was a fortune.

Pennyboy Senior replied, "She is not rigged, sir. Setting forth some lady will cost as much as furnishing a fleet."

An expensive fleet sailed against Spain in the Cádiz expedition of 1625. Women's clothing and accessories can be expensive.

"Not rigged" meant that she had not completed getting ready for Pennyboy Junior's visit.

The door to the study opened. Lady Pecunia sat in state, attended by Statute, Band, Wax, Mortgage, and Broker.

Pennyboy Senior said, "Here she's come at last, and like a galley gilt in the prow."

"Is this Pecunia?" Pennyboy Junior asked.

Pennyboy Senior said to Lady Pecunia, "Please give my promising kinsman, gracious madam, the favor of your hand."

"Nay, of my lips, sir, to him," Pecunia replied.

She kissed him.

Pennyboy Junior said to himself, "She kisses like a mortal creature."

He then said out loud to Pecunia, "Almighty madam, I have longed to see you."

Pecunia replied, "And I have my desire, sir, to behold that youth and shape which in my dreams and waking hours I have so often contemplated, and felt warm in my veins and native as my blood.

"When I was told of your arrival here, I felt my heart beat as if it would leap out in speech, and all my face was on fire. But how it came to pass I do not know."

Pennyboy Junior said, "Oh, beauty loves to be prouder than nature, and nature made you blush! I cannot satisfy my curious eyes, by which alone I'm happy in my beholding you."

He kissed her.

The Canter said to the others, "They pass the compliment prettily well."

The compliment was kissing. They were passing kisses back and forth.

"Aye, he does kiss her," Picklock said. "I like him."

Pennyboy Junior said, "My passion was clear contrary — internally vexed — and doubtful. I shook for fear, and yet I danced for joy. I had such motions as the sunbeams make against a wall or playing on water, or trembling vapor of a boiling pot —"

Pennyboy Senior said to the others, "That's not so good. It should have been a crucible with molten metal; she would have understood it."

In alchemy, the final step of producing a philosopher's stone is Projection: the testing of the power of the philosopher's stone. A base metal is melted, some of the powder of the philosopher's stone is cast into the melted metal, and the base metal is turned into gold or silver.

Pennyboy Junior said to Pecunia, "I cannot talk, but I can love you, madam. Are these your gentlewomen? I love them, too."

Her gentlewomen were her serving-women.

He began to name and kiss them.

"And which is Mistress Statute? Mistress Band? They all kiss intimately; the last stuck to my lips."

Broker identified the last serving-woman whom Pennyboy Junior had kissed: "It was my lady's chambermaid, soft Wax."

No wonder their lips had stuck together: Wax was used as a sealant.

"Soft lips she has, I am sure of it," Pennyboy Junior said.

He had not yet kissed Lady Pecunia's aged nurse.

He said, "Mother Mortgage."

He hesitated and then said, "I'll owe her a kiss, until she is younger."

He then kissed the three younger serving-women again, saying, "Statute, sweet Mistress Band, and honey, little Wax, we must be better acquainted."

Statute said, "We are only servants, sir."

Band said, "But he whom Her Grace is so content to grace we shall obey —"

Wax interrupted, "— and with all fit respect —"

Mortgage interrupted, "— in our poor places —"

Wax interrupted, "— being Her Grace's shadows."

Pennyboy Junior said, "A fine, well-spoken family."

He then asked Broker, "What's your name?"

"Broker."

Pennyboy Junior whispered to him, "I think my uncle should not need you: He is a crafty knave enough, believe it."

A proverb stated, "A crafty knave needs no broker."

He then asked, "Are you Her Grace's steward?"

"No, I am her gentleman-usher, sir," Broker replied.

Pennyboy Junior pretended that he had said he was a gentleman-'usher — gentleman-brusher — someone who brushed or swept the floors.

"What, of the hall?" Pennyboy Junior asked. "You have a sweeping face; your beard is like a broom."

"Sweeping face" can mean "majestic face."

"I have no barren chin, sir," Broker said. "I am no eunuch, although I am a gentleman-usher."

Gentleman-ushers were sometimes thought to be effeminate.

"You shall go with us," Pennyboy Junior said.

He then said to Pennyboy Senior, "Uncle, I must have my princess forth today."

"Whither you please, sir, you shall command her," Pennyboy Senior said.

"I will do all grace to my new servant," Lady Pecunia said.

This kind of servant was a man who was devoted to a woman.

Pennyboy Senior said to her, "Thanks to your generosity in treating him so well. He is my nephew and my chief, the point, tip, top, and tuft — chief — of all our family!"

He then said to Pennyboy Junior, "But, sir, on the condition always that you shall return Statute and Band home, with my sweet, soft Wax, and my good nurse here, Mortgage."

"Oh! Who else?" Pennyboy Junior said.

Pennyboy Senior answered, "Ushered by Broker."

"Do not fear," Pennyboy Junior said.

Lady Pecunia would be well chaperoned.

Pennyboy Senior said, "She shall go with you, whither you please, sir, anywhere."

The Canter said quietly to Picklock, "I see a money-bawd is commonly a flesh-bawd, too."

Picklock quietly answered, "Do you think so?"

Wealthy people do engage in match-making, often in an attempt to gain more wealth.

Picklock said to himself, "Now, I swear on my faith, this canter would make a good grave burgess — magistrate — in some barn."

Beggars gathered in barns like drinkers gather in taverns. The burgess of the barn would be the king of the beggars.

The Canter had shown some good sense in his speech.

Pennyboy Junior said to Pennyboy Senior, "Come, you shall go with us, uncle."

"By no means, sir," Pennyboy Senior said.

"We'll have both sack and fiddlers," Pennyboy Junior said.

Sack is a fortified white wine.

"I'll not draw that charge upon Your Worship," Pennyboy Senior said.

The Canter said quietly to Picklock, "He speaks modestly, and like an uncle."

Pennyboy Senior said, "But Mas' Broker here, he shall attend you, nephew, Her Grace's usher, and what you fancy to bestow on him — be not too lavish, use a temperate bounty — I'll take it as being done to myself."

"I will be princely while I possess my princess, my Pecunia," Pennyboy Junior said.

"Where is it you will eat?" Pennyboy Senior asked.

"Nearby, at Picklock's lodging," Pennyboy Junior said. "Old Lickfinger's the cook, here in Ram Alley."

Many lawyers had offices near Ram Alley.

"Lickfinger has good fare," Pennyboy Senior said. "Perhaps I'll come and see you."

The Canter took Pennyboy Junior to the side, and, along with Picklock, began to persuade him to move the feast.

"Oh, bah!" the Canter said. "An alley, and a cook's shop, gross! It will savor, sir, most rankly of them both. Let your food rather follow you to a tavern."

Lickfinger could deliver the food from the cook-shop to the tavern where Pennyboy Junior would dine.

"A tavern's as unfit, too, for a princess," Picklock said.

"No, I have known a princess, and a great one, to come forth of a tavern," the Canter said.

"Not go in, sir, though," Picklock said.

Picklock was interpreting "come forth" as meaning "born in."

"She must go in, if she came forth," the Canter said. "The blessed Pocahontas, as the historian Captain John Smith calls her because she often saved his life, and great king's daughter of Virginia, has been in the womb of a tavern."

"Been in the womb of a tavern" meant that she had resided in a tavern.

Captain John Smith wrote *The Generall Historie of Virginia* (1624). Pocahontas visited England in 1616 and stayed at two inns: The Bell Savage Inn and an inn across the Thames at Brentford. She attended one of Ben Jonson's masques, and he met her.

The Canter continued, "And, besides, your nasty uncle will spoil all your mirth, and be as disagreeable as the alley and the cook's shop."

"That's true," Picklock said.

"No, truly," the Canter said, "dine in the Apollo Room in the Devil Tavern at Bell Temple, Fleet Street with Pecunia. That's brave Duke Wadloe's place. Have your friends around you and make a day of it."

Simon Wadloe was the innkeeper at the Devil's Inn.

"I am content, truly, to do that," Pennyboy Junior said. "Our food shall be brought thither. Simon the king will bid us welcome."

A song of the time was "Old Simon the King." King Simon was a tippler. The present Simon the King was Simon Wadloe.

"Patron, I have a suit," Picklock said. "I have a favor to ask of you."

"What's that?" Pennyboy Junior asked.

"That you will carry the Infanta — Pecunia — to see the Office of the Staple of News. Her Grace will be a grace to all the members of it."

"I will do it," Pennyboy Junior said, "and I will have her arms set up there with her titles — Aurelia Clara Pecunia, the Infanta — and in the Apollo Room."

Great people often displayed their arms and titles at places they visited.

"Come, sweet princess, let us go," Pennyboy Junior said to Lady Pecunia.

"Broker, be careful of your charge," Pennyboy Senior said.

Broker was the main chaperone.

"I promise you that I will be careful," Broker replied.

They exited.

THE SECOND INTERMEAN: AFTER THE SECOND ACT

"Why, this is duller and duller!" Gossip Censure complained. "Intolerable! Scurvy! There is neither a devil nor a fool in this play! I pray to God that some of us are not a witch, Gossip Mirth, to foretell the matter thus."

The gossips had accurately predicted that no fool or devil would be in the play, and Gossip Censure was saying that she hoped that none of the gossips were witches.

Gossip Mirth replied, "I fear that we are all such, if we were old enough; but we are not all old enough to make one witch."

A stereotype of witches is that they are old and withered. In Ben Jonson's day, boys played all female roles on stage. The combined ages of the four boys playing the gossips would not be enough to make up the age of one witch.

Gossip Mirth then asked, "How do you like the Vice in the play?"

"Which character is the Vice?" Gossip Expectation asked.

Gossip Mirth answered, "There are three or four: old Covetousness, the sordid Pennyboy Senior; he is the money-bawd who is a flesh-bawd, too, they say."

"But here is never a fiend to carry him away," Gossip Tattle said. "Besides, he hasn't a wooden dagger! I'd not give a rush for a Vice that has not a wooden dagger to snap at everybody he meets."

In old medieval morality plays, the Vice character carried a wooden dagger, which he brandished. The Vice character represented evil. Sometimes, the Vice character had a name such as Inequity, which is unfairness, aka lack of justice.

A rush is a plant of little worth. A common cliché of the time stated, "Not worth a rush."

Gossip Mirth said, "That was the old way, Gossip Tattle, when Iniquity came in like Hocus-Pocus the conjuror, wearing a juggler's jerkin, with false skirts like the Knave of Clubs."

The Knave of Clubs is the Jack of Clubs. One meaning of "knave" is "a knight's personal attendant." On playing cards, Jacks wear aristocratic clothing. Apparently, such clothing included long coats with slits on the sides.

Gossip Mirth continued, "But now they are attired like men and women of our own time, the Vices, male and female!"

That was certainly true of Ben Jonson's earlier play *The Devil Is an Ass*.

Gossip Mirth continued, "Prodigality is like a young heir, and his mistress Money (whose favors he scatters like counters) is pranked up like a prime lady, the Infanta of the Mines."

Prodigality, of course, is Pennyboy Junior, and Money, of course, is Lady Pecunia.

Counters are fake coins; think of chips in a casino. "Aye," Gossip Censure said, "therein they abuse an honorable princess, it is thought."

"By whom is it so thought?" Gossip Mirth said. "Or where lies the abuse?"

Gossip Censure said, "It is plain in the giving her the title 'Infanta' and giving her three names. "

The Infanta Isabella Clara Eugenia was the daughter of King Phillip II of Spain. Some people who saw or read the play could think that the Infanta of the Mines, Lady Pecunia, represented her.

People often thought that Ben Jonson's satire was directed against specific people. If that were true, Jonson could get into serious trouble, and so he objected or pretended to object to such interpretations.

"Take heed it lies not in the vice of your interpretation," Gossip Mirth said. "What have Aurelia, Clara, Pecunia to do with any person? Do they any more but express the property of money, which is the daughter of earth and drawn out of the mines? Is there nothing to be called 'Infanta' but what is open to criticism?

"Why not have the 'Infanta of the Beggars,' or 'Infanta of the Gypsies,' as well as the 'King of Beggars' and the 'King of Gypsies'?"

Gossip Censure said, "Well, if there were no wiser people than I, I would sew him in a sack and send him by sea to his princess."

The wiser people would stop her from doing that. If not for the wiser people, she would do that.

Gossip Mirth said, "Indeed, if he — Ben Jonson — heard you, Censure, he would go near to stick the ass' ears to your high dressing, and perhaps to all our high dressings for hearkening — listening — to you."

A high dressing is an elaborate hairstyle in which the hair is combed very high.

Fools were given ass' ears in plays; think of Bottom in Shakespeare's *A Midsummer Night's Dream*.

Never insult a satirist. If you do, people may read insulting things about you hundreds of years later.

Gossip Tattle said, "By our Lady, the Virgin Mary, but he would not do that to mine. I would hearken and hearken and censure, if I saw cause, for the other princess' sake, Pocahontas, surnamed the Blessed, whom he has abused indeed (and I do censure him, and will censure him) by saying she came forth of a tavern — that was said like a paltry poet."

"That's only one gossip's opinion, and my Gossip Tattle's, too!" Gossip Mirth said. "But what says Gossip Expectation here? She sits sullen and silent."

"Truly, I await the sight of their office, their great office, the Staple of News Office, to see what it will be! They have talked about it, but we haven't seen it open yet. I wish Butter the newsman would come in and spread — reveal — itself a little to us!"

"Or the butter-box, Buzz, the emissary," Gossip Mirth said.

Hans Buzz, a Dutchman, was Emissary at the Exchange.

The Dutch had a reputation for loving butter and were called butter-boxes. Dutch people would carry boxes of butter when traveling so that they could add butter to the meals they purchased.

"When it is churned and dished up, we shall hear of it," Gossip Tattle said.

Gossip Expectation said, "If it is fresh and sweet butter; but what if it is sour and wheyish?"

Gossip Mirth said, "Then it is worth nothing, mere pot-butter, fit to be spent in suppositories or greasing coach wheels, stale stinking butter, and such I fear it is, by its being barreled up so long."

Pot-butter is salted butter stored in pots.

Because it was taking so long to see the Staple of News Office, Gossip Mirth expected that there would not be much to see.

"Or rank Irish butter," Gossip Expectation said.

"Have patience, gossips," Gossip Censure said. "Say that contrary to our expectations it proves to be right well-seasoned and -preserved salt butter?"

Gossip Mirth said, "Or to the time of year, in Lent, delicate almond butter!"

During Lent, people ate almond butter instead of dairy butter. Almond butter was sweetened with sugar.

Gossip Mirth continued, "I have a sweet tooth yet, and I will hope for the best, and sit down as quiet and calm as butter, look as smooth and soft as butter, be merry and melt like butter, laugh and be fat like butter — so long as Butter answer my expectation and be not mad butter."

A proverb stated, "Butter is mad twice a year." It is too soft in summer and too hard in winter.

Gossip Mirth finished, "If it is mad butter, it shall both July and December see. I say no more — except *Dixi*."

Dixi means literally "I have spoken" and figuratively "I rest my case."

TO THE READERS

In this following act, the Office of the Staple of News is opened and shown to the Prodigal and his princess, Pecunia, wherein the allegory and purpose of the author has hitherto been wholly mistaken, and so sinister an interpretation been made as if the souls of most of the spectators had lived in the eyes and ears of these ridiculous gossips who tattle between the acts.

But the author — Ben Jonson — asks you thus to mend it: to consider the news here vented to be none of his news or any reasonable man's, but news made like the time's news — a weekly cheat to draw money — and could not be fitter reprehended than in raising this ridiculous Staple of News Office, wherein the age may see her own folly or hunger and thirst after published pamphlets of news, set out every Saturday, but made all at home, and no syllable of truth in them, than which there cannot be a greater disease in nature or a fouler scorn put upon the times.

"And so apprehending it, you shall do the author and your own judgment a courtesy, and perceive the trick of alluring money to the Staple of News Office and there cheating the people. If you have the truth, rest quiet, and consider that

"*Ficta, voluptatis causa, sint proxima veris.*"

***

Ben Jonson translated this Latin passage from Horace's *Art of Poetry* (338) in this way:
"Poet never credit gained
"By writing truths, but things (like truths) well fained [feigned, faked]."
Please note:
The news-books of the time were generally published on Saturday, and they went from new news to old news in six days.

Attempting to verify news can be difficult, and news writers and publishers must decide to which degree the news they write and publish must be verified. A bad news writer and a bad publisher will write and publish unverified "news."

The "news" recounted in the Staple of News Office in Jonson's play is a parody of news.

89

CHAPTER 3

— 3.1 —

Fitton and Cymbal talked together in the Staple of News Office. Lady Pecunia was a rich woman, and Cymbal wanted her for her money. His rival for Pecunia was Pennyboy Junior.

Fitton said to Cymbal, "You hunt upon a wrong scent still, and think the air of things will carry them, but it must be reason and proportion, not fine sounds, that must get you this lady, I say to you, my cousin — my partner — Cymbal.

"You have here entertained a pettifogger, name of Picklock, with the trust of an emissary's place, and he is all for the young prodigal, Pennyboy Junior. You see that he has left us and gone over to the young prodigal's side."

A pettifogger conducts petty cases and shady business.

Fitton did not trust Picklock.

"Come, you do not know him, you who speak like this about him," Cymbal said. "He will have a trick to open us a gap by a trap-door — a sneaky trick — when they least dream of it."

Seeing Picklock coming, Cymbal said, "Here he comes."

Picklock walked over to them.

Cymbal asked him, "What news do you bring?"

Picklock said loudly, "Where is my brother Buzz? My brother Ambler? Where are the register, examiner, and the clerks? Appear and let us muster all in pomp.

The register, Nathaniel the clerk, and the new clerk, Thomas Barber, entered the room.

Picklock said, "Let us be in pomp to put on a show for the rich Infanta, who is coming here straightaway, to make her visit. Pennyboy Junior the heir, my patron, has gotten permission for her to play and amuse herself, with all her train of servants, from the old churl her guardian: Pennyboy Senior.

"Now is your time to make all court to her, so that she may first just know, and then love, the place, and show it by her frequent visits here, and afterwards you must get her to sojourn with you. She will be weary of the prodigal quickly."

"Excellent news!" Cymbal said.

"And the counsel of an oracle!" Fitton said.

"What do you say, cousin Fitton?" Cymbal asked.

Fitton said, "Brother Picklock, I shall adore you for this parcel of tidings. It will cry up and proclaim the credit of our Staple of News Office eternally, and make it immortal!"

Picklock said, "See that your words to her, then, are fair and fit, and entertain her and her entourage, too, with all the *migniardise* — daintiness — and quaint caresses you can put on them."

"You seem by your language no less a courtier than a man of law," Fitton said. "I must embrace you."

Fitton had been suspicious of Picklock, but now he was impressed by the man.

Picklock replied, "Tut, I am Vertumnus on every change or chance; upon occasion, I am a true chameleon; I can change color for it."

He could change his appearance and manner of speaking and acting as needed for whatever goal he wished to achieve.

Picklock continued, "I move upon my axle like a turnstile, fit my face to the parties, and become, straightaway, one of them."

Vertumnus was the Roman god of change; he could change himself to woo the goddess Pomona. The guises he used to court her included fisherman, gardener, reaper, soldier, and old woman.

The two men embraced.

Cymbal said to the register, Nathaniel the clerk, and Tom Barber, "Sirs, up, go to your desks, and spread the rolls upon the table, so."

The register, Nathaniel the clerk, and Tom Barber took their places.

"Is the examiner set?" Cymbal asked.

The register answered, "Yes, sir."

"The Emissaries Ambler and Buzz are both out of the office now," Cymbal said.

"We'll sustain their parts," Picklock said.

They would make the Staple of News Office appear to be a thriving business by seeming to have lots of people busy at work, either inside or outside the Staple of News Office.

Picklock continued, "It does not matter; let them ply the affairs outside. Leave it to us within; I like that well.

"On with the cloak, and you with the Staple of News Office gown."

Fitton put on the Staple of News Office cloak, and Cymbal put on the gown.

Picklock continued, "Preserve your dignity; stoop only to the Infanta. We'll have a flight at Mortgage, Statute, and Band, and it shall be difficult but with some luck, we'll bring Wax to the retrieve."

Trained hawks would fly at their prey, kill it, and then retrieve it — bring it to their masters.

Cymbal, Fitton, and Picklock wanted to get Lady Pecunia's servants on their side.

Picklock continued, "Each man must know his individual province, and discharge it."

Fitton now completely supported Picklock.

"I do admire this nimble stratagem, Picklock," Fitton said.

Cymbal whispered to Fitton, "Cuz — partner. What did I say?"

Fitton whispered back, "You have rectified my error!"

Fitton now trusted Picklock to do his part in their plot.

They were all going to play roles in the Staple of News Office and make it look like a high-status and very successful place of business. By doing so, they hoped to help Cymbal win Lady Pecunia.

— 3.2 —

Some new visitors entered the Staple of News Office: Pennyboy Junior, the Canter, Pecunia, Statute, Band, Mortgage, Wax, and Broker.

"By your leave, gentlemen, what is the news?" Pennyboy Junior said. "Good, good still, in your new Staple of News Office?"

He then said to Lady Pecunia, "Princess, here's the Staple of News Office. This is the Governor; kiss him, noble princess, for my sake."

Lady Pecunia kissed Cymbal.

Pennyboy Junior then asked Thomas Barber, the new clerk of the Staple of News Office, "Tom, how is it, honest Tom? How does your place, and you?"

He said to Lady Pecunia, "He is my creature, princess; this is my creature. I am his patron. I purchased his job for him. Give him your hand to kiss."

Thomas Barber kissed Lady Pecunia's hand.

Pennyboy Junior said, "He was my barber, but now he signs himself *Clericus* — Clerk! I bought this place — this job — for him and gave it to him."

The Canter said, "He should have spoken of that, sir, and not you. Two do not do one office well."

Thomas Barber should have acknowledged Pennyboy Junior's patronage. Pennyboy Junior should not have mentioned it.

"It is true, but I am loath to lose my courtesies," Pennyboy Junior said.

He did not want to miss out on the credit for doing a good deed.

The Canter said, "So are all they who do them to vain ends, and yet you do lose when you pay yourselves."

Proverbs 27:2 states, "*Let another man praise thee, and not thine own mouth; a stranger, and not thine own lips*" (King James Version).

"No more of your moral maxims, Canter; they are stale," Pennyboy Junior said. "We come for news; remember where you are."

He then said, "I ask you to let my princess hear some news, good Master Cymbal."

"What news would she like to hear, or of what kind, sir?" Cymbal asked.

"Any, any kind, so long as it is news, the newest that you have," Pennyboy Junior said. "Some news of state, for a princess."

Cymbal said to Thomas Barber, "Read the news from Rome, there."

93

Thomas Barber read out loud:

"*They write that the King of Spain has been chosen Pope.*"

Actually, Philip IV (Spanish: Felipe IV) King of Spain (1621–1665), never became Pope. Pope Urban VIII was Pope from 1623-1644.

"What!" Pennyboy Junior said.

Thomas the Barber continued, "And Holy Roman Emperor, too, the thirtieth of February."

"Is the previous Holy Roman Emperor dead?" Pennyboy Junior asked.

"No," Cymbal said, "but he has resigned, and trails a pike now under Tilly —"

Actually, Holy Roman Emperor Ferdinand II served 1619-1637. He never resigned and never served as a common soldier under Johann Tzerclaes, Count of Tilly, who was the general of the army of the Catholic League.

Soldiers held a pike — a pole weapon for thrusting — in their hands at the sides, and the end of the pike trailed behind them.

Fitton interrupted, "— for penance."

"These will beget strange turns in Christendom!" Pennyboy Junior said.

If the Holy Roman Emperor and the Pope were the same person, that person would have both ecclesiastical and secular authority and power.

Thomas Barber read out loud:

"*And Spinola has been made general of the Jesuits.*"

"Stranger news!" Pennyboy Junior said.

"Sir, all these news are alike true and certain," Fitton said.

There were two famous Spinolas. One was Charles Spinola the Jesuit (1564-1622), who was martyred in Japan. The other was Ambrogio di Spinola (1569-1630), a Spanish general. The two were sometimes confused.

They began to talk about the Fifth Monarchy.

Cymbal said, "All the prospects of establishing the Fifth Monarchy were held to be but vain until the ecclesiastic and secular powers were united like this, both in one person who is both the Holy Roman Emperor and the Pope."

The Fifth Monarchy is Christ's Kingdom on Earth. An extreme Puritan sect believed that the year 1666 would be the year human beings would cease to rule the earth and Christ would begin to rule for 1,000 years. The Fifth Monarchy has yet to come about.

In history, the Pope and the Holy Roman Emperor were frequently rivals for power. In his *Divine Comedy*, Dante criticized such power struggles. He believed that the Pope should be the spiritual leader and the Holy Roman Emperor should be the political leader. Each leader should be happy with his own sphere of power.

"It has been long the aim of the house of Austria," Fitton said.

"Just see Maximilian's letters to the Baron of Bouttersheim, or Scheiterhuyssen," Cymbal said.

Maximilian I was Elector of Bavaria, and he was the founder of the Catholic League of Imperial Princes.

"Bouttersheim" means, roughly, "Butters-home."

"Scheiterhuyssen" means, roughly, "Shit-house."

Fitton objected, "No, of Liechtenstein — Lord Paul, I think."

Karl von Liechtenstein was a governor of Bohemia, and he presided over the country's conversion to Catholicism.

"Lord Paul" is an inaccuracy made by Fitton.

"I have heard of some such thing," Pennyboy Junior said. "Don Spinola made general of the Jesuits!"

Pennyboy Junior said, "And he is a priest!"

Priest and general seem to be incompatible occupations.

Cymbal said, "Oh, no, he is dispensed — released from his religious vows — now, and so are the whole Society of Jesuits, who do now appear to be the only engineers of Christendom —"

Engineers are 1) schemers, or 2) inventors.

Pennyboy Junior said, "They have been thought so for a long time, and rightly, too —"

Fitton said, "Witness the engine that they have presented to Spinola to travel to the moon and thence make all his discoveries!"

According to this news, Jesuit engineers had invented a rocket for Spinola to travel to the Moon.

Cymbal said to Thomas Barber, "Read on."

Thomas Barber read out loud:

"And Vitellesco, he who was last general, being now turned cook to the Society, has dressed His Excellence — Spinola — such a dish of eggs —"

Mutio (aka Muzio and Mutius) Vitellesco was Superior General of the Society of Jesuits from 1615 to 1645. Spinola had not been made general of the Jesuits. And Vitellesco had not been made a cook.

"Eggs? What, poached?" Pennyboy Junior asked.

"No, powdered," Thomas Barber answered.

"Powdered" means 1) seasoned, or 2) filled with gunpower.

Cymbal said, "All the yolk is wildfire, as he shall need beleaguer and besiege no more towns. Now he can just throw his egg in."

Spinola had undertaken a siege of Breda in the Netherlands in 1624-25. Time wore on, and Spinola grew tired of waiting for Breda to capitulate and so he used incendiary devices — the "eggs" — to set fire to Breda. On 2 June 1625, Breda capitulated.

Wildfire is a chemical mixture that, once ignited, is hard to extinguish.

"It shall clear and clearly consume palace and place, demolish and bear down all strengths before it!" Fitton said.

"It will never be extinguished until all becomes one ruin!" Cymbal said.

Fitton began, "And from Florence —"

Thomas Barber interrupted:

"— *they write that there was found in Galileo's study a burning glass, which they have sent to Spinola, too, to set on fire any fleet that's out at sea —*"

They began to talk about a burning glass by moonshine in the water that could be used as a weapon against enemy ships.

Cymbal interrupted, "By moonshine, isn't that right?"

"Yes, sir, in the water," Thomas Barber said.

"Moonshine in the water" was an idiom for saying that something was unreal nonsense.

"His strengths will be unresistible, if this hold!" Pennyboy Junior said. "Have you no news against him on the contrary?"

Nathaniel the Clerk said, "Yes, sir."

He read out loud:

"*They write here that one Corneliuson has made for the Hollanders an invisible eel to swim the haven at Dunkirk and sink all the shipping there.*"

A man named Cornelius Drebbel was an inventor of weaponry. He had invented a boat that was mostly underwater but allowed the occupant's head to be above the water. The eel sounds much like a torpedo, but invisible.

Dunkirk was a haven for pirates.

Pennyboy Junior asked Thomas Barber, "Why haven't you got this news, Tom?"

Cymbal said, "Because he keeps the pontifical side."

Thomas Barber covered the news about the Catholics.

Pennyboy Junior wanted Thomas Barber to change sides — let someone else cover the news about the Catholics. Pennyboy Junior did not support the Pope, and he felt that the Catholics were against British interests.

"What!" Pennyboy Junior said, "Change sides, Tom. It was never in my thought to put you up against ourselves. Come down from your seat, quickly."

"Why, sir?" Cymbal asked.

"I did not venture my money upon those terms," Pennyboy Junior said. "If he may change, why so. I'll have him keep his own side, sure."

"Why, let him," Fitton said. "It is just writing so much over again."

"For that I'll bear the charge," Pennyboy Junior said. "There's two pieces."

He offered two gold coins to Cymbal.

Fitton said to Cymbal, "Come, do not saddle the gentleman with a position he dislikes."

"I'll take no money, sir," Cymbal said, "And yet he shall have the place."

He was permitting the change of place. And he was saying that he would not take the money. Why? So that he could impress Lady Pecunia with the success of the Staple of News Office.

Unnecessarily, Pennyboy Junior offered more money: "The number of coins shall be ten, then."

Pennyboy Junior said to Thomas Barber, "Up, Tom; and the News Office shall take the money. Keep your side, Tom. Know your own side; do not forsake your side, Tom."

Tom Barber and Nathaniel the clerk changed desks.

Cymbal said to Thomas Barber, "Read."

Thomas Barber read out loud:

"They write here that one Corneliuson has made the Hollanders an invisible eel to swim the haven at Dunkirk and sink all the shipping there."

"But how is it done?" Pennyboy Junior asked.

"I'll tell you, sir," Cymbal said. "It is an automa, runs underwater, with a snug, trim nose, and has a nimble tail — a nimble stern or propeller — that is made like an auger, with which tail she wriggles between the ribs of a ship and sinks it straightaway."

Actually, "automaton" is the singular of "automata."

"Whence have you this news?" Pennyboy Junior asked.

"From a right hand, I assure you," Fitton answered. "The eel boats here that lie before Queenhithe came out of Holland."

Queenhithe Dock was near the Southwark Bridge in London.

"A most splendid device to murder their flat bottoms — their boats!" Pennyboy Junior said.

"I grant you that," Fitton said. "But what if Spinola should have a new project to bring an army over in cork shoes, and land them, here, at Harwich? All his horses are shod with cork, and fourscore pieces of ordnance, mounted upon cork-carriages, with inflatable bladders instead of wheels to run the passage over at a spring tide."

"Is it true?" Pennyboy Junior asked.

"As true as the rest of the news," Fitton replied.

"He'll never leave his ingenious plots," Pennyboy Junior said.

He then said, "I would like to hear now some curious — occult — news."

"As what?" Cymbal asked.

"Magic, or alchemy, or flying in the air, I don't care what," Pennyboy Junior said.

Nathaniel the clerk read out loud:

"*They write from Leipzig* — pardon the use of coarse language — *that the art of drawing farts out of dead bodies is by the Brotherhood of the Rosy Cross produced to perfection, in so sweet and rich a tincture —*"

The Brotherhood of the Rosy Cross refers to the German followers of Christian Rosencreutz: the Rosicrucians.

Fitton interrupted, "— as there is no princess but may perfume her chamber with the extraction."

Even princesses fart, but Fitton meant that princesses could use the farts from corpses to perfume their bedchambers.

Pennyboy Junior said to Lady Pecunia, "There's something for you, princess."

"What, a fart for her?" the Canter asked.

"I mean the spirit," Pennyboy Junior said.

Aristotle divided the soul (or spirit) into three parts: Nutritive, Sensitive, and Rational. The nutritive soul is responsible for nourishment and digestion and excretion.

The Canter said, "Beware how she resents it."

If Lady Pecunia actually used the extracted farts, she would re-scent them.

Pennyboy Junior then asked, "And what news do you have, Tom?"

They began to talk about the perpetual motion.

Thomas Barber read out loud:

"*The perpetual motion is here found out by an alewife in Saint Katherine's at the sign of the Dancing Bears —*"

"What, from her tap?" Pennyboy Junior said. "I'll go see that, or else I'll send old Canter. He can make that investigation."

The perpetual motion was ale flowing from the alewife's taps and down her customers' throats. This alewife kept bears that she brought out to dance for her customers.

The Canter said, "Yes, in ale."

Cornelius (Cornelis) Drebbel presented King James I with what was supposed to be a perpetual clockwork machine.

Noise came from outside. People were coming into the Staple of News Office to buy news.

"Let me have all this news prepared and sealed," Pennyboy Junior said.

The register said, "The people press upon us; if it pleases you, sir, withdraw with your fair princess. There's a room within, sir, to retire to."

The Staple of News Office included some rooms to serve as residences.

"No, good register," Pennyboy Junior said. "We'll remain out here and observe your office and what news it issues."

The register's office or position was called the House of Fame.

Fama is Rumor. Virgil wrote about *Fama* in his *Aeneid* (Book 4, lines 181ff): "Evil moves quickly, and of all evils, rumor moves the quickest. Rumor is the daughter of Mother Earth, who bore her after Jupiter had killed two of her sons: the Titan Coeus and the Giant Enceladus. Mother Earth gave birth to Rumor as a way to get revenge for the death of these sons. Rumor has wings and many feathers. Her many eyes never sleep, and she has many tongues and many ears. By night she flies, and by day she watches and listens. She values lies as much as she values truths."

"My office is the House of Fame, sir," the register said, "where both the curious and the negligent, the scrupulous and careless, the wild and grave, the idle and laborious, all meet to taste the *cornucopiae* — cornucopias — of her rumors, which Lady Fame, the mother of sport and play, pleases to scatter among the vulgar. Baits, sir, for the people! And they will bite like fishes."

"Let's see your office in action," Pennyboy Junior said.

Some news customers entered the room. The first news customer was Dopper, a woman Anabaptist.

A dipper is a believer in immersion in water during baptism, rather than being sprinkled. The Dutch word *dooper* means "dipper."

Dopper asked, "Have you, in your profane shop, any news about the saints at Amsterdam?"

Many Anabaptists were in Amsterdam, a city of religious toleration.

"Yes," the register said. "How much would you like?"

"Six pennyworth," Dopper answered.

"Lay your money down," the register said.

Dopper paid the money.

The register then said, "Read, Thomas."

Thomas Barber read out loud:

"*The saints do write, they expect a prophet shortly, the Prophet Baal, to be sent over to them to calculate a time, and half a time, and the whole time, according to Naometry.*"

Over and over, people throughout history have used numerology to determine the dates of events predicted in the Bible, including the return of Christ. So far, Christ has not returned and all predicted dates of His return have been wrong.

Revelation 12:14 states, "*And to the woman were given two wings of a great eagle, that she might fly into the wilderness, into her place, where she is nourished for a time, and times, and half a time, from the face of the serpent*" (King James Version).

Naometry attempted to predict future events by using the measurements of Solomon's temple at Jerusalem.

"What's that?" Pennyboy Junior said.

Thomas Barber answered, "The measuring of the Temple. A cabal — body of esoteric lore — found out but lately, and set out by Archy, or some such head, of whose long coat they have heard, and, because the coat is black, they desire it."

Archibald Armstrong was court jester to King James I and King Charles I. He mourned, wearing a black coat, when King James I died.

Actually, a German scholar named Simon Studion invented Naometry.

Anabaptists wore black coats.

Dopper said, "Peace be with them!"

"So there had need, for they are still by the ears — at odds — one with another," the register said.

There was need for peace between the secular rulers and the religious people. King James I was Protestant, but in his reign, an Anabaptist named Edward Wightman became the last person to be burned at the stake for heresy in England.

"It is their zeal," Dopper said.

Anabaptists strongly believed in religious zeal. The virtue of Zeal is opposed to the sin of Sloth.

"Most likely," the register replied.

"Have you any other news of that species?" Dopper asked.

"Yes, but it is more expensive," the register said. "It will cost you a shilling."

Dopper offered some money, but she said, "Verily, there is a ninepence; I will spend no more."

The price the register had asked for this news was twelvepence: a twelve-penny shilling.

"Not to hear about the good of the saints?" the register asked.

"I am not sure that man is good," Dopper said.

She may have been referring to the prophet Baal.

The register said to Thomas Barber, "Read, from Constantinople, nine pennyworth of news."

Thomas Barber read out loud:

"They give out here the grand Signor — the Sultan of Turkey — has certainly turned Christian, and to clear up the controversy between the Pope and him, who is the Antichrist, he means to visit the church at Amsterdam this very summer, and quit all marks of the Beast."

Chances, the writer wanted "the Antichrist" to mean the Pope, but as written, "the Antichrist" means the grand Signor.

In Revelation, the damned wore the marks of the Beast. Protestants associated the marks of the Beast with Catholics; Catholics did not.

Revelation 16:2 states, "*And the first went, and poured out his vial upon the earth; and there fell a noisome and grievous sore upon the men which had the mark of the beast, and upon them which worshipped his image*" (King James Version).

Dopper said, "Now, these are joyful tidings! Who brought in this? Which emissary?"

"Buzz, your countryman," the register said.

Hans Buzz, a Dutchman, was Emissary at the Exchange.

"Now, blessed be the man, and his whole family, with the nation!" Dopper said.

"Yes, for Amboyna, and the justice there!" the register said.

On 9 March 1623, the Dutch executed ten Englishmen who were at a trading post in Amboyna. They had confessed — after torture — that they had intended to capture the Dutch castle of Amboyna. A kind of justice was achieved: A plague was said to have killed 1,000 people there shortly after the execution.

The register whispered to Tom Barber, "This is a Dopper, a she-Anabaptist! Seal and deliver her news to her. Dispatch!"

A second customer spoke up as Dopper stepped aside to receive her parcel of news.

"Have you any news from the Indies?" the second customer asked. "Any miracles done in Japan by the Jesuits, or in China?"

In 1624, John Gee's book *The Foot out of the Snare: with a Detection of Sundry Late Practices and Impostures of the Priests and Jesuits in England. Whereunto is Added a Catalogue of Such Bookes as in this Authors Knowledge have been Vented Within Two Yeeres Last Past in London, by the Priests and their Agents* appeared in print. John Gee called the stories of miracles done by priests and Jesuits "old wonder-working tales." Stories about Jesuits in Japan and China tended to be stories of martyrdom rather than of miracles.

Nathaniel the clerk answered, "No, but we hear of a colony of cooks who will be set ashore on the coast of America for the conversion of the cannibals, and making them good-eating Christians. Here comes the colonel who undertakes it."

"Good-eating Christians" could be 1) Christians who eat well, 2) Christians who taste good when eaten, or 3) both.

The third customer, accompanied by Lickfinger, approached them.

"Who?" the second customer asked. "Captain Lickfinger?"

We can assume that "Colonel" and "Captain" were honorary titles. As will become apparent later, Lickfinger thought of cooked food as resembling military fortifications.

Lickfinger said, "News, news, my boys! I am to furnish a great feast today, and I would have what news the Staple of News Office affords."

He considered this feast, prepared for the Golden Heir, to be news.

Nathaniel the clerk said, "We were venting some news about you, about your new project —"

"Venting" means expressing. It can also mean selling, but Nathaniel the clerk had forgotten to collect the money before expressing the news.

The register interrupted, "— before it was paid for. You, Nathaniel, were somewhat too hasty."

Pennyboy Junior asked, "What, Lickfinger, will you convert the cannibals with spit-and-pan divinity?'

Meat was roasted on a spit.

Lickfinger replied, "Sir, for that I will not urge, but for the fire and zeal to the true cause, I have undertaken this:

"With two lay-brethren to myself, no more — one of the broach, aka spit, the other of the boiler — in one six-month period, and by plain cookery, no magic to it except old Japhet's physic (fire is the father of the European arts) to make such sauces for the savages and cook their meats with those enticing steams as it would make our cannibal-Christians forbear the mutual eating one another, which they do, and which they do more cunningly than the wild Anthropophagi who snatch only strangers, like my old patron's dogs there."

Japhet's physic is fire, which was given to human beings by Prometheus, son of Japhet.

The Anthropophagi were a legendary race of man-eaters.

Lickfinger was comparing the Anthropophagi's literal cannibalism to the Christians' figurative cannibalism.

The Anthropophagi ate only strangers, but the Christians — Catholics and Protestants — figuratively ate one another.

Lickfinger's old patron was Pennyboy Senior.

"Oh, my uncle's!" Pennyboy Junior said. "Is dinner ready, Lickfinger?"

"When you please, sir," Littlefinger said. "I was asking for just a parcel of news to supplement the long meal with, but it seems that you are furnished with news here already."

The news could be read out loud in between courses, or it could be posted so that people could read it before or after eating.

"Oh, not half!" Pennyboy Junior said.

He wanted more news.

"What court news is there?" Lickfinger asked. "Any proclamations or edicts to come forth?"

Thomas Barber said, "Yes, there is one that the King's barber has got for aid of our mystery — that is, trade — of barbering, whereof there is a manifest decay."

Trades are mysteries to those who do not know how to do them.

Thomas Barber continued, "There is a precept — an edict — for the wearing of long hair, to run to seed, to sow bald pates with, and the preserving of fruitful heads and chins, to help a craft, almost antiquated."

Men with fruitful heads would allow their hair to grow long and produce seeds, which would be used to sow bald heads and make them fruitful. This would help increase barbers' business.

Some men, however, had heads that would not be fertile fields for the hair seeds.

Thomas Barber continued, "Men who are bald and barren beyond hope are to be separated and set by to be gentlemen-ushers to old countesses —"

Gentleman-ushers had access to high-ranking women. To avoid scandal, those gentleman-ushers could be effeminate, or old.

Lickfinger said, "And coachmen to mount their boxes, reverently, and drive like lapwings with a shell upon their heads through the streets."

Countesses of the time engaged in the affectation of making their coachmen ride bare-headed. The bald coachmen's heads were as smooth as the shells of lapwings. Lapwing chicks were thought to be precocious and to start leaving the nest even while they had part of the shell they had hatched from on their heads.

Lickfinger asked, "Have you no news of the stage? They'll ask me about new plays at dinnertime, and I should be as dumb — silent — as a fish."

"Oh, yes!" Thomas Barber said. "There is a legacy left to the King's Players, both for their various shifting of their scenes and the dexterous change of their persons to all shapes and all disguises, by the right reverend Archbishop of Spalato."

The Archbishop of Spalato had a disagreement with the Pope. He visited King James I to spread his idea of a Universal Church, but the idea never bore fruit. Eventually, he returned to Rome. After the death of Pope Gregory XV, the Inquisition declared Spalato a relapsed heretic, and he was confined to the Castel Sant'Angelo and in September 1624 he died there of natural causes.

Actors are changeable; they play many roles.

The Archbishop of Spalato was also changeable. He disagreed with the Pope, but he later reconciled with him.

Lickfinger said, "He is dead who played him!"

The actor William Rowley, who played the Fat Bishop in Thomas Middleton's play *A Game at Chess*, died in February 1626. The character of the Fat Bishop was based on the Archbishop of Spalato.

"Then he's lost his share of the legacy," Thomas Barber said.

Lickfinger said, "What news is there about Gondomar?"

Thomas Barber answered, "He has a second fistula, or an excoriation at the least, for putting the poor English play that was written about him to such a sordid use, as is said he did, of cleansing his posteriors."

An excoriation is 1) a sore, or 2) a severe criticism.

The Count of Gondomar (1567-1626) did have an anal fistula. Gondomar was satirized in Thomas Middleton's play *A Game at Chess*, which was first staged in August 1624, in the character of the Black Knight. Gondomar had a special chair made so he could sit without discomfort. The chair was mentioned in the play, and Gondomar forced the play to close.

Gondomar is neither the first nor the last person to wipe his butt with the pages of a play.

Gondomar was a Spanish ambassador to England, and he became a friend to King James I. He promoted friendly relations between Catholic Spain and Protestant England. He also favored the beheading of Sir Walter Raleigh on 29 October 1618. Gondomar stayed in London from 1613 to 1618 and from

1619 to 1622. Many English hated him because of his effective promotion of Spanish interests.

Referring to Gondomar's second fistula, Lickfinger said, "That's justice! Justice!"

Thomas Barber said, "Since when he lives condemned to his chair at Brussels, and there he sits filing certain politic — crafty — hinges to hang the states on he's heaved off the hooks."

From 1625-1626, Gondomar was in Brussels on a diplomatic mission to the Infanta Isabella Clara Eugenia, sovereign of the Spanish Netherlands.

In the late 1500s, several Dutch provinces revolted against Spanish rule and declared their independence.

According to Thomas Barber, Gondomar sat on his special chair in Brussels and devised political schemes against the States General of the United Provinces, aka the Protestant Netherlands.

The southern Netherlands, including Belgium, were under southern control, and many Protestants therefore fled to the north.

Hinges are movable joints. Apparently, Gondomar was plotting politic — crafty — hinges that would move the Protestant Netherlands into becoming part of the Spanish Netherlands, with the result that the Protestant Netherlands would be hung out to dry. In addition, he traveled with his special chair. To make it portable, it may have had hinges and hooks.

"What must you have for these news?" Lickfinger asked. "What is the price?"

"You shall pay nothing," Pennyboy Junior, a generous heir, said, "but include their price in with the other items in the bill for the feast."

He then said to Thomas Barber, "There's twenty pieces — twenty coins — that her Grace bestows upon the Staple of News Office, Tom. Write that down for news."

Her Grace was Lady Pecunia, but Pennyboy Junior was paying the money. He wanted her to get the credit and to be mentioned in the news the Staple of News Office published.

"We may well do it," the Register said. "We have not many such news."

Pennyboy Junior wanted it definitely in the news published by the Staple of News Office, so he now made the news more newsworthy by doubling the amount of money.

He put down twenty more coins and said, "There's twenty more pieces, if you say so. My princess is a princess! And put that, too, under the Staple of News Office seal."

Cymbal took Pecunia aside, and he courted and wooed her to the Staple of News Office. He wanted her to take his roof for "covert," a word that means 1) haven, 2) shelter, 3) protection, 4) control, and 5) jurisdiction.

As you would expect, Cymbal wanted Lady Pecunia to make a large investment in the Staple of News Office.

Cymbal said to her, "If it will please Your Grace to sojourn here and take my roof for covert, you shall know the rites belonging to your blood and birth, which few can apprehend. These sordid servants, who are your keepers rather than your attendants, should not come near your presence."

The word "keepers" means guards. Guards can keep someone in custody, or they can protect someone. They are either jail-keepers, or guardians in the sense of guardian-angels.

Cymbal continued, "I would have you waited on by ladies, and your train borne up by persons of quality and honor."

They would lift up the train of her dress so it didn't trail on the floor, and they would make up her train of attendants.

He continued, "Your food should be served in with curious dances, and set upon the board with virgin hands tuned to their voices; not a dish removed but to the music, nor a drop of wine mixed with its water without harmony."

Pennyboy Senior was a miser who accumulated money. Cymbal was a would-be spendthrift who, if he had access to someone else's money, would spend it on luxuriousness. Pennyboy Junior was a prodigal who spent too freely, but who did good deeds with his money, including paying tradesmen well and buying Thomas Barber an office, aka job position.

Lady Pecunia said to Cymbal, 'You are a courtier, sir, or somewhat more, who have this tempting language."

Not all courtiers are good people. The bad ones can persuade other people to do evil.

"I'm your servant, excellent princess," Cymbal said, "and I would have you appear as that which you are. Come forth, state and wonder of these our times."

A person of state is a person of social standing. The word "state" also means splendor.

He continued, "Dazzle the vulgar eyes and strike the people blind with admiration!"

The word "vulgar" means 1) common, or 2) tasteless.

The Canter, who had been listening, said, "Why, that's the end of wealth!"

He was punning. Certainly Cymbal believed that the end — the purpose — of wealth was ostentatious display. The Canter, however, was aware that such ostentatious spending was a way to end — get rid of — all of one's wealth.

The Canter continued, "Thrust riches outward, and remain beggars within; contemplate nothing but the vile sordid things of time, place, money, and let the noble and the precious go. Virtue and honesty — hang them, poor thin membranes of honor, who respects them? Oh, the Fates!"

He was criticizing a life in which riches were thrust outside — money was used for conspicuous spending — and in which other riches — such as virtue and honesty — were ignored.

The Canter continued, "How has all just, true reputation fallen since money, this base money, began to have any reputation!"

While Cymbal was working on Lady Pecunia to persuade her to stay at the Staple of News Office, Fitton was working on Lady Pecunia's waiting-women to convince them to persuade her to stay at the News Office, which he described as a paradise. They were having none of it, and they were jeering him.

"It's a pity the gentleman is not immortal!" Band said

Band was unpersuaded by Fitton's arguments and so she said that it was a pity that Fitton was not immortal because if he were an immortal god he would have the power to make the Staple of News Office as good as he said it was.

Wax said, "As he gives out, the place is, by description — "

Fitton interrupted, "— a veritable paradise, as you would know if you could see it all, lady."

"I am the chambermaid, sir," Wax said. "You mistake. My lady may see all."

Fitton should be showing all of the Staple of News Office to Lady Pecunia, not Wax the chambermaid.

Fitton said, "Sweet Mistress Statute, gentle Mistress Band, and Mother Mortgage, do but get Her Grace to sojourn here."

Picklock said, "I thank you, gentle Wax."

He was referring to her comment that Lady Pecunia may see all of the Staple of News Office.

Mortgage said, "If it were a chattel — a movable possession — I would try my credit."

She would try her credit with her mistress: Lady Pecunia. That is, she would recommend that Lady Pecunia invest in the Staple of News Office.

"So it is, for term of life," Picklock said. "We account it so."

Statute said, "Mortgage means inheritance to Fitton and his heirs, or that he could assure a state of years. If that were to happen, I'll be his Statute-Staple, Statute-Merchant, or whatever he pleases me to be."

"Statute-Staple" and "Statute-Merchant" referred to a contract in which "Statute-Staple" was the mayor of a staple market and "Statute-Merchant" was a merchant of that staple. In the presence of the mayor, the debtor would swear that a debt would be repaid by a certain time. In this contract, if the debtor failed to repay a debt by the appointed time, then the creditor could seize the debtor's land.

A title to a property could be granted for a term of life — until the person dies. Or it could be granted for a term of years — for a certain number of years.

Cymbal and Fitton wanted Lady Pecunia to invest in the property: the Staple of News Office. The investment included the real estate of the Staple of News Office, and Statute knew that Lady Pecunia would like a good investment if she in fact invested in the Staple of News Office.

Cymbal had a term of life contract in the Staple of News Office.

A term of life investment could turn out to be a bad investment if the person with a term of life contract died quickly.

But if Cymbal were to die and the Staple of News Office passed on to Fitton, the contract could stipulate that Lady Pecunia's contract with Cymbal would still apply to Fitton.

"He — Fitton — can expect no more," Picklock said.

Band said, "Fitton's cousin, Alderman Security, whom he did talk of so, just now —"

Statute interrupted, "— who is the very brooch of the bench, gem of the city —"

Band interrupted, "— let he — Alderman Security — and his deputy just assure his life for one period of seven years."

If Alderman Security and his deputy were to insure Cymbal's life for seven years, then the serving-gentlewomen would see about interesting Lady Pecunia in the investment. Of course, the contract would have to be legal, as attested by Alderman Security and his deputy: old Chain.

Stature said, "And see what we'll do for him, upon his scarlet motion —"

Aldermen wore a scarlet gown.

Band said, "And old Chain, who draws — attracts — the City ears —"

Aldermen sometimes wore a ceremonial chain.

Wax interrupted, "— when he says nothing, but twirls his chain like this."

She demonstrated him twirling his chain.

Statute said, "A moving oratory!"

The oratory was both persuasive and in the demonstration of the twirling of the chain, moving.

Band said, "Dumb rhetoric and silent eloquence, as the fine poet Samuel Daniel says."

Fitton said to Picklock, "Come, they all scorn us. Don't you see it? The family of scorn!"

Broker said to the serving-women, "Do not believe him!"

Broker was on the side of Fitton and Picklock. He was willing to make their case to the serving-women and even lie.

He then said, "Gentle Master Picklock, they did not understand. The gentlewomen, they thought you would have my lady sojourn with you at the Staple of News Office, whereas you desire only now and then a visit."

Cymbal and Fitton definitely wanted Lady Pecunia to sojourn at the Staple of News Office.

Picklock replied, "Yes, if she pleased, sir. But her continual residence would much advance the Staple of News Office! I speak but as a member."

As a lady of high social standing, Lady Pecunia's staying at the Staple of News Office would greatly enhance its reputation. Also, of course, Lady Pecunia's wealth would follow her.

Broker said, "It is enough."

He whispered to Picklock, "I apprehend you. And it shall go hard, but I'll so work as somebody shall work her."

Broker was in league with Picklock to persuade Lady Pecunia to invest in — and stay at — the Staple of News Office. He understood that Picklock wanted her to stay at the News Office and he — Broker — would work hard to persuade at least one of the serving-women to help persuade Lady Pecunia to do that.

Picklock said to Broker, "Please, exchange with our master just a word about it."

They stepped aside to talk privately.

Pennyboy Junior said, "Well, Lickfinger, see that our food is ready. You have enough news."

Lickfinger replied, "I need some news about Bethlem Gabor, and then I'm gone."

Gabriel Bathlen was a Prince of Transylvania who first wanted to marry the Emperor Frederick's daughter and when he was rebuffed, he wanted to marry the sister of the Elector of Brandenburg. Bathlen wanted land, and he wanted to marry a woman who would bring him land; in return for marrying such a woman, he would fight on her father's side, whether Protestant or Catholic. The Elector of Brandenburg was Protestant; Emperor Frederick was Catholic. During the Thirty Years War (1618-1648), Bathlen was changeable in his religious and political alliances.

Thomas Barber read out loud about Gabriel Bathlen:

"We hear he has devised a drum to fill all Christendom with the sound, but that he cannot draw his forces near it to march yet because of the violence of the noise. And therefore he is obliged by a design to carry them in the air and at some distance until he is married; then they shall appear."

"Or never," Lickfinger said.

Omens were popularly believed in, including such omens as the appearance of armies in the air.

Lickfinger then said, "Well, may God be with you."

He started to leave, but seeing some people entering the Staple of News Office, he said, "Wait, who's here?"

Two more customers of news entered the room.

Lickfinger said to Nathaniel the Clerk, "A little of the Duke of Bavier, and then —"

Bavier is Bavaria.

Nathaniel said, "He's taken the grey habit of the Franciscans, and he has become the church's miller. He grinds the Catholic grist with every wind; and Tilly takes the toll."

Maximilian I was Elector of Bavaria, and he was the founder of the Catholic League of Imperial Princes.

Johann Tzerclaes, Count of Tilly, was the general of the army of the Catholic League.

The fourth customer asked, "Have you any news of the pageants to send down into the several counties? All the country expected from the city very splendid speeches now at the coronation."

King Charles I was crowned on 2 February 1626, but his reign began on 27 March 1625. London was recovering from the effects of the plague, and the celebrations of the crowning were muted.

Lickfinger said, "It — all the country — expected more than it understood, for they — the pageants — stand mute, poor, innocent, dumb things. They are but wood, as is the bench and blocks they were wrought on, yet when May Day comes, and the sun shines, perhaps they'll sing like Memnon's statue and be vocal."

The pageants were wood, figuratively and literally. They were figuratively wood because they were silent and did nothing. The speakers, because they were silent, were like blockheads — blocks of wood for displaying hats or wigs. They were literally wood because the structures (such as platforms) and furniture (such as benches) were made of wood.

At Karnack in Egypt was a statue of Amenhotep III. When the sun shone on the statue after it was damaged in an earthquake, the statue made a twanging sound like a plunked harp string. Apparently the sun warmed one side, expanding it, and causing friction as it moved against the unwarmed side.

The fifth customer asked, "Have you any forest news?"

Thomas Barber said, "None very wild, sir. Some rumor there is out of the Forest of Fools: A new park is being made there, to separate cuckolds of antler from the rascals. Such men as those whose wives are dead and have since cast their heads — shed their antlers — shall remain cuckolds-pollard."

Parks are enclosed areas.

Rascals are 1) inferior male deer, or 2) inferior male humans.

Cuckolds are men with unfaithful wives; they are said to have invisible horns growing on their heads.

The word "pollard" means "without horns."

The purpose of the park was to separate horned cuckolds from unhorned cuckolds.

"I'll have that news," Lickfinger said.

"And I," Dopper said.

"And I," the second customer said.

"And I," the third customer said.

"And I," the fourth customer said.

"And I," the fifth customer said.

Sex news is always popular.

Pennyboy Junior invited the Master of the Staple of News Office — Cymbal — to dine.

Cymbal replied, "Sir, I desire to be excused; and, madam, I cannot leave my Staple of News Office the first day. But my cousin Fitton here shall wait upon you, and my emissary Picklock."

"And Tom *Clericus*?" Pennyboy Junior asked, referring to Thomas Barber.

"I cannot spare him yet," Cymbal said, "but he shall follow you when they have ordered the rolls."

The news was written on rolls of paper.

Cymbal ordered the clerks, "When you have finished, shut up the Staple of News Office until two o'clock."

Everyone except the clerks exited.

Three jeerers entered the Staple of News Office: Shunfield, Almanac, and Madrigal. They were looking for a free meal somewhere.

Shunfield said, "If you don't mind, clerks, let us ask where shall we dine today? Do you know?"

"Where's my friend Fitton?" Almanac asked.

"He's just now gone out," Thomas Barber said.

"Can't your Staple of News Office tell us what splendid fellows eat together today in town, and where?" Shunfield asked.

Splendid fellows are likely to have money enough to be able to treat others to a meal.

"Yes, there's a gentleman, the brave heir, young Pennyboy Junior, who dines in the Apollo Room in the Devil Tavern," Thomas Barber answered.

"Come, let's go thither, then," Madrigal said. "I have supped in the Apollo Room."

"With the Muses?" Almanac asked.

"No, not them, but with two gentlewomen called the Graces," Madrigal said.

"They were always three in poetry," Almanac said.

"That was the truth, sir," Madrigal said.

The Muses were muses of the arts, including lyric poetry and epic poetry.

The Three Graces were goddesses of beauty, charm, and creativity.

Madrigal's two Graces were possibly prostitutes.

"Sir, Master Fitton's there, too," Thomas Barber said.

"All the better," Shunfield said.

"We may have a jeer, perhaps," Almanac said.

"Yes, you'll drink, Doctor Almanac, if there is any good food, as much good wine now as would lay up a Dutch ambassador," Shunfield said.

They would possibly have a jeer and good cheer — good food and drink.

The Dutch loved butter — and wine.

Thomas Barber said, "If he dines there, he's sure to have good food, for Lickfinger the cook provides the dinner."

"Who?" Almanac said. "The glory of the kitchen, who believes that cookery is a trade that goes all the way to Adam, who quotes Adam's broths and salads, and swears that Adam is not dead yet, but translated — conveyed — in some immortal crust, the paste of almonds?"

Lickfinger believed that Adam, the first man, lived on in the art of cookery.

"The same," Madrigal said. "He believes that no man can be a poet who is not a good cook — only good cooks know the palates and several tastes of the time. He derives all arts out of the kitchen but especially the art of poetry, which he concludes the same with cookery."

Lickfinger valued the art of cookery as highly as he did the art of poetry. Both cookery, as in the case of Adam, and poetry, as in the case of Ben Jonson, could make men immortal.

Shunfield said, "Tut, he maintains more heresies than that. He'll draw the magisterium — the philosopher's stone — from a minced-meat pie, and he'll prefer jellies to your juleps, doctor."

Powdered philosopher's stone was supposed to turn base metals into silver and gold.

Some cooks are so good that they can make metaphorical gold out of an assortment of common ingredients. When Lickfinger created a minced-meat pie, it was if he had created the philosopher's stone.

Juleps are sweetened medicinal drinks.

Almanac said, "I was at an *olla podrida* of his making."

Olla podrida is a Portuguese dish that consists of a jumble or stew of spiced meats and vegetables.

Almanac continued, "The *olla podrida* was a brave piece of cookery at a funeral. Although it was a funeral, by opening the pot-lid, he made us laugh who'd wept all day, and sent us such a tickling into our nostrils as if the funeral feast had been a wedding dinner."

Shunfield said, "Give him allowance, and that but moderate, he will make a Siren sing in the kettle. He will also send in an Arion in a splendid broth of a watery green color, just like the sea color — Arion will be mounted on the back of a grown conger, aka eel, but in such a posture as all the world would take him for a dolphin."

Sirens were mythological monsters, but they sang beautifully.

A dolphin listened to Arion's music and then saved him when he was in danger of drowning in the sea. The dolphin carried Arion on its back to land.

Lickfinger's Arion was possibly an onion.

"He's an excellent fellow, without question," Madrigal said. "But he holds some paradoxes — unorthodox views."

"Aye, and pseudodoxes — false opinions," Almanac said. "But by the Virgin Mary, to be sure, for mostly he's orthodox in the kitchen."

"And he knows the clergy's taste," Madrigal said.

"Aye, and the laity's," Almanac said.

"You're not thinking about the time," Shunfield said. "We'll arrive too late if we don't go immediately."

"Let's leave, then," Madrigal said.

Shunfield said to the clerks, "Sirs, you must get some of this news for your Staple of News Office — news about who dines and sups in the town, where, and with whom. It will be beneficial, when you have news; and as we like our fare, we shall reward you."

The jeerers would use the news to decide whom to sponge off of that day.

The three jeerers — Madrigal, Almanac, and Shunfield — exited.

"A hungry trade it will be," Nathaniel said.

The jeerers lacked money to give to the clerks.

"Much like Duke Humphrey's," Thomas Barber said. "But, now and then, as the wholesome proverb says, it will *obsonare famem ambulando*."

"To dine with Duke Humphrey" was an idiom for "to go hungry." Some gallants would go hungry and spend the meal hour on Duke Humphrey's Walk at St. Paul's. If they were lucky, someone would see them and invite them to dine with him.

The Latin *obsonare famem ambulando* means to get an appetite through walking.

"Shut up the Staple of News Office, gentle brother Thomas," Nathaniel the clerk said.

Thomas Barber replied, "Brother Nathaniel, I have the wine for you — let me buy you a drink. I hope to see us, one day, promoted to be emissaries."

"Why not?" Nathaniel the Clerk said. "By God's eyelid, I despair because I am not a Master!"

He wanted a much higher position than he had.

— 3.4 —

In Pennyboy Senior's house, Broker walked into a room and met Pennyboy Senior, who was startled to see Broker, who was supposed to be with Lady Pecunia.

"What is this now?" Pennyboy Senior said. "I think I was born under Hercules' star! Nothing but trouble and tumult to oppress me!"

Hercules' star was under the influence of the planet Mars, which was named after the Roman god of war.

Pennyboy Senior asked, "Why have you come back? Where is your charge? Where is Lady Pecunia?"

"I have brought a gentleman to speak with you," Broker said.

This can't have made a good impression on Pennyboy Senior. Broker was ignoring his responsibilities to do a favor for someone else — someone who almost certainly was going to ask Pennyboy Senior for money.

"To speak with me?" Pennyboy Senior said. "You know it is death for me to speak with any man."

He was pretending to be ill. If he were ill, he need not engage in social courtesies such as standing when his visitor arrived.

He continued, "Who is he? Set me a chair."

Broker brought him a chair and said, "He's the master of the great News Office."

"What?" Pennyboy Senior asked.

"The Staple of News Office, which is a mighty thing," Broker said. "They talk six thousand a year."

They could talk about making six thousand pounds a year — or they could spread six thousand rumors a year.

"Well, bring your six in," Pennyboy Senior said. "Where have you left Pecunia?"

"Sir, in the Apollo Room," Broker said. "They have scarcely sat down."

"Bring in the six," Pennyboy Senior said.

Broker exited and returned with Cymbal.

"Here is the gentleman," Broker said.

"He must pardon me," Pennyboy Senior said. "I cannot rise because I am a diseased man."

"Rise by no means, sir," Cymbal said. "Respect your health and ease."

"My not rising is not because of pride in me, but because of pain, pain!" Pennyboy Senior said. "What's your errand, sir, to me?"

He then said, "Broker, return to your charge; be Argus-eyed."

The mythological Argus had eyes all over his body.

Pennyboy Senior continued, "Be awake to the affair you have in hand; serve in Apollo, but take heed of Bacchus."

In other words, listen to music, but don't get drunk.

Apollo is the god of music, among other things, and Bacchus is the god of wine.

Broker exited.

Pennyboy Senior said to Cymbal, "Go on, sir."

"I have come to speak with you," Cymbal said.

"It is pain for me to speak, a very death," Pennyboy Senior said, "but I will hear you."

"Sir, you have a lady who sojourns with you," Cymbal said.

Pennyboy Senior pretended to have an affliction in his ears: "Ha? I am somewhat short in my sense of hearing, too —"

Cymbal interrupted, "— Pecunia."

Pennyboy Senior pointed to one ear and continued his sentence, "— on that side, very imperfect; on —"

Cymbal interrupted, "— whom I would draw oftener to a poor News Office I am master of —"

"My hearing is very dead," Pennyboy Senior said. "You must speak quicker."

"Quick" is "living." It is opposed to Pennyboy Senior's very dead hearing, and "quicker" means for Cymbal to speak louder — livelier.

Cymbal said, "Or, if it would please you, sir, to let her sojourn in part with me, I have a moiety we will divide: half of the profits."

This was a bribe.

"Ha?" Pennyboy Senior said. "I hear you better now. How come the profits in? Is it a certain business, or a casual business?

"For I am loath to seek out doubtful courses, or run any hazardous paths. I love straight ways. I am a just and upright man!

"Now all trade totters. The trade of money has fallen two percent in the hundred, but it was a certain trade while the age was thrifty and men were good managers of their financial affairs, looked after their supplies of goods, and had their minds fixed where they ought to be fixed.

"Now all the public riots as if all of them were prostitutes. The public wastes resources by spending money on coaches and on footmen's coats and waiting-women's gowns.

"They must have velvet haunches — with a pox — now taken up, and yet they do not pay the use."

Haunches are a woman's tight-fitting undergarment.

"With a pox" can be emphatic, or it can refer to venereal disease.

"Taken up" means 1) borrowed, or 2) removed.

"Use" means "interest." It can also refer to sex.

This was a topic that Pennyboy Senior felt strongly about. He talked vehemently and loudly.

"Reduce the interest rate?" he shouted. "I am mad — furious — with this time's manners."

"You said just now that it was death for you to speak," Cymbal said.

"Aye," Pennyboy Senior said, "but an anger, a just anger, such as this is, puts life in man."

He regarded his anger as righteous wrath.

He continued, "Who can endure to see the fury of men's gullets and their groins? What fires, what cooks, what kitchens might be spared?"

He became angrier and angrier.

He continued, "What stews, ponds, parks, coops, garners, storehouses? What velvets, tissues, scarves, embroideries, and laces they might lack?"

"Stews" were tanks in which fish were kept until they were cooked and eaten.

Garners are storehouses.

Tissues are fabrics that are made of silk and precious metals.

Pennyboy Senior continued, "They covet things superfluous always, when it would be much more honorable for them to want and buy necessary things! What need has Nature of silver dishes or gold chamber pots, of perfumed handkerchiefs, or a numerous family of household servants to watch her eat?

"Poor and wise, Nature requires food only. Hunger is not ambitious.

"Say that you were the emperor of pleasures, the great dictator of fashions for all Europe, and you had the pomp of all the courts and kingdoms on display for you to make a selection to make yourself gazed at and admired?"

"The pomp of all the courts and kingdoms" was fashionable clothing for people of high social standing.

Pennyboy Senior continued, "You must go to bed and take your natural rest.

"And then, all this show vanishes. Your finery was only shown; it was not possessed. While it was boasting itself, it was then perishing."

While we are asleep, we are not gazed at and admired — or at least we are not aware of it.

Usually, people regard dreams as illusions opposed to reality. To Pennyboy Senior, waking reality, when focused on the pomp of all the courts and kingdoms, was the illusion.

Was Pennyboy Senior really saying what he believed when he said, "Your finery was only shown; it was not possessed. While it was boasting itself, it was then perishing"? He certainly was not telling the truth when he said that talking would be the death of him.

Cymbal said to himself, "This man has healthy lungs."

Pennyboy Senior said, "All that excess appeared as little yours as the spectators'. It scarcely fills up the expectation of a few hours that entertains men's lives."

Splendid clothing is hardly the best thing one can accomplish in life.

After all, shouldn't we be better than our clothing? If people were to judge our clothing to be good and our selves to be bad, shouldn't that make us concerned?

Cymbal said to himself, "He has the monopoly of sole-speaking."

Pennyboy Senior was doing all the talking and not giving Cymbal the opportunity to speak.

Angry, Cymbal said, "Why, good sir, you do all the talking!"

"Why shouldn't I?" Pennyboy Senior said. "Aren't I under my own roof, my ceiling?"

"But I came here to talk with you," Cymbal said.

"Why, if I will not talk with you, sir, you are answered," Pennyboy Senior said. "Who sent for you?"

Cymbal said, "Nobody sent for me —"

Pennyboy Senior interrupted, "— but you came."

He then said, "Why, then, go as you came; here's no man who keeps you here. There, there lies your way. You see the door."

"This is strange!" Cymbal said.

"It is my civility, my code of conduct, when I do not relish the party or his business," Pennyboy Senior said. "I say to you, be gone, sir. I'll have no venture in your ship, the office, your bark of six, even if it were sixteen, good sir."

Investors could invest in a bark: a ship that would travel overseas. To entice people to invest in the risky voyage, rich profits were promised. In this case, even if the venture promised a profit of 16,000 pounds rather than 6,000 pounds, Pennyboy Senior was not interested.

Angry, Cymbal said, "You are a rogue!"

"I think I am, sir, truly," Pennyboy Senior said.

"A rascal and a money-bawd!" Cymbal said.

"Those are my surnames," Pennyboy Senior said.

"A wretched rascal!" Cymbal said.

"You will overflow and spill all," Pennyboy Senior said.

Cymbal called him additional names: "Caterpillar, moth, horse-leech, and dung-worm —"

"— still you lose your labor," Pennyboy Senior interrupted. "I am a broken vessel, all runs out. I am a shrunken old dryfat — a broken barrel good only for dry goods.

"Fare you well, good six."

Cymbal exited the house, and then Pennyboy exited the room.

THE THIRD INTERMEAN: AFTER THE THIRD ACT

"This old Pennyboy is a notable tough rascal!" Gossip Censure said. "Right city-bred!"

Gossip Mirth said, "In Silver Street, the region of money, a good headquarters for a usurer."

Many silversmiths resided on Silver Street.

Gossip Tattle said, "He has rich ingredients in him, I promise you, if they were extracted — a true recipe and formula to make an alderman, if he were well wrought upon according to art."

"I would like to see an alderman in *chimia*!" Gossip Expectation said. "That is a treatise of aldermanity truly written."

"In *chimia*" means to be subjected to alchemical analysis.

"To show how much it differs from urbanity," Gossip Censure said.

"Aye, or humanity," Gossip Mirth said. "Either would appear in this Pennyboy Senior, if he were rightly distilled. But how do you like the news? You haven't mentioned that."

"Oh, the news are monstrous, scurvy, and stale!" Gossip Censure said. "And too exotic and outlandish! Ill-cooked and ill-dished!"

"They were as good yet as butter could make them!" Gossip Expectation said.

Of course, Nathaniel Butter was a prominent newsman of Ben Jonson's time.

"In a word, they were beastly buttered!" Gossip Tattle said. "He — butter — shall never come on my bread more, nor in my mouth, if I can help it."

According to the *Oxford English Dictionary*, the verb "come" has meant "ejaculate" since at least 1604.

Gossip Tattle continued, "I have had better news from the bake-house by ten thousand parts in a morning, or the conduits in Westminster, all the news of Tuttle Street and both the Almonries, the two Sanctuaries, Long and Round Woolstaple — with King Street and Cannon Row to boot!"

Gossip — news — can be found in many places.

King Henry VII had built two almshouses for the poor to the west of Westminster Abbey: the Great and Little Almonries.

Gossip Mirth said, "Aye, my Gossip Tattle knew what fine slips grew in Gardiner's Lane."

The word "slip" can mean 1) twig, and 2) counterfeit. In this context, it means illegitimate children.

Gossip Mirth continued, "My Gossip Tattle also knew who kissed the butcher's wife with the cow's breath, what matches were made in the Bowling Alley and what bets won and lost, how much grist went to the mill and what besides, who conjured in Tuttle Fields and how many, when they never came there, and which boy rode upon the astrologer Doctor Lamb in the likeness of a roaring lion that run away with him in his teeth and has not devoured him yet."

Gossip Mirth was confused, and it showed in her language:

1) Some conjurors conjured in Tittle Fields and they — the conjurors? the spirits? — never came there.

2) A boy rode on Doctor Lamb when Doctor Lamb took the form of a roaring lion and yet the boy was in Doctor Lamb's teeth.

Gossip Tattle said, "Why, I heard about it from my serving-maid, Joan Hearsay, and she heard it from a limb of the school, she says."

"A limb of Satan" is a young rascal or a young imp.

Gossip Tattle continued, "This was a little limb of nine years old, who told her that the master left out his conjuring book one day, and he found it, and so the fable came about. But whether it were true or no, we gossips are bound to believe it, if it is once out and afoot. How should we pass the time else, or find ourselves in fashionable discourse for all companies, if we do not credit all and make more of it in the reporting?"

"For my part, I believe it," Gossip Censure said. "If there were no wiser than I am and it were up to me, I would never have a cunning schoolmaster in England — I mean a cunning man, a schoolmaster, who is a conjurer, or a poet, or who had any acquaintance with a poet."

A cunning man is a conjuror or a smart schoolmaster.

Gossip Censure said, "They make all their scholars play-boys!"

In this context, play-boys are boys who act in plays.

She continued, "Isn't it a fine sight to see all our children made interluders? Do we pay our money for this? We send them to learn their grammar and their Terence, and they learn their play-books!"

Interludes are pauses between play acts.

Terence was a Roman playwright.

Gossip Censure continued, "Well, they say that we shall have no more Parliaments, God bless us."

In August 1625, King Charles I dissolved Parliament. In February 1626, Parliament was recalled, but in June 1626, King Charles I again dissolved it.

Gossip Censure continued, "But if we have, I hope Zeal-of-the-land Busy and my gossip — friend — Rabbi Troubletruth will start up and see that we shall have painstaking — and sometimes painful — good ministers to keep school and catechize our youth, and not teach them to speak plays and act fables of false news in this manner, to the super-vexation of town and country, with a wanion — with a vengeance."

Zeal-of-the-land Busy, who is a character in Ben Jonson's play *Bartholomew Fair*, and Rabbi Troubletruth were Puritans who disliked the theater.

CHAPTER 4

— 4.1 —

Pennyboy Junior, Fitton, Shunfield, Almanac, Madrigal, the Canter, and Picklock were in the Devil Tavern. They had finished eating the noon meal.

"Come, gentlemen, let's take a break from drinking to each other's healths for a while," Pennyboy Junior said. "This Lickfinger has made us a good noon dinner for our Pecunia. What shall we do with ourselves while the women water and the fiddlers eat?"

"Women water" can mean 1) the women freshen themselves with sweet water, or 2) the women urinate.

"Let's jeer a little," Fitton said.

He was referring to the jeering game that he and his friends practiced. The game involved insulting other people — and each other. It was far removed from legitimate satire.

"Jeer?" Pennyboy Junior asked. "What's that?"

"Wait and see, sir," Shunfield said.

Almanac said, "We first begin by jeering at ourselves, and then at you."

"It is a game we are accustomed to play," Shunfield said.

Madrigal said, "We jeer all kind of persons we meet with, of any rank or quality, and if we cannot jeer them, we jeer ourselves."

The Canter said, "It is a pretty sweet society — and a grateful one!"

This kind of "grateful" is "full of grating."

"Please, let's see some jeering," Picklock said.

Shunfield said, "Have at you then, lawyer."

This meant: Prepare to be attacked.

Shunfield continued, "I am going to jeer you. ... They say there was one of your coat in Bedlam hospital for lunatics lately —"

Lawyers wore a distinctive coat that indicated their profession.

"I marvel that all his clients were not there," Almanac said.

"They were the madder sort," Madrigal said.

Picking up on *mad* and *Mad*rigal, Picklock said, "They were all not there except, sir, one like you, and he made verses."

Fitton said, "Madrigal, you have been jeered."

"I know I have," Madrigal said.

Shunfield asked Picklock, "But what did you do, lawyer, when you made love to Mistress Band at dinner?"

"To make love" means "to woo."

Madrigal said, "Why, from being an advocate, he grew the client."

Mistress Band would grow if she were successfully wooed and became pregnant.

"Well played, my poet!" Pennyboy Junior said.

Madrigal continued, "And he showed that the law of nature was there above the common law."

The law of nature governs such things as reproduction. It existed long before Humankind created the common law.

Common law is "the general law of a community," or "[t]he unwritten law of England," according to the *Oxford English Dictionary*.

"Quit, quit!" Shunfield said. "Touché! Touché!"

"Call you this jeering?" Pennyboy Junior said. "I can play at this. It is like a ball at tennis."

Fitton said, "It is very likely that you can play at this, but we were not well started in the game."

Almanac agreed with Pennyboy Junior that the game of jeering was like the game of tennis, "It is indeed, sir, when we speak at volley — fire volleys back and forth — all the ill we can at one another —"

Shunfield interrupted, "— as we this morning — I wish that you had heard us — at the rogue your uncle —"

Almanac interrupted, "— that money-bawd —"

Madrigal interrupted, — we called him a coat-card of the lowest order."

A coat-card is a court-card or face-card in which the figure wears fancy clothing — king, queen, jack (aka knave).

"What's that?" Pennyboy Junior asked. "A knave?"

"Some readings have it so," Madrigal said.

Some manuscripts could use the word "jack" rather than the word "knave."

Different manuscripts could also use the word "knave" to mean different things.

A knave can be 1) the attendant of a knight, or 2) a low, dishonest rogue.

Madrigal continued, "My manuscript uses 'knave' to mean 'varlet.'"

A varlet can be 1) an attendant or servant, or 2) a low, dishonest rogue.

The Canter said, "And your manuscript calls yourself a fool of the first rank, and one who shall have the leading — take the precedence — of the right-hand file under this brave commander."

Madrigal's manuscript was bad enough to identify himself as a fool. The brave commander was probably Pennyboy Junior, host of the feast the jeerers had been enjoying.

The Canter was saying that if Pennyboy Junior was a knave, then Madrigal was the head fool serving under him.

"What do you say, Canter?" Pennyboy Junior asked.

The Canter said sarcastically, "Sir, I say this is a very wholesome exercise, and comely — it is just like lepers showing one another their scabs, or flies feeding on ulcers."

"What is the news, gentlemen?" Pennyboy Junior said. "Have you any news for after dinner? I think we should not spend our time unprofitably."

"They never lie, sir, between meals," the Canter said.

He was punning on the word "lie": 1) They never tell news, aka lies, between meals, and 2) They never lie down between meals, which means that they can stay awake and gather more news, aka lies.

The Canter added, "In preparation for supper — the evening meal — you may have a bale or two of news brought in."

The jeerers began to talk quietly together.

Fitton said to the other jeerers, "This Canter is an old envious knave!"

"A very rascal!" Almanac said.

"I have watched him all this meal," Fitton said. "He has done nothing but mock, with scurvy faces, all we said."

"A supercilious rogue!" Almanac said. "He looks as if he were the patrico —"

Madrigal interrupted, "— or archpriest of canters."

A patrico is a hedge-priest — the uneducated parson of the beggars.

The archpriest is the leading Catholic in England.

A patrico and the archpriest were leading figures of underground organizations.

"He's some primate metropolitan rascal," Shunfield said.

A metropolitan is the leader of an ecclesiastical province, and a primate is the leader of metropolitans. In other words, Shunfield is obliquely saying the Canter is like the Archbishop of *Canter*bury — but for beggars.

Shunfield said, "Our shot-clog makes so much of him."

A shot-clog is a person who is not liked, but who is tolerated because he pays the shot — the bill — for the others. The jeerers regarded Pennyboy Junior as a sucker and a shot-clog. The jeerers were repaying generous hospitality with insults.

Almanac said, "The law and he do govern him."

In other words, Picklock and the Canter govern Pennyboy Junior.

"What are you saying, gentlemen?" Pennyboy Junior asked.

Fitton said, "We were saying that we don't wonder that your man of law — Picklock — should so enjoy your favor; but how does it happen that this rogue, this Canter, enjoys your favor?"

Other people may wonder how does it happen that the jeerers enjoy Pennyboy Junior's favor.

"Oh, speak good words," Pennyboy Junior said. "Speak gentle words."

He did not want the Canter to be criticized.

Fitton said, "He is a fellow who speaks no language —"

Almanac interrupted, "— except what jingling gypsies and peddlers trade in —"

Gypsies jingle because many gypsies sew small bells in their clothing.

Jingling gypsies and peddlers speak cant — specialized language that they understand but most others cannot.

Fitton said, "And no honest Christian can understand it."

The Canter said to all the jeerers, "— why, by that argument you all are canters."

He pointed to the jeerers in turn and said, "You, and you, and you — all the whole world are canters. I will prove it in your professions."

"I would like to hear this," Pennyboy Junior said.

He saw Lady Pecunia coming and said, "But wait, my princess comes. Get ready, Canter, to prove that all the world are canters — I'll call for the proof soon."

He then said to Lady Pecunia, "How is Your Grace?"

Lickfinger, Lady Pecunia, Statute, Band, Wax, and Mortgage walked over to them. The ladies had finished freshening up and Lickfinger had finished cleaning up after the noon meal.

"I hope the fare was good," Lickfinger said.

"Yes, Lickfinger, and we shall thank you for it and reward you," Lady Pecunia said.

Lickfinger and Madrigal had earlier been arguing over the relative importance of cookery and poetry. Now they continued the argument.

"Nay, I'll not lose my argument, Lickfinger," Madrigal said. "Before these gentlewomen, I affirm that the perfect and true strain of poetry is rather to be given the quick — lively — cellar than the fat — greasy — kitchen."

Madrigal was asking this: What is the most important part of a banquet? The food you eat that makes you sluggish, or the wine you drink that enlivens you while also encouraging you to engage in conversation that also enlivens you.

In ancient Athens, people would eat and then following the meal would be a time for drinking and conversing. For example, in Plato's *Symposium*, people ate a meal and following the meal they drank and talked about love.

Intoxicating wine can cause inspiration; heavy food can cause a nap.

Lickfinger responded, "Heretic, I see that you are for the vain Oracle of the Bottle. The hogshead, Trismegistus, is your Pegasus."

Hogsheads are barrels that can contain wine.

In *Pantagruel* V:5, the Oracle of the Bottle is "Trinc," which means "Drink." Panurge, a character in *Pantagruel*, calls the bottle "trismegistian Bottle," which means "thrice-renowned bottle." The priestess tells Panurge that "by wine we become divine."

"Trismegistus" means "thrice-greatest."

Lickfinger continued, "Thence flows your Muse's spring, from that hard hoof."

The winged horse Pegasus struck its hoof on Mount Helicon, home of the Muses, and a spring arose from where Pegasus struck its hoof. Whoever drinks from that spring is poetically inspired.

Lickfinger continued, "Seduced poet, I say to you that a boiler, range, and dresser — kitchen table — were the fountains of all the knowledge in the universe.

"And they're the kitchens, where the master cook — you don't know the man, nor can you know him, until you have served some years in that deep school that's both the nurse and mother of the arts, and hear him read, interpret, and demonstrate!

"A master cook! Why, he's the man of men for a professor! He designs, he draws, he paints, he carves, he builds, he fortifies, he makes citadels of exotic fowl and fish.

"Some he dry-ditches like a dry moat, some he moats round with broths, he mounts marrowbones as if they were cannon, he cuts fifty-angled custards, he rears bulwark pies, and for his outerworks he raises ramparts of immortal crust, and he teaches all the tactics at one dinner. What ranks, what files to put his dishes in — he teaches the whole military art."

Lickfinger was comparing cooking to building a fortification. For example, many forts were built with angles. Doing so meant that often cannonballs would hit the defensive walls at an angle and thus the damage to the wall would be minimized. In addition, angles made it easier for defenders on the walls of the fort to see and fight attackers.

Lickfinger continued, "Then, he knows the influence of the stars upon his meats, and all their seasons, tempers, qualities, and so to fit his relishes and sauces, he has Nature in a pot above all the alchemists or airy brethren of the Rosy Cross — the Rosicrucians.

"He is an architect, an engineer, a soldier, a physician, a philosopher, a general mathematician."

"It is granted," Madrigal said.

Lickfinger continued, "And that you may not doubt that he is a poet —"

Almanac interrupted, "— this fury shows that he is a poet, if there were nothing else, and it is divine! I shall forever hereafter admire the wisdom of a cook."

Almanac, a jeerer, respected cooks.

"And we, sir!" Band said.

Pennyboy Junior, who had been courting Lady Pecunia all the while, said, "Oh, how my princess draws me with her looks and hales me in, as eddies draw in boats or strong Charybdis ships that sail too near the reefs of love!"

Charybdis was a whirlpool that sucked down ships that got too close to it. Jason and the Argonauts and Odysseus and his men had to pass between Scylla and Charybdis. Scylla was a monster whose six heads would each snatch a sailor from a ship and eat him.

Pennyboy Junior continued, "The tides of your two eyes, wind of your breath, are such as suck in all who approach you!"

"Who has changed my servant?" Lady Pecunia asked.

This kind of servant was a male admirer.

Pennyboy Junior answered, "Yourself, who drink my blood up with your beams as the sun drinks up the sea! Pecunia shines more in the world than the sun, and makes it spring wherever she favors! If it pleases her just to show her delicately molded wrists, or bare her ivory hands, she captivates always!

"Her smiles, they are Love's fetters! Her breasts, his apples! Her nipples, strawberries, where Cupid, if he were present now, would cry, 'Farewell, my mother's milk; here's sweeter nectar!'"

Cupid is Venus' son; she breastfed him.

Pennyboy Junior said, "Help me to praise Pecunia, gentlemen. She's your princess; lend your wits."

Fitton said, "She is a lady whom the Graces taught to move!"

"Whom the Hours did nurse!" Almanac said.

The Horae or Hours — goddesses who preside over the seasons — were the first to attend the goddess Venus when she was born from sea-foam.

"Whose lips are the instructions of all lovers!" Fitton said.

"Her eyes are their lights, and her eyes are rivals to the stars!" Almanac said.

"A voice as if Harmony still spoke!" Fitton said.

Harmony is the Music of the Spheres. The ears of the fallen cannot hear it.

"And polished skin whiter than Venus' foot!" Almanac said.

"Young Hebe's neck or Juno's arms!" Fitton said.

Hebe was the ancient Greek goddess of youth, and Juno is called "white-armed Hera" in Homer's *Iliad*. Hera is the Greek name for Juno.

Almanac said, "A hairstyle as large as the Morning's, and her breath as sweet as meadows after rain and just newly mown!"

In this society, the rays of the morning sun were sometimes compared to hair.

"Leda might yield to her, for a face!" Fitton said.

Jupiter, the king of the gods, took the form of a swan and impregnated Leda, who gave birth to Helen, who became Helen of Troy. In a beauty contest of faces, Leda might come in second to Lady Pecunia. Or, possibly, Leda might be seduced because of Lady Pecunia's face.

"Hermione, for breasts!" Almanac said.

Hermione was the daughter of King Menelaus and Helen (of Troy). Hermione married Neoptolemus, the son of Achilles. Helen was the most beautiful woman in the world.

"Flora, for cheeks!" Fitton said.

Flora is the goddess of flowers.

"And Helen, for a mouth!" Almanac said.

"Kiss, kiss them, princess," Pennyboy Junior said to Lady Pecunia.

Lady Pecunia kissed them.

"The pearl strives to compare in whiteness with her neck —" Fitton said.

Almanac interrupted, "— but loses the contest. Here the snow thaws snow; one frost dissolves another!"

"Oh, she has a forehead too dangerous to be looked upon!" Fitton said.

"And glances that beguile the seer's eyes!" Almanac said.

"Kiss, kiss again," Pennyboy Junior said to Lady Pecunia.

She kissed them again.

Pennyboy Junior then asked, "What says my man of war?"

Shunfield, who had been quiet up to now, said, "I say she's more than Fame can promise of her. A theme that's overcome with her own matter! Praise is struck blind and deaf and dumb with her! Lady Pecunia astonishes commendation!"

In other words, words cannot adequately express her beauty.

"Well pumped, indeed, old sailor," Pennyboy Junior said.

"Well pumped" meant that Shunfield's praise was well worked: He had thought up good words to say, although as he said, words could not adequately express Lady Pecunia's beauty.

"Kiss him, too, although he's a sluggard," Pennyboy Junior said to Lady Pecunia.

Captain Shunfield was late in praising Lady Pecunia, who kissed him anyway.

Pennyboy Junior then asked Madrigal, "What says my poet-sucker?"

A poet-sucker is an unweaned poet — a poet who is still a beginner.

Pennyboy Junior added, "He's chewing his muse's cud. I can see that by looking at him."

Madrigal was working on a poem of praise for Lady Pecunia.

"I have almost finished," Madrigal said. "I just lack the conclusion."

"That's the ill luck of all his works always," Fitton said.

"What?" Pennyboy Junior asked.

"To begin many works, but finish none," Fitton said.

"How does he do his mistress' work?" Pennyboy Junior asked.

Madrigal's mistress was Erato, the Muse of love poetry and lyric poetry.

"Imperfectly," Fitton said.

"I cannot think he will finish that," Almanac said.

"That" was the poem Madrigal was now working on.

"Let's hear it," Pennyboy Junior said to Madrigal.

"It is a madrigal," Madrigal said. "I much like that kind of poem."

"And because of that, you have the name Madrigal," Pennyboy Junior said.

"It is his rose," Fitton said. "He can make nothing else."

Ben Jonson knew of a painter who could paint nothing but a rose — a practice he defended by saying that a rose was higher than any other subject of painting.

Madrigal said, "I made it to the tune the fiddlers played that we all liked so well."

Poems often were used as song lyrics.

"Good," Pennyboy Junior said. "Read it, read it."

Madrigal read, "*The sun is father of all metals, you know, silver and gold —*"

"Aye, leave unsaid your prologues," Pennyboy Junior said. "Read your poem!"

Madrigal read his poem out loud:

"*As bright as is the Sun, her sire,*

"*Or Earth, her mother, in her best attire,*

"*Or Mint, the midwife, with her fire,*

"*Comes forth Her Grace!*"

Pennyboy Junior said, "That 'Mint, the midwife' does well."

Madrigal continued reading his poem out loud:

"*The splendor of the wealthiest mines!*

"*The stamp and strength of all imperial lines,*

"*Both majesty and beauty shines*

"*In her sweet face!*"

"That's fairly said of money," Fitton said.

The faces of imperial lines — kings and queens — are stamped on coins.

Madrigal continued reading his poem out loud:

"*Look how a torch of taper light [lit],*

"*Or of that torch's flame, a beacon bright —*"

"Good!" Pennyboy Junior said.

Madrigal said, "Now, there I lack a line to finish, sir."

Pennyboy thought up a line and then said it out loud:

"*Or of that beacon's fire, moonlight —*"

Madrigal thought up the concluding line and then said it out loud:

"*So takes she [Pecunia] place [precedence]!*"

"It is good," Fitton said.

Madrigal then said, "And then I have a saraband."

A saraband is a slow and stately Spanish dance in triple time — three beats to the bar. Madrigal's saraband was composed to that rhythm.

Madrigal recited his saraband:

"*She makes good cheer, she keeps full boards [provides abundant food],*

"*She holds a fair of knights and lords,*

"*A market of all offices,*

"*And shops of honor, more or less.*

"*According to Pecunia's grace,*

"*The bride hath [has] beauty, blood, and place,*

"*The bridegroom virtue, valor, wit,*

"*And wisdom, as he stands for it.*"

"Call in the fiddlers," Pennyboy Junior said. "Nick, the boy, shall sing the saraband."

Pennyboy Junior then said to Lady Pecunia, "Sweet princess, kiss him. Kiss them all, dear madam, and, at the close, deign to call them cousins."

"Cousins" are kin — or friends.

As she kissed them in turn, Lady Pecunia said, "Sweet cousin Madrigal, and cousin Fitton, my cousin Shunfield, and my learnéd cousin —"

The Canter said to himself, "Al-manach, although they call him Almanac."

"Al" is Arabic for "the." Al-manach is "the man — ach." "Ach" is an interjection that expresses disgust and dismay and irritation, among other negative reactions.

Picklock said to himself, "Why, here the prodigal is prostituting his mistress!"

Pennyboy Junior was urging Lady Pecunia to engage in much kissing.

Pennyboy Junior said, "And Picklock, he must be a kinsman, too. My man of law will teach us all to win and keep our own."

He then said to the Canter, "Old founder —"

"Nothing, I, sir?" the Canter said.

The Canter was saying that he did not feel he was worthy to be kissed by Lady Pecunia.

He continued, "I am a wretch, a beggar. She, the fortunate, can lack no kindred; we, the poor, know none."

"Nor shall you know any, as far as I'm concerned," Fitton said.

"I agree with Fitton," Almanac said.

The fiddlers and Nick, the boy singer, entered the room.

"Sing, boy," Pennyboy Junior said. "Stand here."

The boy sang Madrigal's saraband, and the guests danced.

The Canter said to himself, "Look, look, how all their eyes dance in their heads — look at them! — crazed by lust at the sight of their brave idol! How they are tickled with a light air, the bawdy saraband! They are all a kind of dancing machines, and they are set by nature thus to run alone to every sound! All things within and outside them move except their brain, and that stands still!

"Mere monsters here, in a chamber, of most subtle feet! And they make their legs be in tune while walking in the streets!

"These are the gallant spirits of the age, the miracles of the time, who can praise and denigrate men's wits and set whatever rate on things their half-brained fancies please.

"Now, a pox upon them!

"See how attentively he — Pennyboy Junior — learns the jig, as if it were a mystery — a holy rite — of his faith!"

The Canter was hard on the dancing because it was inspired by love of money, but poetry, music, and dance can spiritually uplift human beings. So can food — think of *Babette's Feast*.

Some art is better than other art, but even art that is not the best — or close to it — can be appreciated by at least some people.

The dancers were all struck with admiration of Madrigal.

"A dainty ditty!" Shunfield said.

"Oh, he's a fine, delicate poet when he sets his mind to it," Fitton said.

"And a dainty scholar," Pennyboy Junior said.

"No, no great scholar," Almanac said. "He writes like a gentleman."

Rich gentlemen need not write for money; in this society, some scholars who had graduated from Oxford or Cambridge often did. In Ben Jonson's *Epicene*, Jack Daw — who is a fool — distinguished between poets and versifiers. To Jack Daw, a poet is someone who makes money from poetry. Jack Daw preferred mere versifiers, who did not write for money, to true poets.

This society valued money: It is better to have money and not have to write for money.

Ben Jonson, of course, was a scholar who made his living from his literary endeavors.

"A pox on your scholar!" Shunfield said.

The Canter said to himself, "A pox on your distinction between scholars and gentlemen! As if a scholar were no gentleman. With these, to write like a gentleman will in time become the same as to write like an ass.

"These gentlemen? These rascals! I am sick of indignation at them."

"How do you like it, sir?" Pennyboy Junior asked Fitton.

"It is excellent!" Fitton said.

"It was excellently sung!" Almanac said.

"A dainty air!" Fitton said.

"What says my Lickfinger?" Pennyboy Junior asked.

Lickfinger answered, "I am telling Mistress Band and Mistress Statute what a brave gentleman you are, and Wax here, how much better it would be if My Lady's Grace would here take up residence, sir, and keep house with you."

"What do they say?" Pennyboy Junior asked.

"We could consent, sir, willingly," Statute said.

"Aye, if we knew Her Grace had the least liking," Band said.

"We must obey Her Grace's will and pleasure," Wax said.

"I thank you, gentlewomen," Pennyboy Junior said.

He then said, "Ply them, Lickfinger. Give Mother Mortgage, there —"

Lickfinger finished the sentence, "— her dose of sack. I have it for her, and her quantity of hum — strong ale."

Sack is wine.

Lickfinger served wine all around.

The gallants were all gathered around Lady Pecunia.

"Indeed, therein I must confess, dear cousin, that I am a most unfortunate princess," Lady Pecunia said.

"And you still will be so, when Your Grace may help it," Almanac said.

According to Almanac, Lady Pecunia would cease being unfortunate if she lodged with Pennyboy Junior rather than continuing to stay with Pennyboy Senior.

As a miser, Pennyboy Senior did not treat Lady Pecunia — money — the way she ought to be treated.

Madrigal said, "Who'd lie in a room, with a close-stool and garlic, and kennel with his dogs, who had a prince like this young Pennyboy to sojourn with?"

A close-stool is a chamber pot that is enclosed in a box or a stool.

Shunfield said, "He'll let you have your liberty —"

Almanac said, "He'll let you go forth to where you please, and to whatever company you please —"

Misers keep money shut away from society.

Pennyboy Junior was not a miser.

Madrigal said, "He'll let you scatter yourself — circulate — among us —"

Pennyboy Junior said to Madrigal, "Hope of Parnassus! Your ivy shall not wither, nor will your bays."

Mount Parnassus was regarded as the source of poetic inspiration.

Ivy was sacred to Bacchus, god of wine. The bay laurel was sacred to Apollo, god of music, and poets were crowned with laurel wreaths.

Pennyboy Junior had more respect for Madrigal than he had before Madrigal's song was sung.

Pennyboy Junior added, "You shall be had into Her Grace's cellar, and there know sack and claret all December. Your vein of poetry is rich, and we must cherish it. Poets and bees swarm nowadays, but yet there are not those good taverns for the one sort as there are flowery fields to feed the other.

"Although bees are pleased with dew — ask little Wax who brings the honey to her lady's hive — the poet must have wine. And he shall have it."

Honey is stored in bees*wax*.

Pennyboy Senior — the miser — entered the room.

"Broker!" Pennyboy Senior called. "What, Broker!"

"Who's that?" Pennyboy Junior said. "My uncle!"

"I am abused," Pennyboy Senior said. "Where is my knave, my Broker?"

Lickfinger pointed and said, "Your Broker is laid out upon a bench, yonder. Sack has seized on him, in the shape of sleep."

Broker was drunk and asleep.

"He has been dead to us almost this entire hour," Picklock said.

"This entire hour?" Pennyboy Senior said.

Broker was supposed to have been looking after Lady Pecunia. If he had done his job, perhaps she would not have kissed so many men.

The Canter asked Pennyboy Senior, "Why do you sigh, sir? Because he's at rest?"

"It breeds my unrest," Pennyboy Senior replied.

Lickfinger offered him a drink and asked, "Will you take a cup of sack and see if you can sleep?"

"No, cogging jack — cheating rascal," Pennyboy Senior said. "You, and your cups, too, perish!"

He struck the sack out of Lickfinger's hand.

"Oh, the sack!" Shunfield said.

"The sack! The sack!" Madrigal said.

"A madrigal on sack!" the Canter said.

"Or rather an elegy, for the sack is gone," Picklock said.

"Why do you do this, sir — spill the wine, and rave?" Lady Pecunia asked. "Because of Broker's sleeping?"

"What?" Pennyboy Senior said. "Through sleep and sack, my trust has been wronged."

He had trusted Broker, but Broker had not acted as he should have acted.

"But I am still awake to wait upon Your Grace," Pennyboy Senior said. "Does it please you to quit this strange, lewd, ill-mannered company? They are not for you."

"No, guardian," Lady Pecunia said. "I do like them very well."

"Your Grace's pleasure will be observed, but you, Statute, and Band, and Wax, will go with me," Pennyboy Senior said.

Statutes, bands (bonds), and wax (for sealing documents) are all useful to misers.

"Truly, we will not," Statute said.

Band said, "We will stay and wait here upon Her Grace, and this your noble kinsman — Pennyboy Junior."

"Noble! How noble?" Pennyboy Senior asked. "Who has made him noble?"

Pennyboy Junior answered, "Why, my most noble money has, or shall — my princess, here. She who, had you but kept and treated her kindly, would have made you noble and wise, too; nay, perhaps she would have done for you that which an Act of Parliament could not do: made you honest."

Money, properly used, can do great good. So can a wise, kind, and noble person.

Under King James I, however, money actually could buy a kind of nobility. He sold peerages for money.

Pennyboy Junior continued, "The truth is, uncle, that Her Grace dislikes her treatment and conditions of employment, and especially her lodging."

"Nay, say her jail," Lady Pecunia said. "Never was an unfortunate princess so badly treated by a jailer. Ask my women."

She then said, "Band, you can tell, and Statute, too, how he has treated me, kept me close prisoner, under twenty bolts —"

Statute interrupted, "— and forty padlocks —"

Band interrupted, "— all the malicious engines a wicked smith could forge out of his iron, such as locks and keys, shackles and manacles, to torture a great lady."

Misers keep gold and money locked away.

Statute said, "He's abused your Grace's body."

"No," Lady Pecunia said. "He would have done so, but that lay not in his power. He had the use of your bodies, Band, and Wax, and sometimes Statute's.

"Once he would have smothered me in a chest and strangled me in leather, but you came to my rescue, then, and gave me air."

Statute said, "For which rescue he crammed us up in a closed box, all three — Band, Wax, and me — together, where we saw no sun in one six-month period."

"A cruel man he is!" Wax said.

Band said, "He's left my fellow Wax out in the cold —"

Statute finished the sentence, "— until she was as stiff as any frost, and crumbled away to dust, and almost lost her form."

"There was much trouble taken to recover me," Wax said.

"Women jeerers!" Pennyboy Senior said. "Have you learnéd, too, the subtle faculty? Come, I'll show you the way home, if drink or a too-full diet have disguised — intoxicated — you."

Band said, "The truth is that we have no mind, sir, to return —"

Statute interrupted, "— to be bound back to back —"

Band interrupted, "— and have our legs turned in, or writhed about —"

Wax interrupted, "— or else displayed —"

"Displayed" meant 1) literally lying down with the legs spread open, or 2) figuratively displayed like the pages of a document.

Statute interrupted, "— and be lodged with dust and fleas, as we were accustomed to be —"

Band interrupted, "— and dieted with dogs' dung."

Dogs poop on papers. Since dogs know nothing about which papers are valuable, such papers as bands (legal bonds), if accidentally dropped on the floor, can be pooped on.

Pennyboy Senior said, "Why, you whores, my bawds, my instruments, what should I call you that Humankind may think base enough for you?"

An "instrument" can be a tool, a document, or a woman's genitalia.

"Listen, uncle," Pennyboy Junior said. "I must not hear this of my princess' servants, and in Apollo, in Pecunia's room."

They were in the Apollo Room.

The sun — Apollo is the sun-god — is the alchemical symbol for gold.

Pennyboy Junior continued, "Go, get you down the stairs, home to your kennel as swiftly as you can. Consult your dogs, the *lares* of your family, or, believe it, the fury of a footman and a bartender hangs over you."

The Roman *lares praestites* were guardians of the state, and the Roman *lares familiaris* were household gods. Dogs are loyal guardians and are devoted to the family.

The jeerers all threatened Pennyboy Senior.

"A cudgel and a pot threaten a kind of vengeance," Shunfield said.

"Barbers are at hand," Madrigal said.

"Washing and shaving will ensue," Almanac said.

The jeerers were threatening to cut his hair and beard.

"The well pump is not far away," Fitton said. "If it were far away, the sink — cesspool — is near, or a good jordan — chamber pot."

If necessary, they would shave him using sewer water.

Madrigal said, "You have now no money —"

Shunfield finished the sentence, "— but you are a rascal."

Pennyboy Senior said, "I am cheated, robbed, jeered by confederacy."

The jeerers kicked him.

"No, you are kicked and treated as fittingly as you should be," Fitton said.

"You are spurned from all commerce of men, you who are a cur," Shunfield said.

They began to kick Pennyboy Senior out.

"You are a stinking dog in a doublet with foul linen," Almanac said.

"You are a snarling rascal," Madrigal said. "Get out."

"Out!" Shunfield said.

Retreating, Pennyboy Senior said, "Well, remember, I am cheated by my kinsman and his whore. Bane of these meetings in Apollo!"

Trying to lead him away, Lickfinger said, "Go, sir. You will be tossed like Block in a blanket, if you don't leave."

Block was one of Pennyboy Senior's dogs.

Men and dogs could be punished by being tossed in a blanket.

"Down with him, Lickfinger!" Pennyboy Junior said.

Shaking Lickfinger off, Pennyboy Senior said, "Saucy jack, away! Pecunia is a whore!"

Pennyboy Senior exited, followed by Lickfinger.

Pennyboy Junior said to the musicians, "Play him down, fiddlers, and drown his noise!"

Seeing someone approach, he asked, "Who's this?"

Recognizing the newcomer, Fitton said, "Oh, Master Piedmantle!"

Piedmantle, who had brought the Lady Pecunia her pedigree, entered the room and walked over to them. A pedigree is a genealogical tree or table.

"With your permission, gentlemen," Piedmantle said.

Fitton began, "Her Grace's herald —"

Almanac interrupted, "— no herald yet. He's a heraldet."

A heraldet is a petty herald.

"What's that?" Pennyboy Junior asked.

"A canter," the Canter said.

"Oh, you said you would prove that all of us are canters," Pennyboy Junior said.

Cant is specialized jargon. Beggars and thieves use cant, but many occupations have their own cant. The Canter was going to show that the people present had their own cant.

Piedmantle's cant was in heraldry.

Almanac's cant was in medicine and in astrology.

Shunfield's cant was in military matters.

Madrigal's cant was in poetry and song.

Fitton's cant was the cant of courtiers at the court. Such cant involved business — often fraudulent business. He did favors or pretended to be able to do favors for business people at the court. Fitton was a courtier, but he was also a court gossip.

Referring to Piedmantle, the Canter said, "Sir, here is one who will prove himself to be a canter, immediately. So shall the rest, in time."

Seeing the pedigree that Piedmantle was holding, Lady Pecunia said to him, "My pedigree? I tell you, friend, he must be a good scholar who can know my descent. I am of princely race, and as good blood as any is in the mines runs through my veins.

"I am every limb a princess! The Duchess of Mines was my great-grandmother, and by the father's side I come from Sol. My grandfather was Duke of Or, and he matched — married — in the blood royal of Ophir."

"Sol" and "or" both mean gold. "Sol" is the personified sun, and "or" is the heraldic term for gold.

Piedmantle pointed to the pedigree and said, "Here's his coat of arms."

Lady Pecunia said, "I know it if I hear the blazon."

The blazon is the description of heraldic arms using heraldic terms.

The heraldic terms are, of course, cant.

Piedmantle began to describe the coat of arms in heraldic terms: "He bears, in a field azure, a sun proper, beamy, twelve of the second."

A field azure is a blue background. A sun proper, beamy, is the sun represented by a human face surrounded by twelve sunny rays or beams, and of the second color that had been mentioned: the sun's color — which is or, aka gold. The word "proper" meant having its natural color. In the case of the sun, that color is gold. The first color mentioned was azure.

The Canter whispered sarcastically to Pennyboy Junior, "How far is this from canting!"

Pennyboy Junior whispered to the Canter, "Her Grace understands it."

Cant can communicate, but often a study of the specialized terms must first be made. Lady Pecunia had grown up using these terms and so she had learned them naturally. Piedmantle, however, had to study to become a heraldet, and he was not yet a full herald.

The Canter whispered back, "She can cant, sir."

Pointing to the pedigree, Lady Pecunia asked, "What are these? Besants?"

Besants are small gold circles. Originally, the term referred to large gold coins.

"Yes, if it pleases Your Grace," Piedmantle answered.

"That is our coat of arms, too, as we come from Or," Lady Pecunia said. "What line's this?"

Piedmantle answered, "The rich mines of Potosi, the Spanish mines in the West Indies."

Mount Potosi, which is in Bolivia (not the West Indies), was a rich source of silver.

A good herald ought to have a good knowledge of geography.

Lady Pecunia asked, "And what's this?"

"The mines of Hungary," Piedmantle said. "And this is the mines of Barbary."

"But this, this little branch?" Lady Pecunia asked.

Piedmantle answered, "That's the Welsh mine, that."

"I have Welsh blood in me, too," Lady Pecunia said. "Blaze, sir, that coat."

In other words, describe in heraldic terms the Welsh coat of arms.

Piedmantle said, "That coat of arms bears (if it pleases you) argent, three leeks vert in canton or, and tasseled of the first color: argent."

Leeks are related to onions. They are not normally found in heraldic devices. Vert is the color green. Argent is the color silver.

In non-heraldic terms, the coat of arms of the Welsh mines had a silver background. In a gold square (canton or) were three green leeks. The coat of arms was adorned with silver tassels.

The Canter whispered to Pennyboy Junior, "Isn't this canting? Do you understand him?"

Pennyboy Junior whispered back, "I can't understand him, but it sounds well, and the whole pedigree is splendidly painted. I will have such a scroll, whatever it costs me."

Lady Pecunia said to Piedmantle, "Well, at better leisure we'll take a view of it, and so reward you."

"Kiss him, sweet princess, and give him the title of cousin," Pennyboy Junior said.

"I will, if you will have it," Lady Pecunia said.

She kissed Piedmantle and said to him, "Cousin Piedmantle!"

"I love all men of virtue, from my princess to my beggar here, old Canter," Pennyboy Junior said. "On, on to your proof. Whom will you prove to be the next canter?"

"The doctor here," the Canter said. "I will proceed with the learnéd. When he discourses of dissection, or any point of anatomy, and he tells you of *vena cava* and of *vena porta*, the *meseraics*, and the *mesenterium*, what does he do but cant?"

Of course, the italicized terms were part of the specialized vocabulary of doctors. Often, specialized terms are necessary: Doctors can use them to communicate much information to other doctors and nurses quickly. Giving such information to a patient takes longer because simpler words must be used. More than once, the writer of this book has been spoken to by a doctor but has had to request, "Can you say that in English, please?"

Almanac was an astrologer as well as a doctor. Two kinds of astrology existed. Natural astrology was concerned with predicting tides, seasons, eclipses, etc. Judicial astrology was concerned with the supposed effect of the planets and the zodiac on human beings.

The Canter began to speak about the cant of astrology: "Or if he run to his judicial astrology, and troll — move his tongue nimbly as he speaks about — the trine, the quartile, and the sextile, platic aspect, and partile, with his *hyleg* or *alchochoden*, cusps, and horoscope, doesn't he cant? Who here can understand him?"

Once again, the Canter mentioned many specialized terms, this time those of astrology. One of his points about cant was that specialized terms can be used to deliberately confuse the audience and make the audience think that something non-scientific is scientific.

"This is no canter, though," Almanac said about the Canter.

The Canter was making too much sense and criticizing his "betters" too strongly to be a beggar.

Talking about Shunfield's cant — military jargon — the Canter said, "Or when my muster-master talks about his tactics, and his ranks and files, his bringers-up, his leaders-on, and cries, 'Faces about to the right hand!' or 'The left!' or cries, 'Now, as you were!' and then tells you about redoubts, cats, and cortines, doesn't he cant?"

"Yes, indeed," Pennyboy Junior said.

The Canter then talked about Madrigal's use of the cant of poetry and song, "My egg-chinned — smooth-chinned — laureate here, when he comes forth with dimeters and trimeters, tetrameters, pentameters, hexameters, catalectics, his *hyper-* and his *brachy-catalectics*, his *Pyrrhics, epitrites*, and *choriambics*, what is all this but canting?"

Madrigal said to the others, "The Canter is a rare fellow!"

Shunfield said, "He is some begging scholar."

The Canter had a good knowledge of specialized vocabulary, and he did not have a job. Some scholars are like that.

Fitton said, "He is a decayed — down on his luck — doctor, at least!"

"Nay, I do cherish virtue, though in rags," Pennyboy Junior said.

The Canter said, "And you, Mas' Courtier —"

Interrupting, Pennyboy Junior said to Fitton, "— now he treats of you. Stand forth to him fair."

The Canter said, "You use cant with all your fly-blown — corrupt — projects."

The projects were financial schemes, many of them doomed to fail. Courtiers such as Fitton said that they were able to bring projects to the attention of people who could finance them.

The Canter continued, "You also use look-outs of the politics, and you use your shut faces."

Courtiers such as Fitton learned court gossip from observers at the court, and when they thought it appropriate, they used shut rather than open faces — they used looks that hid their intentions.

The Canter continued:

"You also use reserved — tried and tested and set aside until you need to use them — questions and answers that you play the game with.

"Such as:

"'Is it a clear business? Will it manage well? My name must not be used else. Here, it will dash.'"

"Dash" means founder. When a bill was rejected in Parliament, it was said to be dashed. But "dash" can also mean run or rush.

The Canter continued:

"Or: 'Your business has received a taint; leave off and give it up. I may not prostitute myself.'

"Or: 'Tut, tut, that little dust I can blow off at pleasure. Here's no such mountain, yet, in the whole work that a light purse cannot level — a little money can smooth things over.'

"Or: 'I will carry through this affair for you — give it freight and passage.'"

"Give it freight and passage" means "give me some money." "Freight and passage" refers to money for passage. In other contexts, the word "freight" can mean "cargo."

The Canter continued, "You use such mint-phrases — fancy new phrases. This use of language is the worst of canting because of how much it pretends to have the sense it doesn't have."

In other words, Fitton's cant pretended to have sense and meaning that it did not actually have. Fitton pretended to help people whom he did not really help.

In contrast, doctors' cant does have sense and meaning, and doctors really can help people.

Fitton said to the others about the Canter, "This is someone who is other than he seems!"

"How do you like him?" Pennyboy Junior asked him.

"This man cannot be a canter!" Fitton said.

"But he is, sir," Pennyboy Junior said, "And he shall be still, and so shall you be, too. We'll all be canters. Now I think about it, noble whimsy's come into my brain. I'll build a college, I and my Pecunia, and I'll call it Canters' College. Does this idea sound well?"

"Excellent!" Almanac said.

Pennyboy Junior said, "And here stands my father rector" — he pointed to the Canter and then to the canters — "and here stand you professors — you shall all profess something, and live there with Her Grace and me, your founders. I'll endow it with lands and means, and Lickfinger shall be my master cook."

He looked around for Lickfinger and said, "What! Has he gone?"

The Canter said, "And Lickfinger shall be a professor."

"Yes, he will," Pennyboy Junior said.

The Canter said, "And he will read and teach Apicius' *De re culinaria* to your brave doxy and you!"

Apicius was a Roman gourmand. Another Apicius was credited with writing a book about cooking titled *De re culinaria*.

A doxy is a beggar's mistress. The Canter was referring to Lady Pecunia. In that case, the beggar would be Pennyboy Junior.

Pennyboy Junior said, "You, cousin Fitton, shall, as a courtier, read Aristotle's *Politics*."

By "read," he meant that Fitton would teach that book at Canters' College.

Pennyboy Junior continued:

"Doctor Almanac shall read astrology.

"Shunfield shall read the military arts —"

The Canter interrupted, "— such as carving and assaulting the cold custard."

Pennyboy Junior continued, "And Horace here shall read the *Art of Poetry*."

Horace, the author of *Arts Poetica*, or the *Art of Poetry*, was a Roman poet much appreciated by Ben Jonson. Pennyboy Junior was using the name to compliment Madrigal.

Pennyboy Junior continued, "He shall read his lyrics and his madrigals, fine songs which we will have at dinner, steeped in claret, and, in preparation for supper, soused in sack."

Madrigal would teach his own work at Canters' College.

"Truly a divine whimsy!" Madrigal said.

"And a worthy work fit for a chronicle!" Shunfield said.

The Cantors' College would give them a source of income.

"Isn't it?" Pennyboy Junior said.

"A chronicle to and for all ages," Shunfield said.

"And Piedmantle shall give us all our coats of arms," Pennyboy Junior said. "But Picklock, what would you be? You can cant, too."

"In all the languages in Westminster Hall: Pleas, Bench, or Chancery," Picklock the lawyer said.

The great hall of Westminster Palace housed the Courts of Common Law (Pleas and Bench) and the Court of Chancery.

Picklock continued with a list of cant terms, especially those relating to property, owners, and tenants, used in these courts:

"Fee-farm, fee-tail, tenant in dower, at will, for term of life, by copy of court roll, knight's service, homage, fealty, escuage, soccage, or frank almoin, grand sergeanty, or burgage."

If you, the reader, don't understand these terms, don't worry about it. Neither did most of Ben Jonson's original audience. If the non-lawyers in the audience could understand all these terms, then these terms wouldn't be cant.

"You appear, Κατ' ἐξοχὴν — par excellence — a canter," Pennyboy Junior said. "You shall read all Littleton's *Tenures* to me, and indeed all my conveyances."

Littleton's *Tenures* was a treatise on land law.

Picklock asked, "And make all your conveyances, too, sir? Keep all your courts, be steward of your lands, let all your leases, keep your evidences?"

If Picklock were to have all this legal power, and if he were an unscrupulous man, he could arrange things to favor himself and not Pennyboy Junior.

Picklock continued, "But first, I must procure and pass your mortmain. You must have license from above, sir."

Property held in mortmain could be conveyed only with royal license or permission; such property was controlled by a corporation.

The Canter, who was knowledgeable about legal cant, as he was knowledgeable about so much else, knew that if Picklock could procure and pass a mortmain for Pennyboy Junior, and if he could manipulate Pennyboy Junior into giving him — Picklock — control over Pennyboy Junior's wealth, he could arrange things to favor himself and not Pennyboy Junior.

Of course, if Picklock were both honest and competent, he could be a good steward of Pennyboy Junior's wealth.

"Fear not," Pennyboy Junior said. "Pecunia's friends shall do it."

"But I shall stop it," the Canter said.

The Canter then revealed his true identity. He was not a beggar; instead, he was Pennyboy Junior's father. He had faked his own death in order to find out how Pennyboy Junior would treat his inherited wealth — and Lady Pecunia.

The Canter — hereafter called Pennyboy Canter — said, "I am Your Worship's loving and obedient father, your painstaking steward and lost officer, and I have done this to test how you would use *pecunia* — wealth — and Lady Pecunia when you had her.

"Now that I have seen how you treat her, I will take home the lady to my charge, and these her servants, and leave you my ragged cloak to wear as you travel to Beggars' Bush!"

Beggars' Bush was a tree that was a notable rendezvous for beggars. "To go to Beggars' Bush" was an idiom meaning "to fall into poverty."

Pennyboy Canter continued, "A seat has been built already, and furnished, too, worth twenty of your imagined structures, Canters' College."

The seat was a place by Beggars' Bush for Pennyboy Junior.

Fitton said to the others, "The Canter is Pennyboy Junior's father!"

"He's alive, I think," Madrigal said.

"I knew he was no rogue!" Almanac said.

Pennyboy Canter said to his son, "You, prodigal, was I so solicitous for you to procure and plot with my learnéd counsel, Master Picklock, this noble match for you, and do you prostitute her, scatter your mistress' favors, and throw away her bounties as if they were red-burning coals too hot for you to handle, on such rascals who are the scum and excrements of men?

"If you had sought out good and virtuous persons of these professions, I would have loved you, and I would have loved them — for these shall never have that plea against me or have the opportunity of claiming that I hate their callings — but I do hate their manners and their vices."

Specialized jargon can be used to communicate, or it can be used to deceive. Similarly, people can be good courtiers, soldiers, heralds, almanac-makers (lists of such things as times of tides and seasons can be useful), doctors, and poets — all of these are respectable occupations — or people can be corrupt practitioners of these professions.

Pennyboy Canter continued, "A worthy courtier is the ornament of a king's palace, his great master's honor."

He pointed to Fitton and said, "This is a moth, a rascal, a court-rat that gnaws the commonwealth with broking — unscrupulous — suits and eating grievances!"

He then said, "A true soldier is his country's strength, his sovereign's safety, and, to secure his sovereign's peace, he makes himself the heir of danger, nay, the subject of it, and runs those virtuous hazards and heroic risks that this scarecrow" — he pointed to Shunfield — "cannot endure to hear of."

"You are pleasant, sir," Shunfield said.

He meant: You are making jokes.

Pennyboy Canter, however, was deadly serious in his mocking of Shunfield.

Pennyboy Canter replied, "With you I dare to be pleasant!"

Shunfield would not fight him. Shunfield was the type of person who shuns a battlefield.

Pennyboy Canter then pointed to Piedmantle and said, "Here is Piedmantle. Because he's an ass and I don't love him, does that mean I don't love a herald who is the pure preserver of descents, the fair keeper of all nobility, without which all would run into confusion?"

Seeing a bad herald — one who mistakes a coat of arms for true nobility (a virtuous character) and one who makes a pedigree simply in order to suck up to a wealthy person — made Pennyboy Cantor love good heralds all the more.

Despising a bad herald does not mean one despises heraldry and good heralds.

Pennyboy Canter continued, "If Piedmantle were a learnéd herald, I would tell him that he can give coats of arms and marks of distinction; however, he cannot give honor, no more than money can make one noble — it may give place and rank, but it can give no virtue — and he would thank me for this truth."

Two kinds of nobility exist: one is based on titles, and the other is based on a virtuous character. Sometimes, the two kinds of nobility can be found in one person, but being given — or buying — a title does not make one noble in the virtuous sense.

A person can be given a medal without having earned it.

Pennyboy Canter pointed to Almanac and said, "This dog-leach, this dog-doctor, you title him 'Doctor' — which means 'learnéd' — because he can compile an almanac, perhaps erect a scheme — a horoscope — for my great madam's monkey when it has taken an enema and befouled the ephemerides."

Ephemerides are books of tables of the positions of celestial bodies at various times. The great madam's monkey has excreted solid waste on the ephemerides.

Pennyboy Canter continued, "Do I despise a learnéd physician when I call Almanac a quack?"

If the physician is truly learnéd, Pennyboy Canter would not call him a quack. But Almanac is not truly learnéd and so Pennyboy Canter docs call him a quack.

Pennyboy Canter then said, "Or do I wither the ever-living garland, always green, of a good poet when I say that the wreath of this man" — he pointed to Madrigal — "is pieced and patched together with dirty, withered flowers?

"Away!

"I am out of patience with these ulcers — I call you ulcers so that I will not call you something worse. There is no sore or plague but you to infect the times. I abhor your very scent."

He then said to Lady Pecunia, "Come, lady, since my Prodigal didn't know how to entertain you according to your worth, I'll see if I have learned how to receive you with more respect to you and your fair train of attendants here."

He then said to his son, Pennyboy Junior, "Farewell, my beggar in velvet, for today."

Normally, a beggar in velvet is a courtier who seeks favor from the king. In this case, Pennyboy Junior was wearing fancy clothing, but he had no money because he now had no inheritance due to his father still being alive.

Pennyboy Cantor was leaving, and he was taking Lady Pecunia with him.

Pennyboy Canter pointed at the patched cloak that he had thrown to the floor and said to his son, "Tomorrow you may put on that grave robe and enter your great work of Canters' College, your work, and worthy of a chronicle."

THE FOURTH INTERMEAN: AFTER THE FOURTH ACT

"Why, this was the worst of all!" Gossip Tattle said. "The catastrophe!"

The *catastrophe* is the resolution of the play. Gossip Tattle meant *catastasis* — an extra complication in the play.

Or perhaps she meant that the conclusion of the last scene was a disaster.

"The play's content began to be good just now — and he has spoiled it all with his beggar there!" Gossip Censure said.

"He" means Ben Jonson, the playwright of *The Staple of News*.

"A beggarly jack it is, I warrant him, and akin to the poet," Gossip Mirth said.

The beggarly jack is Pennyboy Canter, and the poet is Ben Jonson.

"Like enough, for he — the Canter — had the chiefest part in his play, if you pay attention to it," Gossip Tattle said.

Gossip Expectation said, "Absurdity on him, for a huge overgrown play-maker!"

Ben Jonson was a heavy man.

She continued, "Why should he — the playwright — make him — Pennyboy Junior's father — live again, when they and we all thought him dead? If he had left him to his rags, there had been an end of him."

Gossip Tattle said, "Aye, but set a beggar on horseback, he'll never lin — cease — until he is a-gallop."

"The young heir grew a fine gentleman in this last act!" Gossip Censure said.

"So he did, Gossip Censure, and kept the best company," Gossip Expectation said.

"And feasted them and his mistress!" Gossip Censure said.

"And showed her to them all! He was not jealous —" Gossip Tattle said.

Gossip Mirth interrupted, "— but very communicative and liberal and generous, and began to be magnificent, if the churl his father would have let him alone."

Certainly, Pennyboy Junior has been generous, but sometimes he has been generous to the wrong people — such as the jeerers, who were happy to eat his food but called him a shot-clog.

And certainly, he has not been jealous. He has allowed many people to kiss Lady Pecunia. Indeed, he has encouraged them to kiss Lady Pecunia.

Of course, other people may object that Pennyboy Junior had allowed unworthy people to kiss Lady Pecunia.

Money may at times be a whore, but we ought not to encourage such whoredom.

Gossip Censure said, "It was spitefully done of the poet to make the chuff — the churl — take him off in his height, when he was going to do all his brave deeds!"

The poet is Ben Jonson. The chuff — a mean-spirited person — is Pennyboy Canter, according to Gossip Censure. The man in his height, about to do all his brave deeds, is Pennyboy Junior.

"To found an academy!" Gossip Expectation said.

"Erect a college!" Gossip Tattle said.

"Plant his professors and water his lectures —" Gossip Expectation said.

"— with wine, gossips, as he meant to do; and then to defraud his purposes —" Gossip Mirth interrupted.

"— kill the hopes of so many towardly — promising — young spirits —" Gossip Expectation interrupted.

"As the doctor's —" Madam Tattle interrupted.

Madam Censure interrupted, "— and the courtier's! I say, I was in love with Master Fitton. He did wear all he had, from the hat-band to the shoe-tie, so fashionably, and would stoop and look invitingly —"

Both hat-bands and shoe-ties could be ostentatious in this society.

"— and lie so, in wait for a piece of wit, like a mousetrap!" Gossip Mirth said.

"Lie" can mean 1) lie in wait, or 2) lie in one's throat.

"Indeed, Gossip Mirth, so would the little doctor. All his behavior was only glister!" Gossip Expectation said.

"Glister" can mean 1) luster, or 2) enema.

She continued, "On my conscience, he would make any party's physic in the world work with his discourse."

Con men, including quacks, are often good with language. It is true, however, that a good bedside manner is helpful to patients and it is true that good doctors cultivate a good bedside manner.

Gossip Mirth said, "I wonder they would suffer it, a foolish old fornicating father — Pennyboy Canter — to ravish away his son's mistress —"

"— and all her serving-women at once, as he did!" Madam Censure said.

"I would have flown in his gypsy's — rogue's — face, in faith," Gossip Tattle said.

"To fly at someone" means "to attack that person."

"It was a plain piece of political incest, and worthy to be brought before the high commission of wit," Gossip Mirth said.

The political incest was Pennyboy Canter's taking Lady Pecunia away from his son: Pennyboy Junior.

"The high commission of wit" is the four gossips.

"The high commission of wit" is also you — the reader of this book. It's a compliment — when it's not sarcastic.

All of you will have to decide whether Pennyboy Canter is justified in taking Lady Pecunia away from Pennyboy Junior.

"Suppose we were to censure Pennyboy Canter," Gossip Mirth said. "You are the youngest voice, Gossip Tattle, so you begin."

"By the Virgin Mary, I would have the old cony-catcher — trickster — cheated of all he has, in the young heir's defense, by his learnéd counsel, Master Picklock," Gossip Tattle said.

"I would rather the courtier had found out some trick to beg him from his estate," Gossip Censure said.

The courtier Fitton could falsely inform on Pennyboy Canter and beg the king for Pennyboy Canter's lands and property. For example, Fitton could lie and say that Pennyboy Canter had spoken treasonous words and then ask the king to give him Pennyboy Canter's lands and property as a reward.

"Or the captain had courage enough to beat him," Gossip Expectation said.

"Or the fine madrigal-man, in rhyme, to have run him out of the country like an Irish rat," Gossip Censure said.

Some Irish believed that bards could kill rats or drive them away with rhymed incantations.

Gossip Tattle said, "No, I would have Master Piedmantle, Her Grace's herald, pluck down Pennyboy Canter's hatchments, reverse — turn upside down — his coat-armor, and nullify him for no gentleman."

Gossip Tattle was describing the ceremony of degradation.

Hatchments are escutcheons or ensigns armorial. They often showed the coat of arms of a deceased person. Since Pennyboy Canter was not deceased, Piedmantle might take away his hatchments.

Coat-armor was a coat of arms depicted on an outer coat and worn over armor. Coat-armor could also be displayed on vests or shields.

Piedmantle would degrade Pennyboy Canter's social status and make him no longer a gentleman and no longer entitled to a coat of arms.

Gossip Expectation said, "Nay, then let Master Doctor dissect him, have him opened, and his tripes taken to Lickfinger, to make a probation dish — a test of cookery — of."

"Agreed!" Gossip Censure said.

"Agreed!" Gossip Tattle said.

Gossip Mirth said, "By my faith, I would have him flat — completely — disinherited by a decree of court, bound to make restitution of the Lady Pecunia, and the use of her body to his son."

"And the use of the bodies of her train of attendants given to the gentlemen," Gossip Expectation said.

"And both the poet and himself — Ben Jonson and Pennyboy Canter — to ask them all forgiveness —" Gossip Censure said.

"And us, too —" Gossip Tattle interrupted.

"— in two large sheets of paper —" Gossip Censure interrupted.

Ben Jonson and Pennyboy Canter would each write their apology on a separate sheet of paper.

"Or to stand in the pillory wearing a piece of parchment, which the court please —" Gossip Expectation interrupted.

The pillory was a form of punishment. An offender's head and hands would be placed in holes in boards called stocks that would limit their movement. The stocks were placed on a pole so that the offender would be standing.

Gossip Censure interrupted, "And those filled with news —"

The parchment Ben Jonson and Pennyboy Canter would wear could list their crimes — that is the news Gossip Censure was referring to.

Gossip Mirth interrupted, "— and dedicated to the sustaining of the Staple —"

Gossip Expectation interrupted, "— which their poet has let fall, most abruptly."

Ben Jonson hadn't written much about the Staple of News Office in the last few scenes.

"Bankruptly, indeed!" Gossip Mirth said.

"You say wittily, Gossip Mirth, and therefore let a protest go out against him —" Gossip Censure said.

"A mournival of protests, or a gleek at least —" Gossip Mirth interrupted.

A mournival is four aces, four kings, four queens, four jacks, or four of anything. A gleek is 1) three aces, three kings, three queens, three jacks, or three of anything, or 2) an insult.

Three of the gossips had been doing a lot of talking recently, but Gossip Tattle had been relatively quiet.

"In all our names —" Gossip Expectation said.

"As a decayed wit —" Gossip Censure interrupted.

"Broken —" Gossip Expectation interrupted.

"Non-solvent —" Gossip Tattle interrupted.

"And forever forfeit —" Gossip Censure interrupted.

Gossip Mirth interrupted, "— to scorn of Mirth!"

Gossip Censure said, "— to scorn of Censure!

Gossip Expectation said, "— to scorn of Expectation!"

Gossip Tattle said, "Subsigned, Tattle."

All were agreed that they would condemn Ben Jonson. As a playwright, he should have provided a good play with *The Staple of News*. In the opinion of the four gossips, he had not done that, and so they would scorn him because he had forfeited the good name of poet.

Gossip Tattle said, "Wait, the actors are coming again."

CHAPTER 5

— 5.1 —

Alone, Pennyboy Junior was wearing the patched cloak that his father had left him.

Pointing to his clothing, he said to himself, "Nay, they fit as if they had been made for me, and I am now a thing worth looking at, just as I said I would be in the morning.

"No rogue at a *comitia* — assembly — of the canters did ever there become his parent's robes better than I do these. I am a great fool and beggar!

"Why don't all who are of those societies come forth and welcome me as one of theirs? I think I should be, on every side, saluted as the Dauphin — Prince — of Beggars! The Prince of Prodigals!

"I, who have so fallen under the ears and eyes and tongues of all, have become the cautionary fable of the time, the subject matter of scorn, and the object of reprehension!

"I now begin to see my vanity shine in this glass, reflected by the foil."

The glass, aka mirror, was the ragged cloak he was wearing on his shoulders. The foil, or contrasting element, was the extravagant clothing he was still wearing under the ragged cloak.

Pennyboy Junior continued, "Where are my fashioner, my feather-man, my linener, perfumer, barber, all that tail of rioters who followed me this morning?

"Not one is here! But there is a dark solitude about me worthy my cloak and patches, as if I had the epidemical disease upon me, and I'll sit down with it."

The epidemical disease was the plague, which London was still recovering from.

He sat on the ground.

Thomas Barber entered the scene and said, "My master! My maker!"

Pennyboy Junior was Thomas Barber's maker in that he had paid for his position as clerk at the Staple of News Office.

"How are you?" Thomas Barber asked. "Why do you sit thus on the ground, sir? Have you heard the news?"

"No, nor do I care to hear any," Pennyboy Junior said. "I wish I could sit here always, and let slip away the next one-and-twenty years, if that would result in having this day forgotten, and the day razed — scraped — out and destroyed, expunged from every ephemerides or almanac!

"Or, if it must stay in existence because time and nature have decreed it, still, then let it be a day of tricking prodigals as if tickling fish about the gills to catch them.

"Let it be a day of deluding gaping — open-mouthed — heirs, setting loose their loves and their discretions.

"Let it be a day of falling from the favors of their best friends and parents, falling from their own hopes, and entering the society of canters!"

"A doleful day it is, and dismal times have come upon us," Thomas Barber said. "I am completely undone and ruined."

"How, Tom?" Pennyboy Junior asked.

"Why, broke! Broke! Wretchedly broke!" Thomas Barber answered.

"What?" Pennyboy Junior said, not understanding.

"Our Staple of News Office is all to pieces," Thomas Barber said. "It is quite dissolved!"

"What?" Pennyboy Junior said, still not understanding.

"It is shivered as if it had been in an earthquake!" Thomas Barber said. "Haven't you heard the crack and ruins? We are all blown up!

"As soon as they heard that the Infanta was taken away from them, whom they had so devoured in their hopes for Lady Pecunia to be their patroness and sojourn with them, our emissaries, register, and examiner flew into vapor; our grave governor Cymbal flew into a subtler air, and he has returned, we hear, to again be the grand captain of the jeerers."

Cymbal's true nature had been revealed: He was the chief of the jeerers and he, along with the other jeerers, had hoped to gain wealth from Lady Pecunia.

Thomas Barber continued:

"I and my fellow melted into butter and spoiled our ink, and so the News Office vanished.

"The last hum — buzz of gossip and news — that it made was that your father and Picklock, the man of law, have quarreled."

Pennyboy Junior said, "What!"

He stood up and said, "This awakens me from my lethargy."

Thomas Barber said, "And a great lawsuit is likely to be made between them.

"Picklock denies that the feoffment, aka the endowment, that your father made of the whole estate to him is a trust.

"Your father says that he did this action as a trust in the event of his death when he first laid this recent device — plan and plot — to test you."

As part of his test of his son, Pennyboy Canter had signed over his assets to Picklock. According to Pennyboy Canter, the document was a trust: Picklock would hold the estate in trust and would deliver it to Pennyboy Junior in the event of Pennyboy Canter's death. Pennyboy Canter meant for the trust to be revocable — he wanted it to last only as long as he was testing his son.

Picklock, however, was saying that the document was an absolute deed — Pennyboy Canter had given his estate away to Picklock with no conditions. If it was in fact not a trust and was in fact an absolute deed, then Picklock has and had no responsibility to do anything whatsoever for Pennyboy Junior.

"Has Picklock then a trust?" Pennyboy Junior asked.

"I cannot tell what the truth is," Thomas Barber said.

So far, it was one person's word against the other person's word: Pennyboy Canter says this, and Picklock says that.

A close examination of the document by a court of law might determine the truth.

Thomas Barber saw Picklock coming and said, "Here comes the worshipful —"

Pennyboy Junior motioned for Thomas Barber to hide himself behind an arras: a wall hanging in front of an alcove. Thomas Barber did so.

Picklock entered the room and said, "What? My velvet — foppish — heir, turned beggar in mind, as in robes?"

Some of Pennyboy Junior's fancy clothing was made of velvet.

"You see what case — condition and clothing — your and my father's plots have brought me to," Pennyboy Junior said.

"Your father's, you may say, indeed, but not mine," Picklock said. "He's a hard-hearted gentleman! I am sorry to see his rigid resolution.

"That any man should so put off affection and human nature, to destroy his own, and triumph in a victory so cruel!

"Your father has quarreled with me because I am your follower and serve you, and he calls me a knave and a traitor to his trust. He says that he will have me disbarred —"

Pennyboy Junior interrupted, "— have you deserved it?"

"Oh, good heaven knows my conscience and the silly — innocent — latitude of it!" Picklock said.

Good heaven does indeed know our conscience and whether it is good or bad.

He continued, "I am a narrow-minded man, and my thoughts dwell all in a lane or line indeed, with no turning or scarce obliquity in them. I still look right forward to the intent and scope of that which he would go from now."

As a narrow-minded man, Picklock's mind is narrowly focused on one thing. His mind makes the lane to that one thing straight as well as narrow. He will not take side trips that lead him away from that one thing. What that one thing is he does not say, and he does not say whether pursuing that one thing is ethical or unethical.

Picklock does say that there is no scarce obliquity in his thoughts. "Obliquity" means deviance from moral conduct. If there is no scarce obliquity in his thoughts, there may be abundant obliquity in his thoughts.

"Had you a trust, then?" Pennyboy Junior said.

Picklock answered, "Sir, I had something that will keep you still lord of all the estate, if I am honest — as I hope I shall be."

One kind of trust is a document giving someone assets to hold in trust for someone else. Another kind of trust is to trust someone.

If you trust someone, you believe that person to be trustworthy and responsible, including morally responsible.

If Picklock had a trust and if he were honest, that might keep Pennyboy Junior lord of the estate. (If nothing else, Pennyboy Junior would eventually inherit the estate.)

Pennyboy Canter, however, could argue that the trust was revocable and that he was revoking it. Picklock would presumably argue that the trust (if it were not an absolute deed giving all of Pennyboy Canter's wealth to Picklock) was irrevocable.

But Picklock says that he hopes he shall be honest. Referring to appearance, being honest means looking respectable, decent, and presentable. If Picklock had a trust, that could keep Pennyboy Junior lord of the estate. But Picklock could then manipulate Pennyboy Junior into giving him control of the estate. (Or he could say that the document was an irrevocable trust in which he would have control of the wealth until Pennyboy Cantor's death.) Picklock would then use the estate for his own benefit, including using it to buy fine clothing that would make him look respectable, decent, and presentable.

Picklock continued, "My tender scrupulous breast will not permit me to see the heir defrauded and, like an alien, thrust out of the blood. The laws forbid that I should give consent to such a civil — legal — slaughter of a son!"

"Where is the deed?" Pennyboy Junior asked. "Do you have it with you?"

"No," Picklock said. "It is a thing of greater consequence than to be borne about in a black box like a Low-Country *Verlof* or Welsh legal brief."

Verlof is a leave of absence or furlough. The Welsh had a reputation for being litigious.

Legal documents were sometimes carried in a black box. But this was a *very* important legal document.

Picklock continued, "It is at Lickfinger's, under lock and key."

"Oh, fetch it here," Pennyboy Junior said.

"I have told him to bring it so that you might see it," Picklock said.

Pennyboy Junior thought and then asked, "Does he know what he is bringing?"

"No more than a gardener's ass knows what roots it carries," Picklock answered.

Pennyboy Junior thought and then said, "I was going to send my father, like an ass, a penitent letter, but I am glad I did not, now."

"Hang him!" Picklock said. "He is an austere and sour grape that has no juice but what is verjuice in him."

Verjuice is the juice of unripe grapes. It is used in cooking.

Pennyboy Junior thought and then said, "I'll show you my letter."

He left the room.

Alone, Picklock said to himself, "Show me a defiance — a challenge! If I can now get father and son to legally fight each other, make my profits out of both, commence a lawsuit with the old man for his whole estate, and go to law with the son's credit, undo and ruin both (both with their own money), it would be a masterpiece of chicanery worthy my lawyer's nightcap — white skull-cap — and the lawyer's gown I wear. It would be Picklock's name in law — that is, worthy of the name of Picklock."

Picklock's true nature has been revealed: He is an unscrupulous lawyer who is willing and eager to seize the wealth of Pennyboy Canter and Pennyboy Junior.

He then called Pennyboy Junior, "Where are you, sir? What is taking you so long?"

Pennyboy Junior returned and said, "I cannot find where I have laid the penitent letter, but I have laid it somewhere safe."

"It doesn't matter, sir," Picklock said. "Trust yourself to my trust. It is that which shall secure you, an absolute deed!"

The absolute deed was the trust Picklock wanted Pennyboy Junior to have in him: Trust Picklock absolutely, and certainly you will have control of the estate.

Picklock continued, "And I confess, it was in trust for you lest anything mortal might have happened to him."

He was admitting that the document was a deed of trust, not an absolute deed.

Picklock continued:

"But there must be a gratuity — a fee — thought on, and aid, sir, for the expenses, which will be great, of the lawsuit against such a mighty man as is your father, and a man possessed of so much land, Lady Pecunia, and her friends.

"I am not able to wage law and go to law against him, yet I must maintain the thing as my own right, always for your good, and therefore must be bold to use your credit to raise money."

Picklock would be using Pennyboy Junior's money — borrowed with Pennyboy Junior's credit — to pursue the lawsuit against Pennyboy Canter. It takes money to wage law.

Picklock claimed that the lawsuit would be for the benefit of Pennyboy Junior, but actually it would be for the benefit of Picklock, who would be serving his own ends, including trying to enrich himself.

The lawsuit might be Picklock versus Pennyboy Canter, in which case Picklock would be saying that the document was an absolute deed giving all of

Pennyboy Canter's wealth to Picklock. In that case, Picklock would be saying — actually, lying — that he would give the wealth to Pennyboy Junior.

Or the lawsuit might be Pennyboy Junior versus Pennyboy Canter, in which case Picklock would be saying that the document was an irrevocable trust in which he would have control of the wealth until Pennyboy Cantor's death.

Of course, Picklock would prefer to have the document regarded as an absolute deed, but he would benefit if it were an irrevocable trust.

Since Picklock had said, "I must maintain the thing as my own right," the lawsuit would be Picklock versus Pennyboy Canter. The other lawsuit could be used, if needed.

Pennyboy Junior said, "Do what you will, so long as we are safe, and the trust will bear it."

"Fear not," Picklock said. "It is he who must pay arrearages — the debts — in the end. We'll milk him and Pecunia and draw their cream down before he gets the deed into his hands. My name is Picklock, but he'll find me a padlock."

Of course, if Pennyboy Canter were to get the legal document in his hands, it would be Game Over. No legal document, no lawsuit to argue over the document.

Pennyboy Canter entered the scene and said to his son, "What are you doing now? Conferring with your learnéd counsel about the cheat? Are you part of the plot to cheat me?"

"What plot?" Pennyboy Junior asked.

"Your counsel there, Master Picklock, knows," Pennyboy Canter said.

He then asked Picklock, "Will you restore the trust yet?"

He wanted Picklock to give him the deed of trust, thereby revoking it.

Picklock replied:

"Sir, be patient and search your memory, and think to yourself: What trust? Where does it appear?

"I have your deed. Does your deed specify any trust? Isn't it a perfect and completed act, and absolute in law, sealed and delivered before witnesses, the day and date emergent?"

"Emergent" means "unspecified." Picklock was denying that Pennyboy Canter had specified a day and date to deliver the estate to his son; however, that date was upon Pennyboy Canter's death. When Pennyboy Canter died, his entire estate was supposed to be given to his son: Pennyboy Junior.

Pennyboy Canter said, "But what about the conversation we had? What about the oaths and vows that preceded the deed?"

"I will tell you, sir, since I am urged to tell you," Picklock said. "As I remember, you told me you had got a grown — huge — estate by griping and grasping means, sinisterly and dishonestly —"

Shocked, Pennyboy Canter said, "What!"

Picklock continued, "— and you were quite weary of your estate. If the parties lived from whom you had wrested it —"

Shocked, Pennyboy Canter said again, "What!"

It sounded as if Picklock were saying that Pennyboy Canter had caused deaths in acquiring his estate.

Picklock continued, "— you could be glad to part with all and give it back to them, for the satisfaction of your conscience. But since they'd yielded to humanity and had died, and since just heaven had sent you, for a punishment

— you did acknowledge it — this riotous heir who would bring all to beggary in the end, and daily sowed consumption wherever he went —"

"You'd cheat both of us, then?" Pennyboy Canter said. "You'd cheat your confederate, my son, too?"

Picklock continued, "After a long, mature deliberation, you could not think where better how to place it —"

Pennyboy Canter interrupted, "— than on you, rascal?"

Picklock replied, "Use whatever name you please in your passionate anger, but with the return of your reason, you will come around and think that I am a faithful and a frugal friend to be preferred."

"Preferred before a son?" Pennyboy Canter said.

Normally, in this society fathers left their property to their sons.

"He is a prodigal, a tub without a bottom, as you termed him," Picklock said.

A proverb stated, "Every tub must stand on its own bottom."

He continued, "For which I might return you a vow or two and seal it with an oath of thankfulness. I do not repent it, neither have I cause, yet —"

He might give a vow to and thank Pennyboy Canter for the estate, but he did not repent Pennyboy Canter's giving the estate to him. The vow could be to do something for Pennyboy Canter's son.

Pennyboy Canter said, "Forehead of steel and mouth of brass!"

He was saying that Picklock had a forehead that was incapable of blushing for shame and a mouth that was capable of saying anything.

Pennyboy Canter continued, "Has impudence polished so gross a lie, and dare you vent it? You engine, composed of all mixed — impure — metals! Get away from here! I will not exchange one syllable more with you until I may meet you at a bar in court before your judges."

Pennyboy Junior's porter arrived. Pennyboy Junior talked to him quietly and received a document and some keys from him. Picklock, who was busy talking to Pennyboy Canter, did not see this.

Picklock said to Pennyboy Canter, "To a court of law it must come before I part with it — your wealth to you, or" — he looked at Pennyboy Junior — "you, sir."

"I will not listen to you anymore," Pennyboy Canter said.

His son said to him, "Sir, listen to me, though. Not simply because I see through his intricate and tangled plots and hidden ends, nor simply because my parts — my shares in the estate — depend upon the unwinding of this so knotted skein, do I ask for your patience. To me he has confessed the trust."

Earlier, Picklock had said to Pennyboy Junior, "And I confess, it was in trust for you lest anything mortal might have happened to him."

But now Picklock denied saying that: "What? I confess it?"

"Aye, you did, you false man," Pennyboy Junior said.

"Stand up to him and confront him," Pennyboy Canter said to his son.

Picklock asked, "Where? When? To whom?"

"To me, just now, and here," Pennyboy Junior said. "Can you deny it?"

"Can I eat or drink, sleep, wake, or dream, arise, sit, walk, or stand, do anything that's natural?" Picklock said.

Yes, he could deny it. To him, lying came naturally.

"Yes, you lie," Pennyboy Junior said. "It seems you can lie and perjure yourself — that is natural!"

"Oh, me!" Picklock said. "What times are these, of frontless carriage — of shameless conduct! An egg of the same nest! The father's bird! It runs in a blood — a family — I see."

Cicero once said, "*O, tempora! O, mores!*" This means, "Oh, the times! Oh, the customs!" It is an expression of despair at how bad the times have become.

"I'll shut your mouth," Pennyboy Junior said.

"With what?" Picklock asked.

"With truth," Pennyboy Junior answered.

"With noise," Picklock said. "I must have testimony before I shut my mouth. Where is your witness? Can you produce a witness?"

"As if my testimony were not twenty witnesses, compared with your testimony," Pennyboy Junior said.

"So say all prodigals, sick of self-love, but that's not law, young Scattergood," Picklock said. "I live by law."

"Scattergood" is a name for prodigals.

"I live by law" can mean 1) I live in accordance with the law, or 2) I make my living through law.

Pennyboy Junior said, "Why, if you have a conscience, that is a thousand witnesses."

A proverb stated, "Conscience is a thousand witnesses."

Picklock said, "No court grants out a writ of summons for the conscience that I know, nor a subpoena, nor an arrest warrant. I must have witness testimony, and of your producing, before this can come to a hearing, and it must be heard on oath and witness."

Pennyboy Junior said, "Come forth, Tom."

Thomas Barber, a witness who had heard Picklock say to Pennyboy Junior, "And I confess, it was in trust for you lest anything mortal might have happened to him," came from the alcove behind the arras.

Pennyboy Junior said to him, "Speak what you heard, the truth, and the whole truth, and nothing but the truth. What did this varlet say?"

"A rat behind the hangings!" Picklock said, seeing Thomas Barber.

Readers will remember the scene in William Shakespeare's *Hamlet* (Act 3, Scene 4) in which Hamlet kills Polonius, who is behind an arras. Hamlet says, "How now, a rat!" and then stabs him.

Thomas Barber said, "Sir, he said it was a trust, an act the which your father had will to alter, but his tender breast would not permit him to see the heir defrauded and, like an alien, thrust out of the blood — the laws forbid that he should give consent to such a civil slaughter of a son!"

Pennyboy Junior said, "And he talked of a gratuity to be given, and aid to the charges of the lawsuit, which he was to maintain in his own name, but for my benefit, he said."

The lawsuit would be Picklock versus Pennyboy Canter.

"It is enough," Pennyboy Canter said.

Thomas Barber said, "And he said that he would milk Pecunia and draw down her cream before you got the trust again."

Pennyboy Canter said to Picklock, "Your ears are in my pocket, knave; go shake them the little while longer you will have them."

Cropping a person's ears was sometimes a legal punishment. Pennyboy Canter was telling Picklock that he would put Picklock's ears in his pocket after they were cut off.

"You do trust to your great purse," Picklock said.

He was saying — that is, lying — that Pennyboy Canter had bribed Thomas Barber to be his witness.

Pennyboy Canter said, "I have you in a purse-net, good Master Picklock, with your worming brain and wriggling engine-head — snare — of maintenance, which I shall see you hole with very shortly — a fine round head, when those two lugs — ears — are off, to trundle — roll — through a pillory."

Purse-nets were nets in the shape of a bag used to catch rabbits.

According to the *Oxford English Dictionary*, "maintenance" means "wrongfully aiding and abetting litigation."

Picklock would end up in a pillory with his earless head trapped in the hole made by a pair of stocks.

Pennyboy Canter asked Thomas Barber, "You are sure that you heard him speak this?"

Pennyboy Junior answered for Thomas Barber, "Aye, and more."

"Much more!" Thomas Barber said.

Picklock said, "I'll prove that your lawsuit against me is maintenance and conspiracy, and sue you all."

"Do, do, my gowned vulture," Pennyboy Junior said. "Crop in reversion."

A gowned vulture is one way to describe a lawyer.

By "crop in reversion," Pennyboy Canter meant "crop my and my son's ears," with "if you can" implied.

Pennyboy Canter continued, "I shall see you quoited — thrown — over the bar, as bargemen do their billets."

In a game of quoits, players threw rings of iron, rope, rubber, etc., at a target.

Bargemen threw their cargo — billets, aka wood cut for fuel — on the quay, aka dock.

Picklock said, "This it is when men repent of their good deeds and would have them in again."

Picklock was saying that Pennyboy Canter's good deed was giving his estate to Picklock — an estate that Picklock said that Pennyboy Canter had gotten immorally.

He continued, "They are almost mad, but I forgive their *lucida intervalla*."

Picklock was planning a defense in which he claimed that Pennyboy Canter and Pennyboy Junior were mentally incompetent. Of course, he would claim that Pennyboy Canter was having a *lucida intervalla* — a period of mental competence — when he signed what Picklock claimed was an absolute deed giving his estate to Picklock.

Although Pennyboy Canter had a witness in Thomas Barber, Picklock believed that he had an ace up his sleeve — the document that Pennyboy Canter had signed.

Seeing Lickfinger enter the room, Picklock called to him, "Oh, Lickfinger! Come here."

He then asked him quietly, "Where's my writing?"

The writing was the document that Pennyboy Canter had signed.

Pennyboy Canter and Pennyboy Junior, who was holding a document and some keys that he had gotten from his porter earlier but had kept hidden, also talked together quietly at a distance from Picklock and Lickfinger.

Lickfinger replied, "I sent it to you, together with your keys."

"What!" Picklock said.

Lickfinger said, "By the porter who came for it, from you —"

Seeing the worried expression on Picklock's face — Picklock had not received the document — Lickfinger added, "— and by the warrant of the token you had given me, the keys —"

The keys were Picklock's keys, which had been used to lock up the document. Picklock had sent a porter to tell Lickfinger to bring him the document, and he had sent his keys so that Lickfinger could open the container and get the document and bring it to him. The keys were a token showing that the request really came from Picklock.

Lickfinger then finished his original sentence, "— and the porter bade me bring it."

"And why didn't you?" Picklock asked.

He had not received the document.

Lickfinger asked, "Why did you send a countermand?"

The countermand was a command revoking a previous command. The first command was for Lickfinger himself to bring the document to Picklock.

"Who, I?" Picklock asked.

"You, or some other you whom you put in trust," Lickfinger said.

"In trust?" Picklock said.

"Your trust's another self, you know," Lickfinger said. "And without trust, and your trust, how should he take notice of your keys or of my charge?"

Actually, Pennyboy Junior had sent his porter to Lickfinger to get the document. (This is a second porter, not the porter whom Picklock had sent.) When Pennyboy Junior had told Picklock that he was going to get the letter he had written asking his father for forgiveness, he had actually been sending the porter to Lickfinger to get the document, which Picklock had said had been locked up. Thus, Pennyboy Junior knew about Picklock's keys, which Picklock must have given to Lickfinger so that he could get the document. Pennyboy Junior had told his porter about Picklock's keys. The second porter's knowledge of the keys and the document had convinced Lickfinger that the second porter had really come from Picklock.

As Picklock and Lickfinger had talked, Pennyboy Junior had revealed to his father his plot of sending for the document by the porter, and that he was in possession of the deed and Picklock's keys. Now Pennyboy Junior and Pennyboy Canter listened to Picklock and Lickfinger talk.

Picklock asked, "Did you know the man?"

Lickfinger replied, "I know he was a porter — and a sealed porter, for he bore the badge on his breast, I am sure."

A sealed porter is a member of the Company of Porters. Their members wore a distinctive badge.

"I am lost! A plot! I scent it!" Picklock said.

"Why, and I sent it by the man you sent, whom else I would not have trusted," Lickfinger said.

"A plague on your trust!" Picklock said. "I am trussed up among you."

"Trussed up" means "ensnared."

Pennyboy Junior, "Or you may be."

Pennyboy Junior meant that Picklock could be trussed up in a noose on a gallows.

"In my own halter," Picklock said. "I have made the noose."

A halter is a noose.

Picklock exited.

"What was it, Lickfinger?" Pennyboy Junior asked.

"A document, sir," Lickfinger said. "He sent for it by a token. I was bringing it, but then he sent a porter, and the porter seemed to be a man of decent carriage."

Porters tend to be men of good carriage; their job is to carry things such as luggage.

"It was good fortune!" Pennyboy Canter said. "To cheat the cheater was no cheat, but justice."

He then said to his son, "Take off your rags and be yourself again. This act of piety and good affection has partly reconciled me to you."

Pennyboy Junior, who wanted to be fully reconciled to his father, began, "Sir —"

His father interrupted, "No vows, no promises. Too much protestation often makes suspected that which we would use to persuade."

In Shakespeare's *Hamlet*, Queen Gertrude said, "The lady doth protest too much, methinks" (Act 3, Scene 2). In other words, she thought that the lady was objecting so much that she was losing credibility.

A proverb stated, "Too much protesting makes the truth suspected."

"Have you heard the news?" Lickfinger asked.

"The Staple of News Office is down," Pennyboy Junior said. "How should we have heard it?"

"But the news about your uncle?" Lickfinger asked.

Because the news was about his uncle, someone could have brought Pennyboy Junior the news.

"No," Pennyboy Junior said.

"He's run mad, sir," Lickfinger said.

Startled, Pennyboy Canter asked, "What, Lickfinger!"

"Your brother is stark staring mad," Lickfinger said. "He has almost killed his serving-maid —"

"Now, heaven forbid!" Pennyboy Canter said.

Lickfinger said, "He would have succeeded except that she's cat-lived and squirrel-limbed. He threw bed-staves at her."

Cats are supposed to have nine lives.

Bed-staves are short wooden sticks; they were used to support a mattress.

Lickfinger continued, "He has set wide his outer doors, and now keeps open house for all the passersby to see his justice.

"First, he has arrested his two dogs because he suspects them of being participants in the plot to cheat him, and there he sits like an old worm of the peace, wrapped up in furs, at a square table, interrogating, examining, and committing the poor curs to two old cases of close-stools" — these are boxes that used to contain a chamber-pot — "as prisons, the one of which he calls his Lollard's tower, and the other his Block-house, because his two dogs' names are Block and Lollard."

Lollard's Tower was a prison for religious heretics; "block-house" was a slang term for a prison.

"This would be splendid content for the jeerers," Pennyboy Junior said.

"Aye, if the subject were not so wretched," Pennyboy Canter said.

"Sure, I met them all, I think, upon that quest," Lickfinger said.

He had met the jeerers going to Pennyboy Senior's house to jeer at him. The jeerers thought that wretchedness was funny.

"Indeed, likely enough," Pennyboy Canter said. "The vicious always are swift to show their natures. I'll go there, too, but with another aim, if all succeed well and my simples work."

Simples are medicines that have a single ingredient.

Pennyboy Canter's aim, aka goal, was to restore his brother to health.

They exited in order to go to Pennyboy Senior's house.

— 5.4 —

In a room of his house, Pennyboy Senior sat at his table with papers before him.

A porter entered the room and Pennyboy Senior asked him, "Where are the prisoners?"

"They are forthcoming, sir," the porter answered, "or coming forth, at least."

Pennyboy Senior said to himself, "The rogue has gotten drunk since I committed the prisoners to his charge."

He then said out loud, "Come here — near me. Yet nearer; breathe upon me."

The porter came near him, and Pennyboy Senior sniffed and said, "I smell wine! Wine, on my honor! Sack, canary sack!"

Canary sack is a sweet wine from the Canary Islands.

He asked the porter, "Couldn't your badge have been drunk with fulsome ale or beer, the porter's element? But sack!"

Ale and beer were cheaper than wine.

"I am not drunk," the porter said. "We had, sir, just one pint, an honest carrier and myself."

"Who paid for it?" Pennyboy Senior asked.

"Sir, I gave it to him," the porter answered.

"What?" Pennyboy Senior said. "And spend sixpence? A frock spend sixpence! Sixpence!"

A frock is a loose garment worn by workmen; it is often called a frock-smock.

As a miser, Pennyboy Senior was outraged that a porter would spend sixpence.

"Once in a year, sir," the porter replied.

"In seven years, varlet!" Pennyboy Senior said.

In seven years at 10 percent interest per year, the interest would roughly equal the principal.

Pennyboy Senior continued, "Do you know what you have done? Do you know what a consumption you have made of an estate? It might please heaven to let you, a healthy and young knave, live some seventy years longer, until

177

you are fourscore-and-ten, perhaps a hundred — say, seventy years. How many times seven in seventy? Why, seven times ten is ten times seven.

"Pay attention to me, I will demonstrate to you on my fingers.

"Sixpence in seven years (because of use upon use, aka compound interest) grows in that first seven-year period to be a twelvepence."

A shilling is twelvepence. It is one-twentieth of a pound.

Pennyboy Senior continued, "That, in the next seven-year period, grows to two shillings.

"In the third seven-year period, it grows to four shillings.

"In the fourth seven-year period, it grows to eight shillings.

"In the fifth seven-year period, it grows to sixteen shillings.

"In the sixth seven-year period, it grows to thirty-two shillings, aka one pound and twelve shillings.

"In the seventh seven-year period, it grows to three pounds and four shillings.

"In the eighth seven-year period, it grows to six pounds and eight shillings.

"In the ninth seven-year period, it grows to twelve pounds and sixteen shillings.

"And in the tenth seven-year period, it grows to five-and-twenty pounds and twelve shillings.

"This money you have fallen from and have lost out on, because of your riotous living, should you live seventy years, by spending sixpence once at the beginning of the first seven-year period.

"But in a single day to waste it! There is a sum that number cannot reach!

"Get out of my house, you pest of prodigality! Seed of consumption, get away from here! A wicked jailor is often worse than the prisoners."

He gave the porter some money and said, "There's your penny: four tokens for you. Out, away!"

A token is a small coin worth a farthing, aka one-fourth of a penny.

The porter exited.

Pennyboy Senior said to himself, "My dogs may yet be innocent and honest. If not, I have an entrapping question or two more to put to them, a cross-examination, and I shall catch them."

He called one of his dogs, "Lollard!"

He then released Lollard from the close-stool that was Lollard's prison.

Pennyboy Senior believed that his dogs were part of the plot to get Lady Pecunia and her serving-women away from him. He believed that his dogs had known that the ladies would leave and not return and that his dogs had done nothing to stop them.

Pennyboy Senior said to Lollard, "Silence! What whispering was that you had with Mortgage when you last licked her feet? The truth, now. Ha? Did you smell she was going?"

He then said an imaginary recorder, "Put down that."

Recorders recorded words spoken during a trial.

He continued, "And not, not to return? You are silent. Good. And when you leaped on Statute? As she went forth? You say, 'Consent'! There was consent as she was going forth? It would have been fitter at her coming home, but you knew that she would not? To your Tower."

He put Lollard in one of the close-stools, saying, "You are cunning, are you? I will meet your craft."

He then called his other dog, Block, and released it from the close-stool that was Block's prison. The dog licked him, and he said, "Block, show your face; stop your caresses.

"Tell me, and tell me truly, what affronts do you know that were done to Lady Pecunia, with the result that she left my house?

"None, do you say? Not that you know, or will admit to knowing?

"I fear that I shall find you an obstinate cur.

"Why did your fellow, Lollard, cry this morning? Because Broker kicked him? Why did Broker kick him? Because he pissed against my lady's gown?"

According to Pennyboy Senior's reasoning, Lady Pecunia may have decided to leave Pennyboy Senior's house because Lollard peed on her dress.

Pennyboy Senior continued, "Why, that was no affront? No? No distaste? You knew of none? You're a dissembling cur."

He put Block in the other close-stool, saying, "To your hole, again, your Block-house."

Pennyboy Senior said, "Lollard, arise."

He released Lollard from the close-stool and said, "Where did you lift your leg up last? Against what? Are you struck dummerer now, and whine for mercy?"

A dummerer is a beggar who fakes muteness, pretending to be unable to speak to gain sympathy and alms.

Pennyboy Senior asked, "Whose kirtle — woman's gown, outer petticoat, or skirt — was it you gnawed, too? Mistress Band's? And Wax's stockings? Who? Did Block bescumber — befoul with feces — Statute's white suit with the parchment lace there, and Broker's satin jacket? All will out. They had offence, offence enough to quit me."

Parchment lace is a kind of decorative trim.

He then said, "Appear, Block! Bah, it — your guilt — is manifest. He shows his guilt. Should he forswear it, make all the affidavits against it that he could before the bench and twenty juries, he would be convicted. He bears an air about him that does confess it! To prison again, close prison!"

He put Block back in a close-stool.

He then said, "Not you, Lollard. You may enjoy the liberty of the house. And yet there is a notion come in my head for which I must commit you, too, and close. Do not repine; it will be better for you."

He put Lollard back in a close-stool.

"This is enough to make the dogs mad, too," Cymbal said, looking into the room. "Let's go in upon him."

He and the other jeerers had been watching Pennyboy Senior. His door was open.

The jeerers — Cymbal, Fitton, Shunfield, Almanac, and Madrigal — entered the room.

"What is it now?" Pennyboy Senior said to them. "What's the matter? Have you come to seize the prisoners? Make a rescue?"

"We have come to bail out your dogs," Fitton said.

"They are not bailable," Pennyboy Senior said. "They stand committed without bail or mainprise — without anyone allowed to go surety for their release. Your bail cannot be taken."

"Then the truth is that we have come here to vex you," Shunfield said.

"To jeer you," Almanac said.

"To bait and torment you, rather," Madrigal said.

"A baited usurer will be good flesh," Cymbal said.

"Baited" means "tormented." A cruel sport of the time was bear-baiting. A bear or bull was tied to a stake so it could not flee, and then dogs were set loose to torment it. Some people of the time thought that baited bull meat tasted better than the meat of a bull that had not been baited.

"A baited" is also a pun for "abated" — "lessened." Pennyboy Senior was complaining about loss of wealth because he had lost Lady Pecunia.

People had given Pennyboy Senior gifts of food when Lady Pecunia was with him. Now that she had left him, those gifts of food may not be forthcoming, and so Pennyboy Senior's weight could also soon be abated.

"And tender, we are told," Fitton said.

"Who is the butcher among you who has come to cut my throat?" Pennyboy Senior asked.

"You would die a calf's death gladly, but it is an ox's death that is meant for you," Shunfield said.

A "calf" is a fool.

Fitton began, "To be fairly knocked on the head —"

Shunfield finished the sentence, "— with a good jeer or two."

Oxen could be killed with blows to the head.

"And from your jawbone, Don Assinigo?" Pennyboy Senior said to Shunfield.

According to the Old Testament book Judges, Samson used the jawbone of an ass to slay a thousand Philistines.

The Spanish word *asnico* means "little ass." Pennyboy Senior was calling Shunfield a little fool.

"Shunfield, he gave you a jeer," Cymbal said. "You have suffered it."

"I do confess a swashing — fiercely slashing — blow," Shunfield said.

He then replied to Pennyboy Senior, "But, Snarl — you who might play the third dog because of your teeth — you have no money now?"

The first two dogs were Pennyboy Senior's pets.

"No, nor no Mortgage," Fitton said.

"Nor Band," Almanac said.

"Nor Statute," Madrigal said.

"No, nor blushet" — rose, aka Rose — "Wax," Cymbal said.

"Nor you no office, as I take it," Pennyboy Senior said.

The Staple of News Office was out of business now.

"Cymbal, he gave you a mighty jeer," Shunfield said.

"A pox on these true jests, I say," Fitton said.

Two proverbs of the time were 1) True jests are the worst, and 2) The truest jests sound worst in guilty ears.

"He will turn out to be the better jeerer," Madrigal said.

Almanac said, "Let's set upon him, and if we cannot jeer him down in wit —"

Madrigal interrupted and finished the sentence: "— let's do it in noise."

The jeerers knew that they had limitations: Almanac and Madrigal acknowledged that their wit — intelligence — was limited. All acknowledged a lack of money.

"I am content to do that," Shunfield said.

"Charge, man of war!" Madrigal said to Shunfield.

"Belay him! Aboard! Board him!" Almanac said to Shunfield.

"We'll give him a broadside first," Shunfield said.

"Where's your venison now?" Fitton asked Pennyboy Senior.

"Where's your red-deer pies?" Cymbal asked Pennyboy Senior.

"With your baked turkeys?" Shunfield asked Pennyboy Senior.

"And your partridges?" Almanac asked Pennyboy Senior.

"Your pheasants and fat swans?" Madrigal asked Pennyboy Senior.

Back when Lady Pecunia lodged with Pennyboy Senior, people often gave him gifts of food.

"Like you, they have turned geese," Pennyboy Senior replied.

"Geese" can mean fools.

"But such as will not keep your capitol!" Madrigal said.

In ancient Roman times, enemy soldiers known as the Gauls were trying to sneak up the Capitoline Hill, but geese sacred to Juno cackled and alerted the Romans to the approach of the enemy soldiers.

Shunfield began, "You were accustomed to have your breams —"

A bream is a kind of fish.

Almanac interrupted, "— and trouts sent in —"

Cymbal interrupted, "— fat carps and salmons —"

Fitton interrupted, "— aye, and, now and then an emblem of yourself, an over-grown pike?"

Pikes were so voracious that they ate other pike.

"You are a jack, sir," Pennyboy Senior said.

"You have made a shift to swallow twenty such poor jacks before now," Fitton said.

Almanac began, "If he should come to feed upon poor john —"

"Poor jack" and "poor john" were phrases that meant dried hake — a kind of fish.

Madrigal interrupted, "— or turn pure Jack-a-Lent after all this?"

A Jack-a-Lent was a stuffed puppet that served as a target for stone-throwing children during Lent and was then burned.

Fitton began, "Tut, he'll live like a grasshopper —"

Madrigal interrupted, "— on dew."

Shunfield added, "Or like a bear, with the licking of his own claws."

Pliny the Elder, author of *Naturalis Historia* (*Natural History*), wrote that grasshoppers had no mouths and lived on dew, and he wrote that during hibernation bears lived by sucking on their own fore-paws.

Cymbal said, "Aye, if his dogs were away."

"He'll eat them, first, while they are fat," Almanac said.

"Indeed, and when they are gone, here's nothing left to be seen," Fitton said.

"Except his kindred — spiders, natives of the soil," Cymbal said.

Almanac said, "He will have enough dust here to breed fleas."

Pliny the Elder wrote that fleas could be brought into being by the sun shining on dust.

"But by that time, he'll have no blood to rear them," Madrigal said.

Shunfield began, "He will be as thin as a lantern; we shall see through him —"

Almanac interrupted, "— and through his gut colon — his belly — and count his *intestina* —"

Intestina is Latin for intestines.

We can count the ribs of a thin person; to count someone's intestines, they must be *really* emaciated.

Pennyboy Senior said, "Rogues! Rascals!"

His dogs began to bark.

"He calls his dogs to his aid," Fitton said.

"Oh, they just rise at the mention of his tripes," Almanac said.

"Let them alone," Cymbal said. "They don't bark for him."

"They bark *se defendendo* — in self-defense," Madrigal said.

According to Madrigal, the dogs are barking because they don't want Pennyboy Senior to get so hungry that he eats them.

"Or for custom," Shunfield said. "As commonly curs do, one for another."

Lickfinger entered the room and said, "Arm, arm yourselves, you gentlemen jeerers! The old Pennyboy Canter is coming in upon you with his forces — the gentleman who was the Canter."

"Let's go hence!" Shunfield said.

"Let's go away!" Fitton said.

"Who is he?" Cymbal asked.

He had not heard that the Canter was actually Pennyboy Junior's father, who had faked his own death.

"Stay not to ask questions," Almanac said.

"He's a flame," Fitton said.

"A furnace," Shunfield said.

"A consumption," Almanac said. "He kills wherever he goes."

The jeerers all ran away.

"See, the whole covey is scattered!" Lickfinger said. "'Ware, 'ware the hawk! I love to see him — Pennyboy Canter — fly."

"Beware the hawk!" meant "Look out! A dangerous figure is coming!"

Pennyboy Canter was coming to fly at and attack the jeerers, but they had escaped by running away.

— 5.6 —

Pennyboy Canter and Pennyboy Junior arrived, along with Lady Pecunia and her train of attendants: Mortgage, Statute, Band, and Wax.

Pennyboy Canter said to Pennyboy Junior, "You see by this amazement and distraction what your companions were: a poor, frightened, and guilty race of men, who dare to stand and face no breath of truth, but, conscious to themselves of their no-wit and no-honesty, ran routed at every panic — frenzied — terror they themselves bred.

"They did that in a place where, elsewise, as confident as sounding brass, their tinkling captain, Cymbal, and the rest dare put on any visor — mask — to deride the wretched, or, with buffon license, jest at whatsoever is serious, if not sacred."

"Buffon license" is licentious buffoonery.

The jeerers were happy to mock wretched people and serious and sacred things; they were afraid to face righteous fury.

"Who's this?" Pennyboy Senior asked. "My brother, and restored to life!"

He had not heard that the Canter was actually his brother, who had faked his death.

"Yes, I am your brother, and restored to life," Pennyboy Canter said, "and I have been sent here to restore your wits, if your short madness is not more than anger conceived for your loss —"

In his *Epistles* I.2.62, Horace wrote that anger is a short madness.

Pennyboy Canter continued, "— which I return to you. See here, your Mortgage, Statute, Band, and Wax, without your Broker, have come to abide with you and vindicate the prodigal from stealing away the lady.

"Nay, Pecunia herself has come to free him fairly, and discharge all ties, except those of love, to her person, to treat her like a friend, not like a slave or like an idol."

The word "friend" can mean "lover."

Pennyboy Canter continued:

"Superstition violates the deity it worships no less than scorn does.

"And believe it, brother, the use of things is all, and not the store.

"Surfeit and fullness have killed more than famine."

186

Pennyboy Canter meant that money must be used wisely and not just stored away — and he knew that that was the way his brother would interpret the two sentences — but the two sentences were ambiguous. The truth of the two sentences is also debatable because extremes are dangerous.

"The use of things is all, and not the store" is ambiguous.

"Use" can mean "interest," as in lending money at interest, and "store" can mean "possessions."

In that case, the sentence means, "Lending money at interest is all, and not having possessions."

But "use" can mean "putting things to work, such as spending money to buy things that you can use," and "store" can mean "savings."

In that case, the sentence means, "Spending money to buy useful possessions is all, and not having savings."

The above two interpretations of the sentence are contradictory. If you believe in Aristotle's theory of the mean between extremes, both sentences are also false.

"Surfeit and fullness have killed more than famine" is also ambiguous.

"Surfeit and fullness" can refer to having 1) too much money, or 2) too many possessions.

"Famine" can refer to having 1) a lack of money, or 2) a lack of possessions.

The ambiguity of the second sentence results in contradictory meanings:

1) Having too much money has killed more than not having enough money.

2) Having too much money has killed more than not having enough possessions.

3) Having too many possessions has killed more than not having enough possessions.

4) Having too many possessions has killed more than not having enough money.

The extremes of both the ambiguous first sentence and the ambiguous second sentence in both pairs of sentences show that Aristotle's ethical theory of the Golden Mean is correct: Avoid excesses and search for the middle.

If you believe in Aristotle's theory of the mean between extremes, you want to avoid the extremes of having too much money or too little money, and having too many possessions or too few possessions.

Being a miser is bad, and being a prodigal is bad. The middle way is liberality: spending and giving what is yours freely but without going to the extreme of being a spendthrift. A person who seeks the Golden Mean will buy things he or she needs and will donate money to charity but will also have an emergency fund. That person will also have a few luxuries when they are affordable and desirable.

Pennyboy Canter said, "The sparrow, with his little plumage, flies, while the proud peacock, overcharged with plumes, is fain to sweep the ground with his grown train and load of feathers."

"Wise and honored brother!" Pennyboy Senior said. "None but a brother, and one sent from the dead, as you are to me, could have altered my character. I thank my destiny, which is so gracious.

"Are there no pains and punishments, no penalties decreed from where you have come to us that smother money in chests and strangle her in bags?"

If Pennyboy Canter had been sent to him from the dead, then he had been to the Land of the Dead, where he had seen usurers.

In Dante's *Inferno*, the usurers are punished in Circle 7. In contrast to the Blasphemers, who take something that ought to be fertile and make it infertile, the Greedy Moneylenders (usurers) take something that ought to be infertile and make it fertile. The definition of usury has changed over time, but originally, as in the Bible, it meant lending money at interest. The Bible is against lending money at interest to relatives or to poor people, although Jews are allowed to lend money at interest to non-Jews; thus, Jews became moneylenders in the Middle Ages. In modern times, usury is charging an unethically high rate of interest.

Because the Greedy Moneylenders have been taking something that ought to be infertile and making it fertile, they are in a burning plain with fire raining down on them. Here they are bent over, just like the Greedy Moneylenders of Dante's time who bent over their tables and counted their money. Hanging from their necks are moneybags. Dante cannot recognize any of the Greedy Moneylenders by looking at their faces; they were so preoccupied with making money that they have lost their individuality.

Pennyboy Canter answered, "Oh, on the usurers are imposed mighty, intolerable fines and penalties, of which I come to warn you, forfeitures of whole estates, if they are known to be immorally acquired!"

"I thank you, brother, for the light you have given me," Pennyboy Senior said. "I will prevent them all by taking action to repent my sins now.

"First, free my dogs, lest what I have done to them and against law is a *praemunire* — a violation of legal process — for, by Magna Carta, they could not be committed as close prisoners, my learnéd counsel, my cook, tells me here — and yet he showed me the way, first."

"Who did? I?" Lickfinger said. "I encroach upon the liberty of the subjects?"

Pennyboy Senior was blaming someone else — someone innocent — for his crime. This is not a good way to repent.

"Peace!" Pennyboy Canter said. "Quiet! Picklock, your lodger, that stentor — that loud-voiced lawyer — has infected you."

True, bad people can infect other people. If you are going to blame someone else, make sure that that person is guilty — blame the right person. But also remember that you have free will, and you can use that free will to resist the influence of bad people. Pennyboy Canter was strong enough not to become a jeerer; Madrigal was not strong enough to resist the bad influence of the jeerers. Pennyboy Senior needs to be strong enough to resist the bad influence of Picklock.

Pennyboy Canter added, "But I have Picklock safe enough in a wooden collar."

The wooden collar was the stocks of a pillory.

Pennyboy Senior continued his reformation:

"Next, I restore these servants to their lady with freedom, heart of cheer, and countenance. It is their year and day of jubilee."

In biblical times, Hebrew slaves were set free in the year of jubilee. In the year 1625, when *The Staple of News* was first performed, a jubilee was celebrated.

Pecunia's train of serving-women said, "We thank you, sir."

Pennyboy Senior then said, "And lastly, to my nephew I give my house, goods, lands, all but my vices, and those I go to cleanse — kissing this lady, whom I give to him, too, and join their hands."

He joined the hands of Pennyboy Junior and Lady Pecunia. The two would be married.

In giving away all his money, Pennyboy Senior was not choosing the Golden Mean, but if he were mentally ill — he believed that his brother was resurrected from the Land of the Dead — it's good that his money is in the hands of a guardian.

Still, by joining the hands of Pennyboy Junior and Lady Pecunia, Pennyboy Senior affirmed that Lady Pecunia — and money — should be properly loved and valued.

Pennyboy Canter said to you, the readers, "If the spectators will join their hands and applaud, we thank them."

Pennyboy Junior added, "And we wish they may, as I, enjoy Pecunia."

Lady Pecunia added:

"And so Pecunia herself wishes that she may always be an aid for their good uses.

"Pecunia does not wish to be a slave to their pleasures or a tyrant over their fair desires, but instead to teach them all the Golden Mean.

"She wishes to teach the prodigal how to live, and she wishes to teach the sordid and the covetous how to die.

"She wishes to teach the sordid and the covetous how to die with sound mind, and she wishes to teach the prodigal how to live with safe frugality."

If the loss of Lady Pecunia can drive Pennyboy Senior mad, then death must be terrifying to misers because the moment we die, our money abandons us. Value money correctly, and you can die with a sound mind.

The prodigal — including Pennyboy Junior — need to value money correctly, too, so that they can live with safe — secure — frugality. Get money, spend money for the things you need and some of the things you want (and donate some money to charity), don't waste money, and have an emergency fund. Safe frugality includes such things as having enough food, being warm enough in cold weather, not being homeless, and having money in the bank.

Art Linkletter once asked a young boy on one of his daytime television programs, "What is happiness?" The boy answered, "A steady paycheck."

Apparently, the boy had lived through times when his parents did not have a steady paycheck.

THE EPILOGUE

Thus have you seen the maker's [the playwright's] double scope [two aims or intentions],

  To profit [instruct] and delight, wherein our hope

  Is, though the clout we do not always hit,

  It will not be imputed to his wit —

  A tree [bow] so tried and bent as it will not start [let fly].

  Nor doth [does] he often crack [break] a string of art,

  Though there may other accidents as strange

  Happen: the weather [disposition] of your looks may change,

  Or some high wind of misconceit [misconception] arise

  To cause an alteration in our skies.

  If so, we're sorry that [we] have so misspent

  Our time and tackle [equipment, arrows]; yet he's confident,

  And vows the next fair day he'll have us shoot

  The same match o'er [over] for him, if you'll come to it.

Notes:

The clout is the center of an archery target: It is the white pin that attaches the target to a structure that holds it up.

Ben Jonson says that his play may not hit the clout, but not through lack of wit (intelligence). An arrow may miss because the bow has lost its elasticity or because the weather or wind makes hitting the clout difficult. A playwright may do his best to write a good play, and yet the play, although the playwright thinks it is good, may fail.

— NOTES —

THE FIRST INTERMEAN: AFTER THE FIRST ACT

*I would fain see the fool, gossip; the fool is the finest man i'the
company, they say, and has all the wit. He is the very Justice o'Peace o'the
play, and can commit whom he will, and what he will, error, absurdity, as
the toy takes him, and no man say black is his eye, but laugh at him. 20*
(First Intermean, 17-20)
Source of Above:
The Cambridge Edition of the Works of Ben Jonson
7 Volume Set. Volume 6.
Ben Jonson (Author), David Bevington (Editor), Martin Butler (Editor),
Ian Donaldson (Editor).
Cambridge University Press, 2012. Print. P. 49.

This is speculation on my part, but I wonder if the Justice of the Peace
mentioned here is a reference to the Lord Chief Justice of England who appears
in *The Famous Victories of Henry V*. The Justice in *The Staple of News* is both
a fool and a man whom "no man will say black is his eye," which means "No
man will impugn his character." Prince Hal in *The Famous Victories of Henry
V* regards the Chief Justice as not worthy of being shown respect, but as King
Henry V he has much respect for him.

— 2.1 —

"Of course a wife and dowry, credit and friends, birth and beauty, are the gift of Queen Cash."

Source of Above: Horace, *Epistles*, 1.6.36-7. H. Rushton Fairclough, Translator. Loeb Classics. Harvard University Press. 1929. P. 289.

https://www.loebclassics.com/view/horace-epistles/1926/pb_LCL194.289.xml?readMode=recto

***

"Indeed, all things, divine and human, serve the beauty of riches — virtue, reputation, honour; and he who hoards it up will be famous, strong, and just."

Source of Above: Horace, *Satires*, 2.3.37. Quoted in

The Cambridge Edition of the Works of Ben Jonson

7 Volume Set. Volume 6.

Ben Jonson (Author), David Bevington (Editor), Martin Butler (Editor), Ian Donaldson (Editor).

Cambridge University Press, 2012. Print. P. 52.

***

Below is another translation of the (slightly longer) *Satires* passage:

"For every thing, virtue, fame, glory, divine and human affairs, are subservient to the attraction of riches; which whoever shall have accumulated, shall be illustrious, brave, just — What, wise too? Ay, and a king, and whatever else he pleases."

Source of Above:

This eBook of *The Works of Horace* belongs to the public domain. Complete book[1].

Authorama - Classic Literature, free of copyright.

http://www.authorama.com/works-of-horace-7.html

Also:

The Works of Horace. Christopher Smart, trans. Wikisource.

---

1.   http://www.authorama.com/book/works-of-horace.html

193

— 2.4 —

"How the rogue stinks, worse than a fishmonger's sleeves"
(2.4.50)
Source of Above:
The Cambridge Edition of the Works of Ben Jonson
7 Volume Set. Volume 6.
Ben Jonson (Author), David Bevington (Editor), Martin Butler (Editor), Ian Donaldson (Editor).
Cambridge University Press, 2012. Print. P. 63.

HORATIUS FLACCUS was a native of Venusium, his father having been, by his own account, a freedman and collector of taxes, but, as it is generally believed, a dealer in salted (541) provisions; for some one with whom Horace had a quarrel, jeered him, by saying; "How often have I seen your father wiping his nose with his fist?"

Source of Above: *The Life and Works of Suetonius*. "Life of Horace." Trans. J.C. Rolfe.
https://archive.org/stream/1thecompleteworksofsuetonius/
1%20-%20The%20Complete%20Works%20of%20Suetonius_djvu.txt

"clapper dungeon"
(2.4.209)
Source of Above:
The Cambridge Edition of the Works of Ben Jonson
7 Volume Set. Volume 6.
Ben Jonson (Author), David Bevington (Editor), Martin Butler (Editor), Ian Donaldson (Editor).
Here are some definitions of "clapper dudgeon":
Cambridge University Press, 2012. Print. P. 70.

A clapperdudgeon, or clapper dudgeon, was a type of con artist common during the Elizabethan era. In order to appear as pitiful and deserving of alms as possible, one would give themselves sores by applying salt, various plants, etc. to their skin, dress in bloody rags and then beg for money.

Source of Above:
ellesleg, "Tuesday Word: clapperdudgeon." Live Journal. 22 April 2014. Accessed 9 May 2021.
https://1word1day.livejournal.com/516149.html

Brewer's: Clapper-dudgeons

Abram-men (q.v.). The clapper is the tongue of a bell, and in cant language the human "tongue." Dudgeon is a slang word for a beggar.

Source of Above:
Dictionary of Phrase and Fable, E. Cobham Brewer, 1894.
https://www.infoplease.com/dictionary/brewers/clapper-dudgeons

A cant name for a beggar born; also used as a term of reproach or insult.

Source of Above: *"clapperdungeon." Oxford English Dictionary.*

The paragraph about Virgil's description of Fama, aka Rumor, comes from my book:

Bruce, David. *Virgil's* Aeneid: *A Retelling in Prose.* Self-Published. 2013. https://www.smashwords.com/books/view/277646 Independently published. Available at major online eBook retailers.

***

"So there had need, for they are still by the ears
One with another."
(3.2.134-135)
Source of Above:
The Cambridge Edition of the Works of Ben Jonson
7 Volume Set. Volume 6.
Ben Jonson (Author), David Bevington (Editor), Martin Butler (Editor), Ian Donaldson (Editor).
Cambridge University Press, 2012. Print. P. 89.
The below information comes from the Wikipedia article titled "British Anabaptism":

Following the death of Elizabeth, James I became the new ruler of England. He continued the policies of his predecessor that valued conformity under the state.[14] As Holland and England continued to maintain trade relations, it was of no surprise that Anabaptist ideas still made their way into England. Under his rule, the last public burning of heretics took place. Edward Wightman was the last to be burned publicly for heresy in England, and he was an Anabaptist. Although James I valued conformity for political reasons, this still shows the value he placed on making a public statement about religious minorities as well.

Source of Above Information: "British Anabaptism." Wikipedia. Accessed 15 May 2021 https://en.wikipedia.org/wiki/British_Anabaptism

The below information comes from the Wikipedia article titled "Edward Wightman":

Edward Wightman (c. 1580 – 11 April 1612) was an English radical Anabaptist[1], executed at Lichfield[2] on charges of heresy.[1][3][2][4] He was the last person to be burned at the stake[5] in England for heresy[6].[3][7]

Source of Above Information: "Edward Wightman." Wikipedia. Accessed 15 May 2021

https://en.wikipedia.org/wiki/Edward_Wightman

---

1. https://en.wikipedia.org/wiki/Radical_Reformation

2. https://en.wikipedia.org/wiki/Lichfield

3. https://en.wikipedia.org/wiki/Edward_Wightman#cite_note-1

4. https://en.wikipedia.org/wiki/Edward_Wightman#cite_note-2

5. https://en.wikipedia.org/wiki/Execution_by_burning

6. https://en.wikipedia.org/wiki/Heresy

7. https://en.wikipedia.org/wiki/Edward_Wightman#cite_note-3

— 4.2 —

In *Pantagruel* V:5, the Oracle of the Bottle is "Trinc," which means "Drink." Panurge, a character in *Pantagruel*, calls the bottle "trismegistian Bottle," which means "thrice-renowned bottle." The priestess tell Panurge that "by wine we become divine."

Note: The edition used is Project Gutenberg's *Gargantua and Pantagruel*, Book V., by Francois Rabelais. Translated into English by Sir Thomas Urquhart of Cromarty and Peter Antony Motteux.

https://www.gutenberg.org/files/8170/8170-h/8170-h.htm#2HCH0045

THE FOURTH INTERMEAN: AFTER THE FOURTH ACT

"*Or to stand wearing a piece of parchment, which the court please —*"
(FOURTH INTERMEAN, line 56)
Source of Above:
The Cambridge Edition of the Works of Ben Jonson
7 Volume Set. Volume 6.
Ben Jonson (Author), David Bevington (Editor), Martin Butler (Editor), Ian Donaldson (Editor).
Cambridge University Press, 2012. Print. P. 135.
Here is some information on pillories and parchment/paper from Terry Bracher's "The Pillory as Punishment" at the Wiltshire & Swindon History Centre website:

[...] sometimes the offender was drawn to the pillory on a hurdle, accompanied by minstrels and a paper sign hung around his or her head displaying the offence committed.

At the Quarter Sessions of October 1626 in Marlborough, "Thomas Edmonds was indicted for making and publisheing Libell which he confessed to be true, and thereupon convicted to goale there to remaine until Saterday next, and then to stand under the pillorie situate in Marlborough for the space of two howres together in the Markett tyme. And then alsoe to have a broad white pap [paper] upon his forehead subscribed with these words in great letters (vizt) for a libel and (then he is to return to prison until the next assizes &c)."

In Devizes in 1615 Nicholas Powell was convicted for deceiving John Smithe of thirty shillings with false letters. He was whipped in the open market "untille his backe doth bleede, and afterwards sett on the pillory." Again paper was placed on his head displaying the crimes of cosonage (cheating) and obtaining money by counterfeit letters.

Source of Above: Terry Bracher, "The Pillory as Punishment." Wiltshire & Swindon History Centre. 10 October 2014
https://wshc.org.uk/blog/item/the-pillory-as-punishment.html

— 5.6 —

The below is a brief description of Aristotle's Mean Between Extremes:

Moral Virtue, and the Mean Between Extremes

Aristotle thought that we can acquire two different kinds of virtue: moral and intellectual. The appetitive element (the desiring element) of the human soul can lead us to moral virtue, if we have desires toward worthy goals and these desires are subjected to the rational regulating principle known as the mean between extremes.

This theory of the mean between extremes is a famous part of Aristotle's thought. He believed in moderation — as most Greeks did. If you have too much or too little of something, you will suffer from an excess or a deficiency of that thing. What you need is exactly the right amount. Thus courage is the mean between the extremes of rashness (excess) and cowardice (deficiency). Applying Aristotle's ideas (but not always his names for the qualities listed), we can make a list illustrating some means between extremes:

1. Courage
Rashness (Excess); Courage (Mean/Virtue); Cowardice (Deficiency)
2. Liberality
Prodigality (Excess); Liberality (Mean/Virtue); Miserliness (Deficiency)
3. Charitable
Overly Generous (Excess); Charitable (Mean/Virtue); Cheap (Deficiency)
4. Weight
Obese (Excess); Normal Weight (Mean/Virtue); Anorexic (Deficiency)
5. Nobility

Vanity (Excess); Nobility (Mean/Virtue); Ignobility (Deficiency)

6. Good Temper

Hot Temper (Excess); Good Temper (Mean/Virtue); Indifference (Deficiency)

7. Truthfulness

Boastfulness (Excess); Truthfulness (Mean/Virtue); False Modesty (Deficiency)

The first example shows that courage is the mean between the excess of rashness and the deficiency of cowardice. Let's say that a person is walking down the street and sees a house on fire. A rash person would shout, "Don't worry, I'll save you," and rush inside the burning building without even bothering to find out whether anyone is inside to be rescued! A coward would ignore the fire and not even call the fire department. However, a courageous person would call the fire department, find out whether anyone was trapped inside the burning building, and render whatever assistance he or she rationally can.

The second example shows that liberality is the mean between the excess of prodigality and the deficiency of miserliness. A prodigal person would leave a $100 tip after eating a $10 pizza (however, this can be a good deed when done by someone who can easily spare the money and wants to help the server. If I give a $100 tip for a $10 pizza, I am being prodigal. If Microsoft founder Bill Gates gives a $100 tip for a $10 pizza, he is doing a good deed / being charitable). A miser would not leave any tip at all. However, a person who is liberal with money would leave a 15 percent tip for good service. (This example refers to the USA; most other countries don't have tipping.)

The third example shows that being charitable is the mean between the excess of being overly generous and the deficiency of being cheap. An overly generous person will give away all of his or her money to charity, not saving enough to live on. A cheap person will never give money to charity. However, a charitable person will pay his or her bills, keep enough money to live on (and keep some to save), but also give a portion that he or she can afford to charity.

The fourth example shows that normal weight is the mean between the excess of obesity and the deficiency of anorexia. An obese person pigs out every night (and every morning, and every noon, and two or three other times a day). An anorexic person will do 100 sit-ups after chewing a stick of sugarless gum.

However, a person who maintains his or her normal, healthy weight will eat three square meals a day, and is willing to eat cake and ice cream at birthday parties (and salad for lunch the next day).

One point to notice is that not all activities have a mean between extremes. Some activities are already excessive in themselves. Thus, adultery is always wrong. You will never be able to commit adultery with the right person at the right time and in the right manner. (You should never say, "I don't want to commit too little adultery or too much adultery; I want to commit exactly the right amount of adultery"!)

Also, the mean can vary among people (see liberality above). In determining how much food to eat, the mean for a 300-pound weightlifter will be much greater than the mean for a 100-pound secretary. Also, a wealthy person such as Microsoft founder Bill Gates can afford to give much more money to charity than a college student can.

The way we acquire moral virtue, according to Aristotle, is through imitation and acquiring good habits. If we act the way a brave person acts, we will become brave. If we act the way a truthful person acts, we will become truthful. If we act the way a noble person acts, we will become noble.

Source: David Bruce. *Philosophy for the Masses: Ethics*. Self-Published. 2009.

https://www.smashwords.com/books/view/374071

— **5.6** —

Pennyboy Senior says this to his brother, Pennyboy Canter:

Wise and honoured brother!
None but a brother, and sent from the dead,
As you are to me, could have altered me.
I thank my destiny, that is so gracious.
Are there no pains, no penalties decreed (35)
From whence you come to us that smother money
In chests and strangle her in bags?

(5.6.31-37)

Source of Above:

The Cambridge Edition of the Works of Ben Jonson

7 Volume Set. Volume 6.

Ben Jonson (Author), David Bevington (Editor), Martin Butler (Editor), Ian Donaldson (Editor).

Cambridge University Press, 2012. Print. P. 155.

In Chapter 5, scene 6, I described what Dante writes in his *Inferno* about the punishment of the Greedy Moneylenders (Usurers). That description was taken from this book:

Source: David Bruce, *Dante's* Inferno: *A Discussion Guide.* Self-Published. 2009.

https://www.smashwords.com/books/view/342391

From the same book is a description of the punishment of the Hoarders and Wasters of Money in the Fourth Circle of the Inferno:

The Incontinent: The Wasters and the Hoarders

As the god of wealth, Plutus is an appropriate guard for the Wasters and the Hoarders, who were incontinent when it came to managing money. The Wasters are Spendthrifts, who spent every penny they could, saving nothing for emergencies. The Hoarders are Misers, who saved every penny they could, spending little even to make themselves comfortable. These two opposed groups are condemned to roll great weights at each other. Each group sets off in an opposing direction around the Circle, and then they meet and crash the weights together, one group crying "Why hoard?" (*Inferno* VII.30) and the

205

other group crying "Why waste?" (*Inferno* VII.30). Then they roll the weights back and meet again on the other side of the Circle. These two groups were opposed to each other in life; now they are eternally opposed to each other in death. In addition, Dante does not recognize any of the souls here. These souls were undiscerning in life — they did not know what true wealth is. Now, in death the souls are unable to be discerned by the living Dante. (He does recognize that some of the souls were monks by their haircuts, but he does not know their names.)

Note: The brief quotations are from Mark Musa's translation of Dante's *Inferno*.

APPENDIX A: ABOUT THE AUTHOR

It was a dark and stormy night. Suddenly a cry rang out, and on a hot summer night in 1954, Josephine, wife of Carl Bruce, gave birth to a boy — me. Unfortunately, this young married couple allowed Reuben Saturday, Josephine's brother, to name their first-born. Reuben, aka "The Joker," decided that Bruce was a nice name, so he decided to name me Bruce Bruce. I have gone by my middle name — David — ever since.

Being named Bruce David Bruce hasn't been all bad. Bank tellers remember me very quickly, so I don't often have to show an ID. It can be fun in charades, also. When I was a counselor as a teenager at Camp Echoing Hills in Warsaw, Ohio, a fellow counselor gave the signs for "sounds like" and "two words," then she pointed to a bruise on her leg twice. Bruise Bruise? Oh yeah, Bruce Bruce is the answer!

Uncle Reuben, by the way, gave me a haircut when I was in kindergarten. He cut my hair short and shaved a small bald spot on the back of my head. My mother wouldn't let me go to school until the bald spot grew out again.

Of all my brothers and sisters (six in all), I am the only transplant to Athens, Ohio. I was born in Newark, Ohio, and have lived all around Southeastern Ohio. However, I moved to Athens to go to Ohio University and have never left.

At Ohio U, I never could make up my mind whether to major in English or Philosophy, so I got a bachelor's degree with a double major in both areas, then I added a Master of Arts degree in English and a Master of Arts degree in Philosophy. Yes, I have my MAMA degree.

Currently, and for a long time to come (I eat fruits and veggies), I am spending my retirement writing books such as *Nadia Comaneci: Perfect 10*, *The Funniest People in Comedy*, *Homer's* Iliad: *A Retelling in Prose*, and *William Shakespeare's* Hamlet: *A Retelling in Prose*.

By the way, my sister Brenda Kennedy writes romances such as *A New Beginning* and *Shattered Dreams*.

APPENDIX B: SOME BOOKS BY DAVID BRUCE

Retellings of a Classic Work of Literature

Arden of Faversham: *A Retelling*

Ben Jonson's The Alchemist: *A Retelling*

Ben Jonson's The Arraignment, or Poetaster: *A Retelling*

Ben Jonson's Bartholomew Fair: *A Retelling*

Ben Jonson's The Case is Altered: *A Retelling*

Ben Jonson's Catiline's Conspiracy: *A Retelling*

Ben Jonson's The Devil is an Ass: *A Retelling*

Ben Jonson's Epicene: *A Retelling*

Ben Jonson's Every Man in His Humor: *A Retelling*

Ben Jonson's Every Man Out of His Humor: *A Retelling*

Ben Jonson's The Fountain of Self-Love, or Cynthia's Revels: *A Retelling*

Ben Jonson's The Magnetic Lady, or Humors Reconciled: *A Retelling*

Ben Jonson's The New Inn, or The Light Heart: *A Retelling*

Ben Jonson's Sejanus' Fall: *A Retelling*

Ben Jonson's The Staple of News: *A Retelling*

Ben Jonson's A Tale of a Tub: *A Retelling*

Ben Jonson's Volpone, or the Fox: *A Retelling*

Christopher Marlowe's Complete Plays: Retellings

Christopher Marlowe's Dido, Queen of Carthage: *A Retelling*

Christopher Marlowe's Doctor Faustus: *Retellings of the 1604 A-Text and of the 1616 B-Text*

Christopher Marlowe's Edward II: *A Retelling*

Christopher Marlowe's The Massacre at Paris: *A Retelling*

Christopher Marlowe's The Rich Jew of Malta: *A Retelling*

Christopher Marlowe's Tamburlaine, Parts 1 and 2: *Retellings*

Dante's Divine Comedy: *A Retelling in Prose*

Dante's Inferno: *A Retelling in Prose*

Dante's Purgatory: *A Retelling in Prose*

Dante's Paradise: *A Retelling in Prose*

The Famous Victories of Henry V: *A Retelling*

From the Iliad *to the* Odyssey: *A Retelling in Prose of Quintus of Smyrna's* Posthomerica

George Chapman, Ben Jonson, and John Marston's Eastward Ho! *A Retelling*

George Peele's The Arraignment of Paris: *A Retelling*

George Peele's The Battle of Alcazar: *A Retelling*

George Peele's David and Bathsheba, and the Tragedy of Absalom: *A Retelling*

George Peele's Edward I: *A Retelling*

George Peele's The Old Wives' Tale: *A Retelling*

George-a-Greene: *A Retelling*

The History of King Leir: *A Retelling*

Homer's Iliad: *A Retelling in Prose*

Homer's Odyssey: *A Retelling in Prose*

J.W. Gent.'s The Valiant Scot: *A Retelling*

Jason and the Argonauts: A Retelling in Prose of Apollonius of Rhodes' Argonautica

John Ford: Eight Plays Translated into Modern English

John Ford's The Broken Heart: *A Retelling*

John Ford's The Fancies, Chaste and Noble: *A Retelling*

John Ford's The Lady's Trial: *A Retelling*

John Ford's The Lover's Melancholy: *A Retelling*

John Ford's Love's Sacrifice: *A Retelling*

John Ford's Perkin Warbeck: *A Retelling*

John Ford's The Queen: *A Retelling*

John Ford's 'Tis Pity She's a Whore: *A Retelling*

John Lyly's Campaspe: *A Retelling*

John Lyly's Endymion, The Man in the Moon: *A Retelling*

John Lyly's Galatea: *A Retelling*

John Lyly's Love's Metamorphosis: *A Retelling*

John Lyly's Midas: *A Retelling*

John Lyly's Mother Bombie: *A Retelling*

John Lyly's Sappho and Phao: *A Retelling*

John Lyly's The Woman in the Moon: *A Retelling*

John Webster's The White Devil: *A Retelling*

King Edward III: *A Retelling*

Mankind: *A Medieval Morality Play* (A Retelling)

Margaret Cavendish's The Unnatural Tragedy: *A Retelling*

The Merry Devil of Edmonton: *A Retelling*

The Summoning of Everyman: *A Medieval Morality Play* (A Retelling)

Robert Greene's Friar Bacon and Friar Bungay: *A Retelling*

The Taming of a Shrew: *A Retelling*

Tarlton's Jests: A Retelling

Thomas Middleton's A Chaste Maid in Cheapside: *A Retelling*

Thomas Middleton's Women Beware Women: *A Retelling*

Thomas Middleton and Thomas Dekker's The Roaring Girl: *A Retelling*

Thomas Middleton and William Rowley's The Changeling: *A Retelling*

The Trojan War and Its Aftermath: Four Ancient Epic Poems

Virgil's Aeneid: *A Retelling in Prose*

William Shakespeare's 5 Late Romances: Retellings in Prose

William Shakespeare's 10 Histories: Retellings in Prose

William Shakespeare's 11 Tragedies: Retellings in Prose

William Shakespeare's 12 Comedies: Retellings in Prose

William Shakespeare's 38 Plays: Retellings in Prose
William Shakespeare's 1 Henry IV, aka Henry IV, Part 1: *A Retelling in Prose*
William Shakespeare's 2 Henry IV, aka Henry IV, Part 2: *A Retelling in Prose*
William Shakespeare's 1 Henry VI, aka Henry VI, Part 1: *A Retelling in Prose*
William Shakespeare's 2 Henry VI, aka Henry VI, Part 2: *A Retelling in Prose*
William Shakespeare's 3 Henry VI, aka Henry VI, Part 3: *A Retelling in Prose*
William Shakespeare's All's Well that Ends Well: *A Retelling in Prose*
William Shakespeare's Antony and Cleopatra: *A Retelling in Prose*
William Shakespeare's As You Like It: *A Retelling in Prose*
William Shakespeare's The Comedy of Errors: *A Retelling in Prose*
William Shakespeare's Coriolanus: *A Retelling in Prose*
William Shakespeare's Cymbeline: *A Retelling in Prose*
William Shakespeare's Hamlet: *A Retelling in Prose*
William Shakespeare's Henry V: *A Retelling in Prose*
William Shakespeare's Henry VIII: *A Retelling in Prose*
William Shakespeare's Julius Caesar: *A Retelling in Prose*
William Shakespeare's King John: *A Retelling in Prose*
William Shakespeare's King Lear: *A Retelling in Prose*
William Shakespeare's Love's Labor's Lost: *A Retelling in Prose*
William Shakespeare's Macbeth: *A Retelling in Prose*
William Shakespeare's Measure for Measure: *A Retelling in Prose*
William Shakespeare's The Merchant of Venice: *A Retelling in Prose*
William Shakespeare's The Merry Wives of Windsor: *A Retelling in Prose*
William Shakespeare's A Midsummer Night's Dream: *A Retelling in Prose*
William Shakespeare's Much Ado About Nothing: *A Retelling in Prose*
William Shakespeare's Othello: *A Retelling in Prose*
William Shakespeare's Pericles, Prince of Tyre: *A Retelling in Prose*
William Shakespeare's Richard II: *A Retelling in Prose*
William Shakespeare's Richard III: *A Retelling in Prose*
William Shakespeare's Romeo and Juliet: *A Retelling in Prose*
William Shakespeare's The Taming of the Shrew: *A Retelling in Prose*
William Shakespeare's The Tempest: *A Retelling in Prose*
William Shakespeare's Timon of Athens: *A Retelling in Prose*
William Shakespeare's Titus Andronicus: *A Retelling in Prose*
William Shakespeare's Troilus and Cressida: *A Retelling in Prose*
William Shakespeare's Twelfth Night: *A Retelling in Prose*
William Shakespeare's The Two Gentlemen of Verona: *A Retelling in Prose*
William Shakespeare's The Two Noble Kinsmen: *A Retelling in Prose*
William Shakespeare's The Winter's Tale: *A Retelling in Prose*